A novel by
CAROLE MASO

The Art Lover

NORTH POINT PRESS
San Francisco   1990

This book is an invention, an act
of the imagination, and in no way
should be mistaken for reality, the
place where much good invention
originates.

LIBRARY OF CONGRESS
CATALOGING-IN-PUBLICATION DATA
Maso, Carole.
    The art lover : a novel / by Carole
    Maso.
        p.   cm.
    ISBN 0-86547-427-3
    I. Title.
PS3563.A786A86   1990
813'.54—dc20   89-25512

For Gary Falk, who saw hoops of gold.
1954–1986

The Art Lover

Spring 1985

1

A girl in a striped bathing suit sits at the water's edge. She digs deeply in the sand and from the vast beach makes shapes: an arch, a pyramid, two towers. Not child, but not yet adult, she is at that tender age of becoming.

A man further back on the beach, now getting up, calls to her. He calls something out as if it were pure song. "The sun" I think is what he says. She turns. No. "Alison!" He is saying her name. "Alison." Although there is only a slight physical resemblance, the man can only be her father. You can tell by the way he moves toward her. As she stands up now I can see the intricate jigsaw shapes their bodies make to fit together. They will gnaw off an arm if necessary to properly fit, bleed at a joint, tilt the head, or nod a little too deeply just to maintain the vaguely heart-shaped vacuum that must always exist somehow between them. They move closer for a moment as if to compensate for someone lost or gone away, someone missing. Wordlessly they move to shield each other from things yet to come, as if the body were capable of anything. Not big things necessarily, perhaps just against the sun which shines at times so brutally, or some small disappointment, the denial of a promotion, or a B on a test instead of an A—or protection against the collapsing walls of the sand city. They shift to greet each other. They turn at the last moment to maintain the correct distance.

"Father," she calls him now as she drags a pail of sand motioning. Arm up toward him. Arm back. Hand in the sand. Closer now. "Daddy." His hand on her shoulder. His hand dip-ping into the water, moving back and forth, back and forth, clarifying the world. Daddy.

The day is slightly chilly. It is early spring. In the distance a wall of yellow—the forsythia in bloom. In the distance an umbrella, a hat. And now out of the water another girl rises. It is as if she has been created by the man's back-and-forth motion in the water. She cries with delight. Clearly she is a member of this family of father and daughter.

"Alison!" she calls to the girl. "Come in." She laughs and dives into a wave. "Both of you!" she shouts. "I'll be your porpoise." They watch her body arc through the cool blue. When she finally comes out, I see she is a woman really, a young woman, and that she resembles the father more than the younger girl. She drips all over them, and they shout, "Candace, no!" The father moves away. She steps closer.

"Stop, it's freezing cold," he says.

"What do you expect? It's still May." She laughs, wrapping herself in towel after towel.

"Your lips are blue," he says.

"And my hair is red," she laughs.

"We should go in and change." He collects tape recorder, suntan lotion, book, towel. "Our picnic dinner awaits us."

"*One more minute,*" Candace says, wrapping her hand tightly around his arm, then releasing him. With a finger, Alison presses teeth into the top of her sand tower.

"A cornice," Candace says. "How very postmodern of you. Now all we need is a moat." She digs deep into the sand, scooping out handfuls and throws them at her father.

"Candace!" he cries.

Alison pours water into the moat, then smoothes the curving walls. Fortifies all sides. Makes a gum-wrapper flag. "Where's Mom?" she asks.

"Over there," Father says, turning. Headless, half-headed, under an umbrella, on the other side of the beach, she is reading.

"Mother," Alison calls. "Come see! Come see!"

2

The woman walks across the large lawn, over a stream where trillium grow and into a meadow. Her long skirt billows in the wind. Under her arm she carries a large blue blanket. She unfolds the blanket, extends her arms and the blanket balloons, then waves, then settles on the grass. She sits on the edge of the blue square and looks at the summer house she loves, just opened for the season. She is waist high in grass.

I know by the trees, the gentians at her feet, the quality of light, that it is spring. This is the Berkshires and spring comes slowly here, not like in the cities. Here there is some holding back, the sense that we are on the verge of something, a promise of some sort. There is something vaguely sexual in the air, in the laugh of the woman.

She breathes deeply and sighs. She is in love with light. Her eye caresses each blade of grass, each lavender shadow. She stretches her legs out. There are ants, I'm sure, the first ones of the season, now near her ankle. Does she hum a song? Something about her suggests to me she's not from our time. What? A glance? A way of dressing? I think she sings a Bach cantata and its high alleluias rise up and float across the field. Her daughter waves to her from the edge of the field, calling her name, calling her back over and over to this world.

The woman smiles as the girl bounds down the steep farmhouse steps and runs across the lawn to her, carrying a basket. The man emerges from the house, crosses the lawn, the stream, the meadow to his family. Only the older daughter is missing now. One suspects, I suspect, she watches from far off, like any teenager. Soon she too will descend the steep stairs and join them for a picnic in the meadow. There is asparagus from the garden, salmon and fiddleheads. Chèvre and pears.

One wants to keep this family well. Seeing them this way from some distance I can tell they are talking, but I can't make out what they say. They laugh and their laughter is carried toward me on the breeze. The teenage daughter, holding bunches of lilacs, crosses the stream now, crosses the meadow, kneels down, putting her arms around her father's neck, and gives him a kiss. The family come no closer than this, they hang back, keep their distance. But I have faith in them. And so for now the light is what I notice most, and certain familiar gestures. The jug of wine being lifted over and over. The mother pointing to the sky. The younger girl pinwheeling around the family doing cartwheels, her legs blurring. The man reclines in the purply grass. I can almost hear their mild laughs, their swoonings. The mother saying "comet" under her breath. I can almost smell the evening as it arrives.

They are still just a lovely picture, a word picture of a family really, picnicking in the meadow near their summer house in Massachusetts, though it is not yet summer. And while the figures appear static, they are not in fact—it is only my wish for them: that they stay together, that the light remain. Dusk comes quickly. Still there is laughter, sighs, rapture, a jug of wine, enough love to last.

I cannot guess yet how remote I, the onlooker, I the one who is telling their story, have become, how cautious. If there is a clue in this scene of something about to go awry, I do not see it. I overlook it. Or perhaps I prefer not to see. If I could tilt this tableau, flip it so that the house and the lake are nearest me and the family becomes small in the meadow, perhaps what I would see is the city of sand collapsing now, the overripe sunfish gone to the bottom of the lake for the night, the white house ghostly and luminous in this light. But something prevents me from doing this. Only one thing stands out now, dwarfing everything—the family, the beautiful pink of the salmon's head in the grass which is so green, the Berkshires themselves, which look like an ocean in this light—oddly, in all of this there is only one thing that cannot be ignored—and that is the enormous starburst in the arch over the farmhouse door.

A Few of the Things I Know About You

You were elegant, graying, distinguished, with a slight paunch.
You were cerebral, exacting, lively, passionate.

You were not old.

You were critical, cold at times, a little monstrous. Melancholy only on occasion. Intelligent. Your grayish eyes traversed great distances of time and space.

You liked Brahms, Mahler, Stravinsky. You had a genuine appreciation for life and also a deep cynicism that struck me more often than not simply as good sense.

You had many passions. Women found you irresistible.

You were not old.

Things are not in our control.

One need not look very far to see what I am talking about.
Look on any day of the week, on any page of the newspaper.
For example:

Cape Canaveral, Florida — Wherever it is going, whatever it is carrying, however long its planned mission, the Space Shuttle *Discovery* took off this afternoon on the first flight of American astronauts dedicated exclusively to secret military objectives.

For example:

Methyl isocyanate has escaped from a Union Carbide tank in Bhopal, India, killing more than 2,000 people.

I read this in the newspaper. I die a little with this news, accompanied by a photograph of mother and child.

Things are not in our control.

We see close up and also from a great distance, and we are dizzied by the constant shift in perspective.

We see close up. Walk down any street on any day in New York City. Men lie drunk and destitute on the streets. Women too, their shopping bags filled with their whole lives. This is not only on the Bowery anymore or other so-called bad sections of the city. Go to Madison Avenue. Everywhere a hand reaches out for money. From the gutter a hand at my ankle.

And now my father is dead. From the grave, a hand. I have come back to his house to settle what can be settled. A townhouse on West Eleventh Street in Manhattan. I am surrounded by his things—his papers, his extensive library, his coffee mug, his pipes, his brandy glasses. So little goes with the body of a man. So much is left behind. Canvases, paints, diplomas, honorary diplomas. In the bedroom closet three pairs of women's shoes, all different sizes. On his bureau his pocket watch. His second pair of glasses. His whole life before me—only he, strangely missing.

I am back in New York, his New York, my New York, after a full year away. I walk the streets. I have started reading the papers again.

It has become almost possible to skip the bad parts of the newspaper altogether. One can be reasonably well assured that in the Living section of the *New York Times* or the Home section or the Weekend section, one will be in relatively little danger. Beware though and proceed with care through Tuesday's Science section. Occasionally a Sudden Infant Death Syndrome baby will be slipped in or some detailed account of the latest antisocial behavior: autoerotic death, for instance. Finally, distrust most those stories that seem most innocuous, regardless of what section they appear in. For example: an article about a circus unicorn. Great, you think. Harmless. You're reading. OK. But the unicorn turns out to be a goat whose horns were diabolically fused together to make one mythic horn, center head.

I did not get to him in time.

In time for what? one wonders. We had cared for each other. We had, it seemed, been saying good-bye our whole lives. From the time I was little and he called me his cherub. Even then he was saying good-bye, putting me into a painting, holding me afar and admiring.

Max, I had wanted a firmer grasp.

"She held very still," you always said.

You lived a good life. I believe, I have faith that you are in heaven. You were kind and generous, in your own way. I picture God's hand in yours.

I suspect that there are lots of new things to see up there, to comment on, lots of places to turn your intelligent, discerning eye. I believe you are in heaven.

Some days I notice on the Bowery that the men have lifted themselves up, at least for a moment, out of the gutter, the doorway, the broken stoop, have torn a shirt into strips for rags, have bought or stolen a bottle of Windex and have begun cleaning the windshields of cars stopped at red lights, for change.

Another day I hear that a most unlikely fellow, the leader of a rock band called The Boomtown Rats, has come up with a way to help feed the people of Ethiopia.

And buried in each Sunday *Times* is a map of the stars accompanied by a little star story. You can, if you like, simply by looking up into the sky, chart them with this handy diagram. This is one perfectly safe and reliable part of the paper.

But sometimes even the sky is dangerous. I look up and see your face in the stars.

"A neat trick," you'd say.

I've been watching a building go up on the West Side. I'm especially fond of it because it looks like a tube of lipstick to me, though the fact of the matter is it's made of mortar and steel or whatever, it has no windows, the people who will have to work there day after day will not get any light, there's probably inadequate ventilation and who knows about the fire exits. But still I love that building. I want things to be beautiful.

I get stuck too easily. Sometimes it takes so long just to finish one sentence in the newspaper. For example: "Because it is too early for peach picking in Western Georgia . . ." I stopped, just wanting to be there, imagining the roundness of the young fruit, feeling the early heat.

I have gotten distracted far too easily my whole life. The past year, away in the country at the Cummington Community of the Arts, I was stopped so often by blue flowers on the side of the road or by the ostrich plume fern or a stone wall. Or by a certain composer's interesting face or body. One loses one's way so easily. One is blue-petaled at the least suggestion, passing a field of gentians on the way down the hill to the mailbox. Staying there even as I take the mail from the box and attempt to separate it. One becomes irretrievably lost in the music, or the musician. One loses a certain analytic perspective.

I am a lover of detail, a marker—it's a way of keeping the world in place. One documents, makes lists to avoid becoming simply petals. I am like you, Max: a looker, an accountant, a record keeper, a creator of categories, a documenter. For evidence I rip flyers from telephone poles, save every scrap of paper I get. Listen carefully. Organize. Reorganize.

I open her clenched hand. In her palm a swirl of green, a fiddlehead fern, a small emerald of hope. No.

I am trying to regain my analytic perspective.

I began foreseeing his death in that recurring New England shape, that architectural sunrise, that starburst over every door, in the gate, in the churches. In the farmhouse I lived in. In the center of town. I started photographing it. There is a need for evidence. I saw the starburst in my face. I had a picture taken of it. In this pattern, this cool geometry, there was something about to explode. It moved inside my father's head. He had a stroke and died. I did not get there in time.

One wonders. In time for what? We loved each other so much we felt it necessary, in preparation, to say good-bye our whole lives.

One becomes a blue flower, a mountain, a gate, a stream. The landscape is not stationary; it follows you around. And the dead? We shall see, I suppose.

"She held very still."

She does, she holds very still.

The landscape changes moment to moment like your face once did as you read, as you looked at a painting, as you gazed out the window. I often wondered if you were thinking of Mother, but I never asked. You would often catch me staring at you. I would say, "How much your face changes, Max." You would say, "It is essentially a matter of light."

I am back in your Village apartment, your enormous art history library before me. A few blocks away your students are just getting out for the year. Distinguished Professor of Art History, Chairman of the Department, you were always everyone's favorite, though you could not see why and regarded their affection with some suspicion. Even the beautiful ones—you kept a skeptical, a healthy, you called it, distance. You had many lovers, I know, but none of them were your students.

I picture God's hand in yours.

But other times I think no, you were not old enough to die. There was a certain spring to your walk. You must have sensed something. You were a sensitive man, but you gave us no warning. You were not that old. And there were children to consider.

"Children, indeed," you would have said. I, the youngest at thirty. My brothers far away, having learned the lessons of art and distance you taught well.

I believe in one God the Father Almighty. And I have faith that you are in heaven, content with new visual stimulus.

You were not that old. There were many women after my mother. Right up until the end. You were a sensitive man. You must have sensed it. Did a young large-breasted woman lying over you whisper death in your ear? Did you try to ward death off, pumping yourself into her?

"No."

I did not get to you in time.

"Caroline, please."

You lived such a civilized life. Life of beautiful food. Goat's cheese, artichoke life, asparagus in the afternoon. Wine-cellar life. Academic life. Book life. Life of the mind. And of the body. All those women, Max. Exotic, perfumed, the lovely white-throated night women, giggling, sighing, a shoe falling off a perfect foot, a silk stocking. Young pretty women, patting me on the head. I did understand. Oh, yes. I never questioned that you missed my mother. But she was dead, and you were a prac-tical man of desire.

Can I miss the mother I barely knew? A woman I only vaguely recall? A patterned dress, a scent of spices, dark hair that fell around white shoulders. Is it possible to miss her, this phantom mother? No, I think not, you would say.

You mourned her and the part of your own life that followed her into the earth. This closet filled with paints, charcoals, pa-per, linseed oils, half-drawings, paintings of her, untouched all these years. With her death you closed that door for good, never stretching a canvas again, never picking up a brush.

"She held very still," he said. "She was a wonderful model. She never moved."

It was in this studio of this apartment, forty years ago that you would break for absinthe or sherry with my mother, first your lover, then your wife, never taking your eyes off her as she refilled the glasses and stretched her back. "She was always very still.

"How I cried for her abbreviated life!"

You must have loved her very much, Max. Was it hard for you, her terrible sadness? Did you try to put it on canvas, put it at arm's length, where it was manageable?

One wonders continually how to send an atheist like you to heaven.

It is most inconvenient of him to resist my best efforts.

For all I know he will never rise from this place.

It may seem ridiculous, but I go up to the roof, star map in hand, and look to the heavens. On a clear night it is still possible to see a constellation, a falling star, a lunar eclipse from West Eleventh Street.

"One gives up with a model like her. She was too perfect. She was a painting by Matisse. It was so hard to see her otherwise."

Max, it is time for wild leeks in West Virginia. Mustard seed in the Napa Valley. Sorrel in New York. You taught me all this. It's time for fiddleheads, those tender shoots of the ostrich fern in Western Massachusetts.

I think of death breaking like a star in your head.

I am going to write now, because I am a writer. I have already written one novel, published when I was twenty. I have seen it turned into a movie, have won several prestigious awards. I have just returned from an artist colony at the edge of the Berkshires. I went for a month, but I stayed for a year. I tried to write poetry. Had I not seen his death in the form of the rising sun everywhere, I might have stayed forever.

"Because it is too early for peach picking in Western Georgia, the boys who are missing cannot be considered safe. Twelve already murdered in Atlanta."

Do you denounce Satan?

Yes.

And all his teachings?

Yes.

For all I know you will never ascend into heaven.

I am going to write now. It is a way of telling the truth. Or nearing the truth.

The absolute truth? The literal truth?

Well, yes. Well, no. But something of the whole. Something of what it means to be alive.

I think of the family of father and mother, of two daughters, Candace and Alison, just a word picture for now.

Writing too can keep the world at a distance. One uses "one" instead of "I." One does not look long enough, or one becomes frightened, fainthearted. One turns flesh too often into words on a page. Turns Ethiopia into a gem on the tongue. The temptation is to make it beautiful or perfect or have it make sense. The temptation is to control things, to make something to help ease the difficulty. One checks oneself as often as possible, but death still whispers in my father's ear in the form of a beautiful woman just about my age.

But death is not a beautiful woman.

One wants not to have to struggle so much.

For all I know he will never ascend into heaven.

Writing helps, if you are intent on the truth.

She was a painting by Matisse, but she took sleeping pills.

The Truth Is, Max

After tearing the first page from the first book it becomes infinitely easier to tear the next one and then the next one. Now that I am in charge of the disposition of the estate, I have a certain right, an obligation even, to make use of it, especially the impressive art history library. After all I am the only one here, David in Italy and Grey still in Greece.

3

Maggie

My sabbatical starts today, sitting on a pale blue blanket watching these figures gather before me. Notice how the space continually changes as one by one they enter the plane. Someone has rendered each detail with such exactness and precision, the curl on the young girl's brow, the neck of the man, the gentians at their feet.

The question in my mind persists. It remains as each one comes closer now. Two figures first. What is the unifying motive here? A girl and a man, moving as they are in a landscape of light? How to compose in pyramidal form a girl, a man, and if I include myself, a woman, intimately linked? The issue is complicated by the rock formations, the forest, the meadow, the house. But how I love these questions! Such are my notions of happiness.

Note the graceful lines of the young girl's body, the folds in her flowing shirt. But the solution cannot be a purely intellectual one—there are other factors. See the tenderness, the eloquence of the gesture between father and daughter, the father tentatively extending his arm, the daughter moving toward him. Now comes a flare of light, almost fire light from the upper quadrant and here is the second girl. Older, a young woman. The man and the young woman embrace, then fall away from each other. Observe the half-smile of the man as he looks toward the viewer. It is at once tender and sad, a little mysterious as if he knows in advance all that is before him. The older daughter in some indefinable way brings movement and vivacity to the scene, but still the man's look remains unchanged. In contrast to the young woman's, his expression is a sadder, deeper, a more profound expression than it would carry alone. As the older girl moves off, the pyramid becomes rather wide at the base, wider than deep, and the man is not fully knit into the group and this is an added tension. His form becomes a little vague; he seems to be disappearing into the background even as he moves toward the pyramid's apex.

To watch these shifting forms fall into order and balance—there is no greater joy than this. Light and dark mingle more freely now with the source of light lowering. To steady the chaos, the quickness with this vision. To stabilize the scene. It is the youngest now who moves. There is such gentleness in her face as she comes nearer and extends her arms, one arm toward the viewer, one toward the wayward man, rescuing him from obscurity, and forcing the viewer to participate. She is the unifying element, standing at the base now, one arm in either direction. The resolution lies somewhere in her wide shoulders, which are immense, much larger than the shoulders of a girl her age could physically, realistically be. And yet it does work. Note the beautiful, soft upturned arm, the skin at the wrist, the delicate fingers as they reach, reach for something.

Yes. But what disturbs? A touch. Sound returns, drowning my thoughts.

"Mom," the balancing figure says, her arms still outstretched. She comes closer, bends down. She is holding a swirl of green.

"Yes, my love?"

"Look," she says, tickling me. "Oh look, lady ferns!" she smiles.

4

Alison

Mom and I were talking about lady ferns when Dad came over carrying his tiny tape recorder in one hand and a jug of wine in the other. I was telling her how the lady fern differs from the maidenhair fern and that the fragile fern is bright and green and small and appears in early spring between crevices, often disappearing in summer and reappearing in fall.

"I should have *named* you Fern!" she laughs.

"Well, well," Dad smiles, sitting down next to us. "What a sight: two of my lovelies languishing in the grass." His eyes sort of twinkled when he looked at me, dimmed when he looked at Mom and then brightened again when he looked at me. It had something to do with light and shadow and the angles at which we sat is what Mom would have said, but she didn't seem to notice.

I got up out of the range of his eyes and walked into the forest. "Look!" I shouted, running back to them.

"What is it, Fern?" Mom asked.

"Fiddleheads!"

"Oh my," Dad said. He closed his eyes. To be in the Berkshires in time for fiddleheads.

"We're here in time to watch all the ferns unfurl," my mother sighed. "Henry, this was one of your finest ideas. To simply pick up and leave. To begin the summer a month early."

"I should have thought of it sooner," he whispered in her ear. "Oh my, all these years, Maggie." Dad took her arm. His eyes were glassy like the lake. I cartwheeled away from them. The meadow was filled with wildflowers, meadow grass, humming and chirping. The air was so sweet, particularly after New York. "I bet I can cartwheel without stopping all the way to the edge of the forest," I said. When I got there I plucked more fiddleheads and brought them to my parents who languished, as Dad liked to say, in the tall grass.

He smiled. "Fiddleheads!" he called out like an ice cream man. "Fiddleheads, get your fiddleheads!" he said. "Fiddleheads."

"The Fiddlebricks, I mean the Philbricks, did you hear, they've seen bears this year. A mother and her cub. Just before we got here."

"What kind of bears?" I asked. "I've never seen a bear, I mean, not a bear in the real woods."

"Don't you remember the bear, Ali?"

"Oh, Henry. How could she possibly remember?"

"I never saw a bear. I would have remembered. Really. It's not something I would forget," I said.

Dad stood up. "Stand up for a minute, Ali, would you?" he said. "I want to see how long it's been since the last bear. Let's see how tall you are."

I came up nearly to the middle of his chest. I was pretty tall, and almost thirteen years old. He hugged me. "The last time I saw a bear," he said, "you were curled like a fiddlehead inside your mother. How tall are you now?"

"Almost five feet."

"Nearly five feet ago we saw the bear." He touched my head. "Long brown hair ago. Seven thousand cartwheels ago."

"Tell me about it," I said. "Why haven't I heard about the bear before?"

"I was pregnant with you. We were taking our evening walk around the loop. Candace was with us, she was, oh, about five or six. It was a little misty, very beautiful. Do you remember the

light, Henry?" He nodded. "And your father was humming as
usual and Candace was dancing as usual and then out of nowhere what crosses our path but a bear, a large brown bear!
And it walked right up to your father, and I was behind him
and Candace was wrapped around my leg and it looked right
at him."

"I could feel his bear breath," Dad said. "He was that close.
'Please let us live,' I pleaded with the bear, looking into his eyes.
'Let us live.' And the oddest damned thing happened. He just
turned around and walked into the woods." Dad kissed me.
"What can I say? You've unfurled," he said.

"Five feet ago, seven thousand cartwheels ago, we saw the
bear. Oh, Ali," he said and he squeezed my hand. "Let's eat.
Where's Candace?"

Mom looked up to Candace's window. "I see an orange
shape," she said.

Dad pours the wine. Candace shouts something from her
window and then comes down from her room on the top floor.
Dad raises his glass to her. She runs through the field to us with
an armful of lilacs. She takes long deep breaths.

"Oh, it's simply *too* beautiful here! And lilacs twice in the
same season! Once in New York and once in Massachusetts."

Dad pours her a glass of wine and smiles. She is his firstborn
and he loves her best.

"I'm going to make a costume out of lilacs and pale blue rib-
bons." She holds two lilacs up to her breast. Who would not
love her best?

"I'll dance a rite of spring this year."

Mom opens the picnic basket. Out comes salmon, goat's
cheese, asparagus, pears.

"Right from the asparagus patch," I say.

"I love the purple tips of asparagus," Dad says. "And what
beautiful fish."

"I wish the fish didn't have to come with a face," Candace
says. "It's staring at me! Look, Dad, I swear."

"Eat, Candace, you are so thin."

"Mother," she says. "I am not one of your Renaissance Madonnas. I have fuchsia hair. I have three holes pierced in my ear."

Candace begins to sing a bit of a Talking Heads song as if to convince her, but it's all beyond Mom. Dad sings along.

"Oh, Dad, you haven't used my voice in one of your compositions for years. You could put it through the synthesizer. It doesn't have to sound like me. I don't care, as long as it *is* me."

"The asparagus patch was the first place I went when I got here," I say, eating an asparagus.

"Shh," Dad says. "There's a sound we haven't heard in a while. Listen. The wind blowing through the leaves of the trees."

"Don't you think these first leaves look exactly like stars?" Candace says.

"Yes, I do," I say, wishing I could see more often what Candace sees.

"We'll bring out the telescope later," Mom says. "There're sure to be lots of stars tonight."

"I want to learn the spring sky," I say. "Soon we'll begin to watch for the comet."

Candace dances away, having eaten her few morsels. "Candace," Dad says, "come back." Dad looks sad, like with each step to come Candace will be dancing away from him.

"I'll dance a rite of spring this year," she sings.

"Oh, I almost forgot about the weasel walk," I say. "We're *sure* to see bears if we do the weasel walk!"

"The weasel walk?" Dad asks smiling.

"The weasel walk is a way of stalking, like a weasel, so you can get up close to animals like bears. You crouch down and hold your arms close to your body. Then you start moving slowly, watching all the time. You lift one foot and come down on the foot's outside ball, then you roll to the inside and apply your weight. Then you lift the other foot. Like this."

"I can do the cakewalk," Dad says.

"I can do the foxtrot," Candace smiles.

"What?" I ask tentatively, afraid she'll make fun of me, which is so often her way.

"Dinner was wonderful," Dad says.

We lie on the blankets. "I hear a wood thrush," I say.

"You're right, Ali," Dad says with delight. He takes out his pipe and his small tape recorder, which he carries everywhere. "I've meant to record the birds," he says, "for a piece I'm working on."

"And there's a robin. And another wood thrush."

"You've got a very sophisticated ear, Ali."

Candace sighs. "Nature," she says.

Mom smiles. "Oh, my many-colored-haired daughter."

"Could we have a little quiet," Dad says.

We lie in the grass. Dad lights his pipe. "OK," he says and he begins his tape. We sit and listen to the birds and the wind in the leaves.

It seems as if Dad can see sound, as if it has shapes. He can change bird calls into music.

I lie on my back looking at the clouds. One looks like a fish, one looks like the sad face of a woman and then it turns into some kind of cat.

As the sun goes down it seems hundreds of birds swoop, dive, in the blue- and yellow-flowered grass. "Over there," I point. "Is that a Wilson's warbler or a goldfinch?"

Mom runs her hands through Candace's spiky hair. Their eyes are closed. Dad looks at Mom and Candace, then closes his eyes and listens to the sounds of the world. He turns off the tape and stands up.

"I've forgotten something inside," Dad whispers. "I'll be back, Ali," he says, and he gives me a bear hug.

5

Candace

Dad says I've got lots of time to decide what I want to do. He says I shouldn't rule anything out at this point, but I'm already eighteen. He laughs when I say that, but when *he* was eighteen he had already composed *two* operas! He calls it "that old Mozart thing." An andante and allegro at six. A symphony at eleven. Dead at thirty-five. Sometimes I think I'd be happy to have that life. A brilliant flame in the dark, coming from nowhere and as quickly extinguished. Oh, but to burn, however briefly. To leave something behind. A few poems. To compose something so heartbreakingly beautiful, so unbearably beautiful, or dark, or frightening, or hilarious. To be Rainer Werner Fassbinder. To have a vision. To be Byron, to be Keats, or Sylvia Plath.

You wouldn't want to die young really, a strange voice somewhere inside says.

This summer I'll cut my hair off. This summer I'll be Jeanne d'Arc. I'll write the script, I'll play her life. I'll burn for what I believe.

"I want to know what you know, Vincent van Gogh," I sing out the window. "Marilyn Monroe. Antonin Artaud." Maybe I'll be a singer in a band. I'll call myself Jeanne Dark. Or a composer—imagine really being a composer. "Igor Stravinsky!" I call out the window. Maybe I'd use a Synclavier like Dad and Laurie Anderson. Dad says one composer in a family is enough though, and he's probably right.

How gorgeous they look out there sitting in the grass! How happy I am to be here again with them. To roam in the woods, to walk the loop, to find mushrooms. I think it was last year that Dad put a mushroom brush in Mom's Christmas stocking. And now we're back again with all the animals, the cows and my favorites, the sheep. I remember when I was little telling all my friends in New York that I had seen sheep. They had never seen sheep, so my best friend Steven said, "I know, I'll draw you sheep," and he took out his crayons and drew the most beautiful sheep I'd ever seen, real or not. *"Dessine pour moi un bobcat,"* I asked him next. *"Le chat sauvage."* (Mom was teaching us French that year.) "What do they look like?" Steven asked. There were bobcats, we heard, in the Berkshires, but we had never seen one. They have *les yeux jaunes et beaucoup de fur.* Thick, I told my friend who drew as I spoke.

And now to be back here again! The ferns, the smell of the earth, the smooth beach, the dark trees. How blatantly sexual everything seems since Pierre, the exchange student last winter. I want to make love all night with the dogs howling, the bobcat's eyes glowing, the rain pounding. Pierre and I could bring the animals right up to the windows with our passion, their fur pressed up against the screen. The moth wings madly beating. The bobcat clawing deep welts in my brain.

"Candace!" Dad shouts.

"I'm coming!" I shout back.

There he is, pouring wine. There she is, composing the scene. And Alison collecting fiddleheads in a basket. How I love them. How good they are. They endure endless hours of me talking about the future. They keep me near and at the same time bid me farewell. That is what real love is.

I will go to France, meet Pierre, call myself Colette. I will go to England and be Pru. I will go to Italy and a dark man will purr "Francesca" in my ear. I will paint. I will dance. In America my stage name could be Candace California or maybe Candace Indiana. Yes, Candace Indiana! I practice my signature all the time.

If I were in New York now I might be at the Pyramid Club or at the Cat Club. I might be at the Palladium. I could build the model city, I bet.

I change out of my bathing suit and dance naked in my princess room. That's what Dad calls it. My only adornment a fluorescent Eiffel Tower dangling from my ear. Maybe I could design clothes. I wish I was a little taller, a little more angular, I think, looking in the mirror.

"Come down," they call.

"A performance artist!" I shout, testing it out on them.

There is so much out the window past my tiny family huddled in the meadow. In the distance sheep dot the field, black and white cows, surely a bobcat. And a wild dog, a wolf perhaps, just beginning to really howl.

Post-Delirium

How strange to be working on a novel again after all this time, Max. I haven't written any fiction since *Delirium* "burst onto the scene" almost ten years ago. A "smashing debut," "filled with promise," "an extraordinary talent," a child of brilliance, yes, genius, yes, etc. Where did that book come from?

Afterwards the agents, the editors, the parties, the job offers. I retreated. No more novels, I decided. Why? Do you want the facile explanation? How often I sound like you, Max: "the facile explanation." Novels seemed just a little too dangerous.

"Anything you do well is going to be dangerous, Caroline."

I tried working for causes for a while. Nuclear disarmament, world hunger. Putting up posters, taking them down. Calling up people, having them hang up. I hated all the chaos, all the disappointment. The broken lives, the fighting. So then I went to film school at NYU where, as you recall, I made one strange little film after another. I don't know, I thought film would be easier somehow. I wanted to make documentaries. I wanted to gather evidence. I wanted to record the truth. What the bums were saying. I rode the subways alone all night, filming. Talk about dangerous, Max! But what I got down—that didn't seem to be the truth either.

Besides, I missed language. I missed words. So I tried poetry, and when I was accepted at an artist colony as a poet, it made me feel like one. Poetry seemed quieter, kinder. *Delirium*, a book of "complicated sexuality and rage." "A ravishing account of a girl's travels in Europe." Too noisy for me.

"To think you could have complete control, Caroline."

Max, there's something to it. All these things I've collected: directions, maps, photographs, all kinds of odd scraps. Max, I've kept everything. Like it might come in handy someday. Maybe it's a way of having a private life, a life of my own. One no one else could possibly get to or decode.

"Yes, very touching, Caroline."

Max, my passion for documentation—

"Please," he says, "not the facile explanation."

open eyes have the stare of dea...
One of Giotto's most poignant figures is that of the Magdalen in the *Noli Me Tangere* (fig. 52). Christ, in his first appearance after resurrection, meets the Magdalen, who reaches out to touch Him. Kneeling and stretching out her arms toward Christ, her entire figure conveys a sense of almost unbearable yearning and emotion (fig. 53). The very idea that she cannot, must not, touch Him is used by Giotto to suggest the idea of not only the transcendent nature of Christ but the very human tragedy of two people at a fateful and final moment, separated by an enormous gulf although they are close enough to touch.
The figures of the Magdale   d Christ in thi

A Few More Things About You

You were at once amused, proud, a little baffled. "This is *mein Kind*," you said, "coming out of Columbia with a bachelor's degree and an entire novel under her arm." I overheard you tell somebody once, "She always liked to make things. Absurd little animals of clay—whole zoos of animals, entire cities in the sand, postage stamp–sized paintings, plays and ballets, stories for children when she herself was a child."

I was determined not to be like Mother, Max.

"Oh, my dear. To think you could do it through sheer will!"

Veronica Speaks

I loved you, but I could not even do the minimum required of a mother—I could not stay alive for you, Caroline. I cried every night as I rocked you to sleep. You must have grown up thinking my sobbing was a song.

A Letter from Henry

Dear Maggie,

I was watching you sitting on the blue blanket in the grass. You looked more lovely than I can remember. Even lovelier than 25 years ago. 25 years! Jesus, where has the time gone? You made it seem like a day—one long, brilliant day. You looked so happy and good and beautiful sitting there that I almost changed my mind for a minute. I looked hard, looked at you and our daughters, radiant in this marvelous place, and still, God forgive me, I loved another woman and made up an excuse to get up and call her.

This may be only temporary, but I don't expect you to forgive me. I'm as shocked as anyone.

I know it's cowardly not to tell you to your face, but the last image I wanted was you with your head raised looking up at the night sky.

I can't say I'll ever be back. My only virtue in this whole matter is that I have summoned up the small courage to be truthful with you and myself.

I will write you from West 4th near Washington Square, where I will be staying until I find a place. The West 11th Street apartment is yours of course. And the summer house.

Love always,
Henry

Sky Watch | This week at 10 P.M.

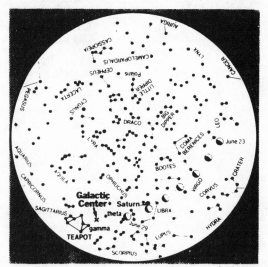

As the Moon enters our map this week, we can look ahead to the Teapot, an asterism just east of the tail of the scorpion. These are actually some of the stars of the zodiacal constellation Sagittarius, the archer. On the galactic equator about half way from the archer's gamma to the theta of Ophiuchus is a place that has figured in astronomy news in recent weeks. Nothing particularly interesting strikes our eye, but here lies the center of our galaxy, 30,000 light years away. Astronomers using radio waves to penetrate interstellar haze and dust detected a hot spot in this place and named it Sagittarius A, which has been studied intensely. Recently two teams found evidence that the galactic center may be a black hole containing as much matter as a million Suns. Other galaxies seem to have them, why not ours?

To use the map, hold it vertically before you, with the direction you are facing positioned at the bottom. The outer circle represents the horizon; the zenith, the spot directly overhead, is near the center of the map. The map is accurate for 10:40 tonight, by Saturday it will be accurate for 10 P.M.

By Franklyn Astronomer Emeritus, The Hayden Planetarium — The New York Times. June 23, 198_

Summer

Things That Are Gone

I am back in your city of fire-eaters, jugglers, magicians, fortune-tellers, three-card montes. I don't know how you've stood it all these summers since the country—unicyclists, parrots—twenty or so years now, in this madness that descends on Greenwich Village each year, soon as the weather turns.

Oh, I know there was an occasional fling that took you to Montauk or Cape Cod, but it was the exception, just somewhere you found yourself, not something you sought out. I see you puzzled mostly, sitting on a wooden deck high above the sea with a lobster in front of you, and some beautiful woman at your side insisting you wear the lobster bib. She directing your attention to something she found terribly moving: a sunset probably. And you so out of your element.

Your element: a trip around the corner on a Saturday night for the Sunday *Times*. A stroll to Dean & DeLuca's. But this city in summer, Max! It's preposterous! It's always shocking, I don't care how long you've been here. The great assault. I walk the same ten blocks—territorial like you—it's a small town, but a town where absolutely anything can happen.

I walk to the butcher, the baker, the candlestick maker. I remember them all, of course, and they me. All still here. The pet-store owners, the dog walkers, the dogs. Dogs are bad enough, but in the summer, in this city!

"Is that a seeing-eye dog or is that a normal dog?" the deli man asks. "Because we don't allow normal dogs in here."

"It's a seeing-eye dog."

I am back on your lunatic fringe. Two people hand me a

small pink card. They want to be my friend. They are trying to talk to me. I hand them a quarter.

So why do I stay? To put things in order, is that it? I could sublet the place and think about it some other time, but something keeps me here—I've been away too long. Deep in the middle of nowhere. This is as good a place as any to write a book, if it's a book I'm writing. It's kind of nice to think of writing prose after all this time, *Delirium* finally out of my system, I think. Besides, there are movies here. And fire-eaters.

Summers at Cummington were another story, Max. It's amazing how much you can change in just one year. I became a nature lover! In love with the birds, the plants, the earth. Out my window all that green, and a tractor in the middle of it. Out my farmhouse window my view was of Leon and Olive Thayer, farmers aged eighty-seven and eighty-five. A few sheep. That's it. I finally understood the Williams poem you liked to recite. The one we always laughed at.

so much depends
upon

a red wheel
barrow

glazed with rain
water

beside the white
chickens.

Max, remember that?

But what to do with this bombardment of images and sounds? Ice cream vendors, torch-song singers, neon, the insane, roses for sale on every corner, evangelists, drug dealers, creeps of every kind, incense sellers, caricaturists, dog walkers.

A dog named Artemis. A dog named Cindy. Here, Cindy! A black dog named Gustave.

Everything changing.

The candlestick maker told me that his partner, the other

candlestick maker, is in the hospital with AIDS. Acquired immune deficiency syndrome. "It's primarily a gay disease now. You get it," he said, "through the exchange of bodily fluids. Five thousand have already died, and no one has survived." Where have I been, I wonder? He puts my two white candles into a bag and a free votive candle. He asks me to say a prayer for the candlestick maker.

Some things are still here.

Things that are still here:
The Minetta Tavern
The Corner Bistro
The Lion's Head
The Figaro
Aphrodisia
Beasty Feast

Some things are new.

Things that are new:
Caffe Passione!
Akitas of Distinction
Cafe Cremolata
The Little Mushroom Cafe
The K train

The disciples of the Reverend Sun Myung Moon are still here chanting, "Roses, roses," vacant-eyed as ever.

"Dove Bars!" a shy ice cream vendor sings. When you look at him he stops. Then you hear him again. "Dove Bars, Dove Bars," he sings sweetly. Dove Bars are new.

"Hey, I know how to grow these!" I shout, pointing at the lettuce at the Korean grocer's. I am becoming a part of this city again. Its loudness.

It is loud. A radio goes by. "I'm not lost but I don't know where I am," David Byrne sings, "I got a question."

"Please help me."

"I am recently widowed."

"I have no food."

"I am unemployed."

"I am a blind man."

"I need a quarter for the subway."

"I need a dollar, sweetheart. God bless you."

After a year I've forgotten all the ways people beg for money. You forget their different speeches. They're everywhere, Max. There seem to be more than ever. Thank you. God bless you. Such good manners!

"I am a Vietnam vet."

"My dog needs an eye operation."

I hope I don't dole out money based on the literary merit of each story. I hope I've got better standards than that. How, though, to decide on the neediest? Is it the one-legged? Is it the woman with three children in tow? Or the man who mutters to himself in classical craziness: "My brother, the emperor Caesar and I have determined you to be an enemy of the crown and to be executed. Will someone please do something"?

What is a fifty-cent story then? A seventy-five-cent one? Who is the most convincing? The man who mutters? The guy who made a collage picturing his family, the charred house, the record of all he's lost? Or the man who says, "Come on, give a dollar to a no-good motherfucker"?

Bruce in an armchair is parked outside Bloom's Shoes for the summer, bums being territorial like everyone else. Buy him a beer and he will remember any kindness he can. A man on the street once who gave him a twenty-dollar bill, the day his father took him to a baseball game.

A man, the same man every day, feeds the pigeons in Father Demo Square. A modern-day Saint Francis. Picture Giotto.

If you wait it out, the brute heat will clear just about everyone off the streets, I think I remember you saying. All the tourists, all the dogs, everything. But not the homeless, Max. Why were they always invisible to you? And so many more of them in the years since Reagan.

There are lots of things to see on the street. You can see famous people if you're sharp. I'm not too good at this. A few times I saw Wendy O. Williams from the Plasmatics in Balducci's, but who could miss her with her blonde mohawk haircut? And there are always those kind-looking Mafia bosses who touch the melons so tenderly. Also the neighborhood regulars. Grace Paley. Donald Barthelme. Brooke Adams. This one. That one. Stanley Kunitz.

Lots of your old lovers, Max.

Some people wish I were famous. "Hey, didn't you write *Delirium*?" "Hey, weren't you in that Amos Poe movie?" "Aren't you Madonna!?"

Well, it's good to be back, in a way. Back to the streets where I'm recognized. Back to civilization.

To mistake me for Madonna. A singer, Max. Yes, it's her real name. She's Italian.

"To mistake a German French-Canadian American for Madonna."

People are desperate to connect. "Weren't you in that Amos Poe film?" "I could swear I met you at the Cat Club." "The Lion's Head." "The White Horse Tavern." So many animals, Max. "Didn't I see you at Arnold's Turtle?" "Elephant and Castle?"

"Well, yes, maybe Elephant and Castle, it's very near the apartment."

Someone hands me a pink card.

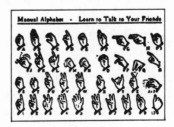

I am trying to talk to you.

Let's start over. You liked *Delirium* a lot. I would even say you were proud of it in your way. You defended it, even after your students started asking you if you were the father in the book, the stuffy professor of archeology she goes to visit that wild summer in Greece. To mistake Max Chrysler, distinguished professor of art history, for Arthur Simpson, harsh, a little hateful, the remote archeologist, digging for parts of the world that got lost.

Artistic license, you told them. "It's called taking liberties." A pause. "Fiction," you said, "have you heard of it?" "Are you calling your daughter an artist, then?" the NYU faculty asked you. "Yes, I am," you said. And when I went on the Johnny Carson show, you, for the first time in your life, rented a television.

I'm really back, Max. You were there for me, but where was I when you cried out in the night against the jugglers? I did not get to you in time. I pass the Film Forum. The Vandam Theater is now called the Thalia Downtown. Remember? It's where we sat all weekend, eight hours Saturday, eight hours Sunday, to watch Fassbinder's *Berlin Alexanderplatz*. "Yes," you whispered to me. "A masterpiece. Undeniably. A work of art," you said with reverence.

I was out of film school by then. I had realized that making films was dangerous too. "Anything you do with your heart is dangerous," you said. "It comes with the territory."

My ambitions were not great, though. I liked best talking the language of film with you: f-stop, room tone, Nagra, wild sound.

How many New York Film Festivals did we go to together? Twenty-three? All of them except last year's, because I was away at Cummington. I was only four hours away. Why didn't I come?

How we loved looking up at where the director and actors sat. When I was a little girl, I dreamt of sitting up there. Maybe that's why I went to film school, so that someday we might sit up in the director's box together. I should have come last year.

I never learned to read the signs right. Or rather I never learned to read the signs fast enough.

All of New England cracking open like a sunburst. Yes, even last summer and fall.

I see that the Antonocci apartment, the site of my first love affair with Anthony Antonocci on Carmine Street, is now the Caffe Passione! (Exclamation point theirs.)

Categorizing helps. Putting things in columns helps.

Hand the bum on Eighth Street a quarter. He'll say: "Thank you for keeping me employed another day. It is the only job I will never be fired from."

Many things have changed in the year I've been away. Many things are new. Fashions, I notice, have changed. At Cummington fashion stood still, along with almost everything else, except the seasons and, hopefully, art.

Can you hear me, Max? Shall I speak louder?

Lists help. Columns. Especially when keeping track of things that are gone.

Some things thought to be gone have only moved.

And then, of course, there are the things that are lost. Lots of things are lost. Torn from a lamppost on Seventh Avenue:

LOST PARROT

TYPE: RED SPECTACLED AMAZON
NAME: GARIBALDI
AGE: 5 YEARS
COLOR: MOSTLY GREEN
LANGUAGES: NONE
WHEN: MONDAY 22, 1985 3.30 PM
WHERE: PRINCE ST./THOMPSON
MARKINGS: SILVER BRACELET ON LEFT PAW

CONSPICUOUS REWARD FOR
INFO LEADING TO HIS WHERE:
ABOUTS . 555-6090 or "LA LUNA"

"Taxi," someone shrieks. Sirens. A symphony of sounds. A fire truck goes by. "I saw the figure five in gold," you used to say dreamily whenever a fire truck passed. A mutter. A sigh. "Roses, roses." Dogs wheezing on their leashes. Rap music. Imagine hearing all the interior monologues going on in all those people's heads in the street.

"No."

Imagine. Each of these people has a name, most have addresses. What if they all said them out loud in unison? The cacophony.

"Please, Caroline, it's bad enough out here already."

Another fire engine. An ambulance. A police car. A fire engine. I think of the Williams poem he loved.

Among the rain
and lights

I saw the figure 5
in gold
on a red
firetruck

A siren. A St. Vincent's Hospital ambulance.

I pass a newsstand. I haven't seen a magazine in ages. This bright one calls to me. On a field of red, black letters say AIDS and there's a small picture of a gaunt Rock Hudson. I am here in your city of AIDS. At Cummington I kept dying at bay for an entire year. At arm's length, until you, Max. And now suddenly here in the West Village people are dying everywhere around me. I look from one person to the next.

I pass the new cafes. The invariable parrot on the shoulder of some modern-day pirate. The poseurs, with notebooks, looking up with cigarettes. The earnest aspiring actresses with their thimblefuls of talent.

Note on the Bird Jungle door: Meg who found bird, we located owner, PLEASE CALL!

Today I saw a conventioneer of some sort lost on the subway, Max.

"How did you know he was from a convention, my dear?"

Blue jacket, checked pants, white patent leather shoes, straw hat, name tag.

"Yes, I see now."

"Where are you going, little conventioneer?" I asked him.

"I'm lost," he said. He was hot and tired. "I can't remember what convention I'm supposed to be at."

"Doesn't it say on your tag?"

He looked down. "No."

"My suggestion is to get on an E train and ride it somewhere and then ride it back again. It's cool in there and it will come to you—where it was you meant to go."

"Yes, thank you."

"An E or an F train."

The E finally arrived and he stepped into the swimming-pool coolness of the train and waved.

"What a sad story. A conventioneer with no convention," Max says.

He wasn't waving at me.

"Ah, it gets sadder."

He was waving at someone else, his wife perhaps, in a straw hat, too, and a convention tag. Or maybe he was waving to his friends, somewhere in this city right now, the other tile or air conditioner salesmen, or whatever. He's waving, Max. He's lost.

Max shrugs his shoulders. "You've always got another one of these stories, Caroline—every day."

"Please help me."

"I am recently widowed."

"I have no food."

"My dog needs an eye operation."

"I am a Vietnam vet."

"I am the Emperor Caesar."

"I am unemployed."

"Hello, the man before you is stone deaf," says the tape slung around the man's shoulder. "He is legally blind. Won't you help him?"

"Dove Bars," the sweet call of the season. "Roses, roses," this summer's call. Sirens.

"Is that a seeing-eye dog or is that a real dog? Because we don't let real dogs in here," the store owner says. "It's a seeing-eye dog," the man responds.

I pass the mailboxes in the foyer. Whittiker, Davis, Pelligrino. I have never met Whittiker, Davis, or Pelligrino, I am quite sure. The place does not seem that familiar. The names don't ring a bell.

Categorizing helps.

Things that are new:
Whittiker, Davis, Pelligrino
The Milk Bar
The Banana Republic
Hallo Berlin

Things that have multiplied:
Patisserie Lanciani
Vinyl Mania
Elephant and Castle
The Magic Carpet

Things that have moved:
The Pink Teacup
Three Lives Bookstore
Formerly Joe's
One of the candlestick makers
Reminiscence

Categorizing helps. Especially when thinking of things that are gone.

Things that are gone:
The Unicorn Store
Feu-Follet
The Middle of Silence Gallery
The wing of St. Vincent's where my mother died
The entire Antonocci family

You

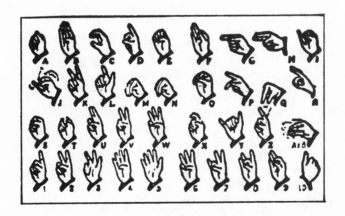

Jesus and the Star

"Look at this painting he's done of me. It's fascinating, don't you think?" Jesus says. "Look at that strange star. I do seem to remember an amazing light shone on my infant face."

"It looks like the comet," Alison says. "My mother and I are hoping to see it this year."

He runs his hand across the Arena Chapel wall. "Here I am just after I was born. Do you think I really looked like that?"

"Isn't she beautiful?" he says, gazing off.

"Why is she so sad?"

"I will die in an oven in Auschwitz. I will be humiliated and killed in Soweto. I will suffer with a young woman who swallows pill after pill, seeing no way out."

What are you talking about? Alison thinks.

"I will die a horrendous death over and over and over again in a plague in the late twentieth century."

"It's unbearable to think," Alison says.

"Such a strange star breaking over my head."

He runs his hand over the chapel wall. "Look at my mother in a mantle of blue. And Joseph—"

"Whatever happened to him?"

Jesus shakes his head. "I don't know," he says. "He just left. I miss him."

He presses his face next to the face of Joseph that Giotto has painted. "He was very kind," Jesus says. "He taught me how to build a house for the birds."

"That's nice," Alison says.

"Such a strange star this is, breaking over my head."

More Green, Less Blue

I pass by the mailboxes quickly: Whittiker, Davis, Pelligrino, and enter the coolness of the house. I put on the "Transcendental Etudes" and close the shutters, shutting out the fire-eaters, the dancing bears, the tattooed ladies—the street festivals on every corner.

I go into your library where it is dark and quiet.

I understand a little. How hard it was to leave these books, their beautiful bindings, their cool, soothing appraisals of painting, sculpture, architecture.

It was a way to love too. It was the way, I see now, you loved us, a bit removed—but it was love nonetheless.

Where did your days of painting go? The days when all you wanted to do was paint her? Before our births? Your palette of bright colors, she sitting, standing, lying for hours. Oh yes, there was something dangerous here too, you detected it instantly, but you were young and she with her almond-shaped eyes, her chestnut hair, was happy to do the thing she did best: to be still and allow you into her life in one of the few ways still possible.

She called you an artist and she loved the idea of living with an artist, though you were no artist, you told her, merely a dreaming student. She loved being a bohemian in the Village with you. "She would dance, Caroline, with dangling earrings sometimes. She could be red and yellow and green some days. She was capable of that for a few hours before she fell away again, back into gray. She was a painting by Matisse, a painting, or one of those achingly beautiful line drawings. After a while I could not see her any other way. Lying on the striped divan. Her pantaloons. Her breasts. But I didn't have the ability to approximate her beauty—the talent, I believe we call it."

Was it really that, Max, or was it too frightening to go to the place she was, where, as you know, sooner or later the artist must go?

"I wanted so badly to get her right. To get at the truth of her, the place where likeness turns into intimate recognition. But she was out of my league."

Or did you want to turn her into paint and canvas? Put her out there where she was manageable?

"I did my best, Caroline."

I don't doubt that, Max, that you loved her, that you did what you could.

She was a painting by Matisse, but she took sleeping pills.

"She was way out of my league, Caroline."

I put on the "Five Sarcasms" by Prokofiev. I go into the kitchen, open the cabinets, eye all the gourmet foods. There are green peppercorns, pink peppercorns, star anise, Greek oregano, herbes de Provence, Spanish saffron. There are four kinds of mustard, plum chutney, tomato chutney, champagne vinegar, balsamic vinegar, tarragon vinegar. Rice wine, sesame oil, walnut oil. Little bags of morels, chanterelles, Trompettes de la Mort. Pignolis, hazelnuts, currants, dried apricots. Irish oatmeal, couscous, blue corn meal, biscotti di vino, olivada, pizzocheri, toasted seaweed sheets, sea salt, a tiny tin of Russian Beluga. What I realize is that I knew him. I am finding no secrets. Nothing I don't already know. Nothing shocks here. I knew him and I loved him for what he was. Little nests of pasta everywhere.

Actually, there are a few surprises. For instance, he always hated to eat Mexican food out in New York and yet here in the apartment are two books of matches from Carramba! (Exclamation point theirs.) Did he take his last lover to Carramba!?— the one I see on the street a lot, walking her dog, each time she sees me, bursting, yes, bursting into tears. I don't want him dead either. He probably didn't even love you. Then again, did he take you to Carramba!? Maybe he loved you. No.

This one who keeps crying, Max. I have trouble keeping up with her. One day she has sort of reddish hair, then another day it's brownish and poufy, then the next day honey blonde with a permanent. Did she want that blonde, wide-eyed, ringletted, innocent look, even at thirty, that phoney-baloney, burrito eater, margarita drinker?

A woman at thirty is allowed to act like a child if she can find someone twice her age. But thirty is grown, or as grown as we ever get.

Max, I never knew you to eat Mexican food out.

Forgive this anger coming out of nowhere—in a book of matches, in a change of hair. The day I got here, there was a glass bowl on the floor in the kitchen. The only thing I can think is her dog must have been thirsty.

"Poor thing's parched, is it?" you must have said in your sarcastic way, shaking your head and looking for some old bowl. When I came in that day, there it was on the kitchen floor, a small glass bowl, half filled with water. It was only then that I finally cried.

I never said I wasn't angry.

I'm not really sure why I'm staying here, where you are everywhere. I could stay at the Vermeer Hotel or the Rembrandt, be moved by Van Gogh Movers. I could stay at the Hotel Chelsea, or how about the Algonquin? Do I really want to dig up your life like a dog at a bone? Found: more paints, and still more canvases in a third closet. Found: a childhood Bible of my mother's inscribed "This Bible belongs to Veronica Le Bourveau, given to her by her parents on the occasion of her confirmation." Written in French.

Who told her not to move?

Found: lots of mail of mine you never forwarded, tossed on the bottom shelf of your night table.

From the liquor cabinet, I take out my port. You told me you put down a case of port for each of us at our births, to be drunk after our twenty-first birthdays. "We had no money. I mean really no money, me disinherited for trying to paint, your mother with nothing really. But we made it a point about the port. We both agreed, *they shall not live unlovely lives.* There is so much that is crass, brutish, ugly. We shall show them what pleasure is. What beauty is. One does not need endless amounts of money for such things. This is a good life. This has been a good life, despite everything."

Why all these conversations going on in my head now, Max? What is the point of all this?

"Are you complaining?"

Yes. No.

This port is delicious, Max. Thank you for thinking of the three of us. A letter from David reports on his restoration work on *The Last Supper*, he and his Italian wife standing up there all day on a scaffold. Grey's in Greece on a dig. I'm not sure how he's doing. David hasn't heard from him lately either.

"Keep track of him, Caroline."

I'll try.

What the red magazine with the dying Rock Hudson on the cover says that I've been putting off reading since I got in the house is that he had something called acquired immune deficiency syndrome (AIDS), lymphadenopathy-associated virus (LAV), human T-cell lymphotropic virus-III (HTLV-III). It seems the virus specifically attacks the T-4 lymphocytes, a subgroup of white blood cells. Origins: Unknown. The Green Monkey of Africa? Maybe. Prognosis: Grave. Up through July 1985, some 12,067 cases recorded in the United States. Six thousand already dead. No one has ever been known to recover.

Rock Hudson went to France to receive HPA-23. I've had no TV for a year. Hardly any newspapers. This is ridiculous. I'm going to call the TV rental place. Why didn't you ever write to me about this, Max? The whole neighborhood dying. Didn't you notice?

"Yes, but why didn't you ever open a paper, my cherub, or turn on the radio?"

Night descends. I put on *Eine Kleine Nachtmusik*. I open the shutters slightly. The light looks like the long thin bones of my neighbors, falling across the street.

I open the closet door again. The drawings are lovely, Max. The arm of the woman raised, then the arm down, no hat, then a fringed hat, a man in the background, then the man forward holding the woman's hand. The man alone. The woman erased. Where did she go? The woman back with a new face, serene, lying on a striped divan. Then the woman with two faces. Then everything darker. Then everything obliterated. Then here, July 9th, you begin again: The woman, her arm raised, her arm down. The woman smiling.

How pretty she is there on the window seat. In a light blue dress with a tie. Dark, dark hair waving to her shoulders. Not unhappy, not so remote. Max, did you try to paint her into a life?

Another painting. In this one her half-motion is stopped. Her figure has turned sculptural, gained weightiness, become immovable. Her face grays, the expression slackens. What to do? What to do? "More red!" I imagine you cried, looking at her. "More green, less blue."

What the Light Looked Like

There were many things I wanted to tell you. Nothing pressing, but still things I wanted you to know. There are lots of Cummington stories—how I got up at dawn to stalk elusive birds, worked in the garden, learned the names of all the flowers and trees. Yes, this is your same high-heeled daughter talking, the one afraid of spiders, the same one who long ago took a walk in a field of buttercups (this is your story, Max) and said they looked like a thousand tiny taxicabs. Oh my God, you said. What have I done? This was one of our big stories, the ones every family has, one of those stories that stick.

It was on that same day too that I remember hearing for the first time of "What the light looked like." It came from your love of seeing, your love of simile and metaphor. Your love of me, too, I'd like to think. It was just the two of us then, the boys already up the Hudson at boarding school. Mom gone, just you and me, delirious with grief.

"Let's play a game," you said as we drove home one Sunday from the boys' school. "Look over there. What do you think the light looks like?" I shrugged. "To me," you said, "the light looks like twin elephants. See," you pointed, "there are their trunks, their bodies, their tails. Foreheads together." "But, Daddy," I think I said, "that's what the highway looks like." "No," you said, "it's the light falling on the highway that makes it look that way. On another day in a different light you would see no elephants." I thought I understood. You were always my best teacher, Max. It was a way to try to learn to see.

We played what the light looked like for many years. We played it for the rest of your life. It kept us near when we were far apart, kept us looking. We decided to keep notebooks of what the light looked like on certain dates and in certain places. It was a lovely notion, Max—that sometime in the future on a particular date and time and place, if the conditions were right, I could look out and just perhaps see something of what you saw.

The Robe of Christ

I realize, Max, that one must imagine the robe of Christ in order to touch it.

"Why would you want to touch it?"

A woman who suffered from a plague thought if she could but touch his garments she would be made whole.

"I see."

It's purple. It's velvet. It's got ermine on the collar.

"Ermine, really?"

Well, what do you think?

"I hope it's a hospital-green bathrobe. And that his crown is a sort of shower cap. What the surgeons wear."

Don't be funny, Max. There are roses—don't you see them?—blood red arranged around his head.

Jesus begins to shake his head. "No. Don't be absurd. There are no roses around my head," he says. "Make the roses disappear. See better."

Your robe is made of linen. It's off-white, there's a rope for a belt— No, the robe is brown and woven. It's a sort of caftan— there's a hood, protection, I hope, from the sun, from foul weather. It feels like burlap. Does it scratch? When he moves it makes a sound. It sounds like peaceful sleep, mysterious and even. It's got a lot of folds in it. It must be dark in there. It's filled with pockets. It smells a little like sheep.

I put my hand out to touch its border. It's softer than I thought. It feels a little like felt. Sheep could sleep there. It's got a sweet smell. The hem just brushes the ground.

Jesus smiles. "Your faith has made you whole."

A Shepherd Drawing Sheep

Another story from back then. It was right after Mother died.
You sat down on the edge of my bed.

"A long time ago, a shepherd boy was sitting in a field with
his sheep," you said. "It was such a lovely day and the sheep
were so beautiful that he decided to draw them. But he didn't
have a pencil and paper, so he drew them on a boulder with a
stone."

"Is it because he loved his sheep?"

"Yes, indeed."

"And so that he could keep them? So they would not go
away?"

"Yes, my cherub."

And you said, Max, that into the field where the young boy
was drawing walked a man, a painter named Cimabue, who
saw that the boy was drawing sheep like angels and he took
the boy and he taught him all that he knew. That boy drawing
sheep in the field was Giotto. He would become one of the
greatest painters ever to live.

Candace Goes to New York

"I loved him more than the rest of you did," she said, sobbing
now. And for whatever reason, whether because the words
sounded so absurd or because no one felt like arguing, or simply because they were the truth, no one said anything at the bus
station, not Maggie, not Alison. They didn't try to talk her out of
leaving. They watched their lilac dancer, their lover of life, their
passion flower, pass unexpectedly on that warm morning from
adolescent to adult, right before their eyes.

She was full-grown in an instant. They saw a carefree, a
reckless life even, suddenly directed by rage.

"How thoughtful of him to wait for you to go on sabbatical," she sputtered, looking at her mother. "How convenient."

"He's ruined our lives only if you allow him," Maggie whispered.

"I won't make it easy for him. I suppose he's expecting it to be easy. Well, he's in for a real surprise. And if you think I'm going to NYU now, where he'll be, you're crazy!"

Still they said nothing. They just let her rant, her sentences interrupted by cries.

She choked. "Coward," she said. "He snuck out behind our backs. I'm not going to make it easy for him. He didn't even say as much as good-bye."

Alison remembered how his eyes dimmed. And how he had hugged her just before going into the house. It was not a good-bye exactly, she thought. No. It was not exactly a good-bye. She felt suddenly breathless. Not angry but sad. That he had not exactly said good-bye. She bowed her head for a moment and looked up to see Candace boarding the bus. Finally she spoke.

"Candace," she said.

"Don't call me that! It was his mother's name." She scowled, forsaking the woman she had cared for so deeply, and she fell into her younger sister's arms and cried.

On the bus from Northampton to New York, Candace decided to keep her name, become rational, a detective, a spy, destroying her father's life as he had destroyed hers. Her goal was set. The future was no longer nebulous. She was not seduced by the headiness of the season, the cows in every pasture, the smell of hay and rain and lilacs. They had come early this year, she thought, and she began to cry again. Where would she be this Father's Day? she wondered. This Bastille Day? On West Eleventh Street, she thought, in the family apartment. And where would he be?

She would find him. And when she found him . . .

She took out an empty notebook. She wrote Strategies on the first page.

Candace Calls Alison

"He's got this tiny studio on Carmine Street on the ground floor. Gates on both windows—depressing. There's just a mattress on the floor. I don't know where all his stuff is. Maybe in the closet? But picture it: Dad in this little room. I don't even know where his music is. There's just a mattress on the floor and— this is the weirdest thing of all—next to the mattress there's a little glass bowl, half filled with water. Just Dad, a mattress and a fucking bowl of water."

———————

"Her name is Belinda Hansen, but, get this, her nickname is Biddy. Probably from when she was a child. Too cute even then, huh? But somehow it stuck because along with Iddy it exactly describes the size of her brain."

———————

"You can follow her career through the class notes of her college's alumni magazine. She went to Wheaton, class of '77. How did I find out? I've got a murderer's eye for detail."

———————

"She's an actress who never acts. She goes to a lot of classes though. Changes hairstyles a lot. Sits in cafes. "Those who have talent are obligated to pursue it, and those who do not have it are obligated not to!" (Max, stay out of this.)

———————

"I looked into her apartment from the fire escape. Clearly, Father is taking a vacation from standards, overlooking everything, including the Billy Joel album on the turntable, the garish display of relatives' photos and photos of the dog, large five-by-fives of the face of the dog. The fish (no face) overcooked and stuck to the bottom of the pot, the floury sauce slightly burned. The answering machine taking messages for toothpaste-commercial auditions, mouthwash commercials, dog food commercials.

"And the sex is pathetic. She's constantly saying, 'Just hold me, honey!'"

"OK, Candace," Alison says.

"It's pathetic. In the middle of the summer Biddy is sleeping in one of those long Victorian gowns with high collars, long sleeves and lace. It's ridiculous."

———————

"She's a vegetarian, and she goes on little vegetarian crusades. She eats granola, yogurt, raw bee pollen, rice cakes. She can tell you stories about calves put into pens where they are not allowed to move their legs, so the meat stays tender."

"Oh my."

Stay out of this, Max.

"She would give up her career to go save stray dogs. I eat everything now, Alison. Veal. Lamb. Every one of her innocents. I eat the cutest bunnies from Ottomanelli's you've ever seen."

———————

"There is something decidedly morbid in using your own dear mother's death to bring tears to your eyes on stage when no tears will come. Her only authentic emotion, I suppose. But would *you* dig up my fingers, Ali, up from the garden, like a dog, tasty as they might be? Nutritious too."

"You're going too far, Candace."

"Would you?"

"Candace."

"Would you dig up my fingers, exhume my body? I don't

know. Something is rotten in the state of Denmark. She's Scandinavian. Swedish, I think."

The dog divides neatly into pieces, like a chicken.

"Why did he have to leave?"

———————

"He's become a cliché. A man who leaves his wife for a younger woman. Another middle-aged man who is afraid to die. A coward."

———————

Jesus and the Beautiful Woman

He hears himself saying, "You smell like jasmine, like myrrh. Honey and mushrooms and nuts." His voice begins to swim. "You are precious, precious," he says. "You glow like the star at my birth."

He's frightened by his own passion—this woman, this dark Jewish woman, appallingly beautiful, musky—her pendulous breasts, her full hips.

She kneels down. She offers to anoint his bare feet.

Jesus weeps.

She offers to wrap him in her hair. To take him somewhere far away . . . Her open body like a boat.

He pricks his finger on something sharp. He starts to bleed.

"I would anoint you with oil," she murmurs. "I would feed you cheese in a leaf." Jesus shudders. "I am wet," she says. "I am wide and deep."

"I'm thirsty," he whispers. "Please."

She presses her finger to her full lips and then to his. He does not pull away.

2. Vermeer: *Woman in Blue Reading a Letter.*
18¼ × 15½ in. Rijksmuseum, Amsterdam

Maggie Asks Alison

"One loves art more than life; it's better than life, don't you think, Ali? It doesn't disappoint so," she sighed. "It's not so frightening," she said, her eyes filled with terror.

1. Overleaf: Vermeer: *Head of a Young Girl.*
18¼ × 15¾ in. Mauritshuis, The Hague

I⊤ ɪꜱ ᴀʟᴡᴀʏꜱ the beauty of this portrait head—its purity, freshness, radiance, sensuality—that is singled out for comment. Vermeer himself, as Gowing notes, provides the metaphor: she is like a pearl.[1] Yet there is a sense in which this response, no matter how inevitable, begs the question of the painting, and evades the claims it makes upon its viewer. For to look at it is to be implicated in a relationship so urgent that to take an instinctive step backward into aesthetic appreciation would seem in this case a defensive measure, an act of betrayal and bad faith. It is *me* at whom she gazes, with real, unguarded human emotions, and with an erotic intensity that demands something just as real and human in return. The relationship may be only with an image, yet it involves all that art is supposed to keep at bay.

Faced with an expression that seems always to have *already* elicited our response, that not only seeks out but appropriates and inhabits our gaze, we can scarcely separate what is visible on the canvas from what happens inside us as we look at it. Indeed, it seems the essence of the image to subvert the distance between seeing and feeling, to deny the whole vocabulary of "objective" and "subjective." And yet few paintings give their viewer such a feeling of being held accountable. If what follows may at times seem arbitrary or impressionistic, I can only say that I have tried to remain open to the painting's address, to keep it continually in view and—a more difficult matter—answer to its look as well.

The Omniscience of Jesus

The lilies trumpet his arrival. The birds sing his praises. He could speak back to them. He could speak in any language ever invented, but he does not drop a single foreign word into his speech.

He could tell us things: to look for the names Bach, Brahms, Mahler, or that the world is not flat. He could tell us in advance what we'll regret. He could show us exactly how a Synclavier will work, but he's not a show-off. He's very modest. Though he will be painted again and again, he does not seem to be posing.

But he's starting to say strange things like "she has lost enough," or "a star explodes in my head," or "the hour is at hand." He doesn't know what to say anymore or leave unsaid.

The Second Page of a Letter Never Sent

Oh, don't think I don't admire you out there
in the goddamned middle of nowhere.

I look out my office window, Caroline, and
it's a veritable three-ring circus and my ten-
dency is to exaggerate this but, Jesus, there really
are roller skaters, fire-eaters, unicyclists,
parrots, snakes, magicians, torch-song singers,
belly dancers. I miss you. A visit would be nice.
I remember you sane. Much saner than this at any
rate.
Love,

Max

Alison Labels the Trees

Summer was here and the trillium and violets had given way to Indian paintbrush, daisies, firecrackers, to raspberries, monarch butterflies, oranges and reds. She missed him. She had thought he loved them. She thought he loved them still. But how to explain it, then? How could he cause such deliberate and terrible pain and still love them? She turned the question over and over in her mind. No answer came. There *was* no answer, she believed now.

"Mom," she had said that day in spring, in an adult voice already, a voice which seemed about to announce some unbear-

able sorrow, though not shocking or surprising—quietly, some
inevitable sadness. She spoke calmly, because somewhere it had
already been accepted. "Mom," she had said, looking at her
mother who held the letter in her hand, reading it again and
again, folding and unfolding it.

"What is it, Alison?" her mother had asked.

"It's Daddy."

"Daddy?"

"It's Daddy, isn't it?"

"Daddy."

"He's gone away, hasn't he?"

She walked to her mother's side now. "It's a beautiful drawing," she said.

"Poussin," Maggie smiled. "It's a real beauty. How lucky to
be able to copy something as lovely as this into a notebook. To
copy his genius. To feel his hand guiding mine. Such balance
and grace. Such proportion, harmony."

She wanted to ask her mother what she thought, did he love
them at all anymore, and if he did how could he have done such
a thing? But she did not dare ask her. Even with Poussin guiding her mother's hand, it trembled. What to do? She had left the
Renaissance behind and begun to wander from one painter to
the next searching for solace.

Alison thought of the étude for the left hand her father loved
to play. Never a very good pianist, he joked that he should be
able to play with two hands what others could play with one.
Written for two pianists who had lost the use of their right
hands. If he were here, she'd ask him to play that one-sided
étude now. She'd ask him who wrote it. She closed her eyes.
Saint-Saëns, she thought, that's it. She could almost hear it.
How beautiful, she thought, for the pianists with no right
hands. What happened to those hands, Daddy?

Alison went for a long walk and listened to the wind blowing
through the leaves. There were so many trees here, she thought,
perhaps she should label them so as to keep all the names
straight. It could be a project for her and her mother. Summer

stretched out before them like a challenge. Alison filled each day with such projects. If she could label the trees. If she could know the names of the parts of the sink. It was comforting somehow. After she labeled the trees, making a small white card for each one, she made a list of plants. It was an odd list, she noticed, but she continued with it anyway.

She imagined her mother and father were holding hands when they saw the bear. Keenly she watched for the bear's return. Surely it would be a sign of luck. If she could only see it.

They were doing the best they could. In the evenings they would still go out and look at the stars. With her mother strangely absent, Alison alone would try to identify the constellations of the summer sky. Her mother had taught her to find one bright star, one distinguishing star and move from there. There was Vega, and Arcturus, the reddish star. Alison tried to trace Cygnus with her finger in the sky. She looked down at her book. But was it Cygnus? Or perhaps Hercules? And wasn't all this part of the Northern Cross? It was so hard to tell without her mother's help. Well, there was Cassiopeia, that much she was sure of. Maggie just looked up at the beautiful sky, identifying nothing.

There were fireflies everywhere and it made it seem like the stars were all around them—at their feet, at their hands, right within reach; they seemed to be drifting in space. How beautiful the country is, Alison thought. This heaven of stars. This world of nameable trees.

"Tomorrow's the Balloon Festival in Cummington," she said, looking up at the sky still. At dawn the hot-air balloons would be pumped up. Hundreds of them—their brilliant, huge heads rising up over barns, lighter than air. The family had gone every year since Alison could remember. She was sure it was her first memory of the world. A sun, a stripe, a great curve, a basket rising. "Can you say 'balloon'?" her father asked Candace, who screamed it back with delight. "Balloon! Balloon!"

Last year the morning of the balloon fest had been particularly hazy. The dark orange sun burned through the fog casting a strange and wonderful light, illuminating all who had gathered to watch the great balloons be inflated. Farmers, women, children, cows and goats, sheep, a few horses. Alison picked a favorite balloon, as she had every year, and watched it fill up. But this year was different. As it rose high, above the trees, high above the beautiful countryside, Alison realized her lips were moving, though there were no words yet. She simply watched it float up higher and higher, growing smaller and smaller, and she whispered, "This is my son, in whom I am well pleased," and caught off guard by such a sentiment, she began to cry. She trembled and could not stop crying, and Candace was there and comforted her, Alison, who never cried.

"Let's go in now," her mother said, the stars still blazing overhead. Alison nodded and took her mother's hand. She was tired. Tomorrow the two of them would get up at dawn and go to the Cummington Farm, same as every year since Alison could remember. People pointing. People looking up. The strange, graceful balloons rising like some enormous hope.

It was about three o'clock that morning when Maggie made her nightmare run through the house, leaving a trail of light, her long robe billowing behind her like a white balloon. "Is your father back yet?" she asked, sweating, turning on one lamp after another, running from room to room in her sleep.

Alison, awakened by her mother, did not remember much of her own dream, but thought she knew something now she hadn't known before. It was this: that bears have poor eyesight, but great noses. And so that even that summer evening long ago, with all of them together walking down the path, the bear must not really have seen Father very clearly, or any of them. When he looked at her family, he saw only a blur. Henry, Maggie, Candace, Alison—they were only a smell.

Candace's Dream

Alison's List of Poisonous Plants

Plant	Toxic part	Symptoms
Hyacinth Narcissus Daffodil	Bulbs	Nausea, vomiting, diarrhea. May be fatal.
Castor bean	Berries (seeds)	One or two castor bean seeds are near the lethal dose for adults.
Lily-of-the-valley	Leaves, berries	Irregular heartbeat and pulse, usually accompanied by digestive upset and mental confusion.
Rhubarb	Leaf blade	Fatal. Large amounts of raw or cooked leaves can cause convulsions, coma, followed rapidly by death.

Yew	Berries, foliage	Fatal. Foliage more toxic than berries. Death is usually sudden, without warning symptoms.
Elephant ear	Any	Can be fatal.
Wild and cultivated cherries	Twigs, foliage	Fatal. Contain a compound that releases cyanide when eaten. Gasping, excitement, and prostration are common symptoms that often appear within minutes.
Burning bush	Leaves	Potentially dangerous.
Mock orange	Fruit	Potentially dangerous.

Cummington in Summer

The long, slow spring that year turned into a summer of vibrant green and the artists came en masse. Poets, painters, playwrights, performance artists, novelists, composers. All wild to work, to talk and to share, share, share. Neurotics, psychotics, manic-depressives by the dozens. Nymphomaniacs, homosexuals, not to mention bisexuals by the dozens, a few heteros and a rising contingent of snobbish asexuals. Repressed divorcées, unrepressed mothers of two, unwedded single parents of one. They brought their children. They came armed with bug sprays, flashlights, mosquito nettings, contraceptive foams and moved into the Frazier farmhouse (my house), the Vaughn stone house and the cabins in the woods: the Astro Cabin, the Hexagon, the Red Cabin, the Dome. They moved into the Sculpture Studio, the Music Shed, the Red Barn. They moved their children into the Children's Barn. The children had names like Olympia, Gabriel, Cleopatra, Yoho, Chantal, Narcissus. They came from Boston and Maine, the backwoods, the Live Free or

Die State, the Sunshine State, the Show Me State, the great state
of California. Mostly, they came from New York. They were suc-
cesses, failures. Macrobiotics. Feminists. Teachers on sabbatical, teachers on summer vacation. Waiters and waitresses who
served every imaginable type of cuisine: Middle Eastern, Thai,
Northern Italian, French-Vietnamese, nouvelle cuisine. Literary
waiters (The Algonquin, The Russian Tea Room) and those who
catered to the tourists (The World Trade Center, Mama Leone's).
Hip waiters (The Odeon, The Milk Bar) and lots more from that
cultural mecca, New York (The Kiev, Indochine, The Magic Carpet, etc., etc.).

There were word processors and other temporary agency
workers of every imaginable kind. Phone-sex employees, ex-
Jesuits out of work, scene painters, medical-text illustrators, au
pairs, and me, the author of *Delirium*, a best-seller in paperback,
a major motion picture. All of us thrown together suddenly on
these one hundred acres of land, in one common pursuit: ART.
Working and working and then passionately not working.

Inseparable ties formed overnight. Vows of love declared in
nearly every cabin. Dramas of enormous proportion.

We were left breathless at precipices, needing more than we
ever needed, it seemed. A couple makes love in the graveyard
under the northern lights. "Shit, is that the police?" the one
from New York asks, looking at the floodlights in the sky.

L. wants N. but all she can think of is T., and it goes on like
this.

How to keep order in a community of thirty artists and as-
sorted children (Octavio, Zoe, Yoho, Olympia, Milano, Lorelei,
Cleopatra, etc.) for the summer. The community had worked
out a detailed set of rules. Round sponges for pots. Square
sponges for surfaces. The labeling of leftovers a must—all food
containers marked with masking tape divulging the contents
and the date: Lentil soup 7/7. Stir fry 7/15. Brown rice 7/3.

From down the hill, artist/gardeners come with bags full of
lettuces, snow peas. All artists do chores here, it's part of the
philosophy of the place. It's a communal life, yes, in the eighties.

It's simple: artists help run things, artists do chores—office work, cooking, working in the children's program, going on the milk-and-egg run, whatever your preference. Two city girls show off the carrots they've picked. One muses on carrot picking. "It felt familiar somehow, it felt like, it felt like . . . what? It felt like, what? I know, it felt like taking out a tampon!" she says, so pleased with herself. She's a poet, after all.

It was that garden I think I loved most. Planting things in rows. Watching them grow. Weeding. Keeping order. The Maestro Peas. The Champion Radish. The Jubilee Sweet Corn. Often I'd take the children up there. My Early Wonder Beets! Miracles everywhere. Food growing in dirt. Children giggling.

Sometimes I slept over in the Children's Barn as a chore. After dinner I'd go to my sleep-over room at the bottom of the barn with a book to read, with letters to write, while mothers or fathers would get their children ready for bed. In each room of the big barn a bedtime story, a song, a prayer, children in feet pajamas—the nights often chilly even in August. The smell of toothpaste and powder, everywhere, then finally sleep. I loved the dreaming barn. The sounds of children murmuring in their sleep. The still small worries of their nights. A nightmare. A cry. Octavio says "Jupiter" in his sleep. I get up and hold him close. I love his little curly head. I take back the part about small worries. "Where is mother?" he howls. "Sleep," I tell him and he sinks back into the galaxy. I check on the other children. Linger there. You take your job far too seriously, the artists who are awake for breakfast say, after my report of the previous night's events.

My affair with the Children's Counselor led me on trips to the aquarium, the dinosaur museum, the creamery. But my favorite trip of all was to the Smith College greenhouse. "Oh to make love, here, on the mossy floor in the humid air," the children running up and down the aisles, feverishly picking what they should not touch.

There were always a lot of possibilities in these summer groups. Who could resist Hawk, just back from a vision quest in New Mexico? Who could resist the Minister's Daughter? Cummington in summer was a show a night, a thrill a minute, better than New York. Who could resist the Handywoman? Sometimes a chore was to help assemble a sink, or clean the leaves from the drains, or clean out the chimneys—all impossibly erotic. Who could resist being covered with ash or leaf-slime or grease? Who could resist the guy who fixed foreign cars in Florence? And meanwhile, my father, that same summer back in New York busy romancing the NYU librarian, the exchange student, the summer intern, the waitress at the Cafe Degli Artistes.

Who, I ask, could pass up Normal Boy, from Vermont, who stayed that summer in the Astro Cabin, near the apple tree where the deer roamed in the early morning? Normal Boy, with his muscles and boyish face. The Astro Cabin, with the fantastic skylight where at night you could see all the stars. "God," I said, lying on his bed while he sat diligently at his typewriter. "It looks like a planetarium."

"What a dumb New York thing to say," he says. "Why did you stop writing novels anyway?" he asks as he broods over his.

"First," I tell him, "you must make a commitment like love to it," I say. And I can't do that right now. "Second, you must have something to say." I realize it's starting to sound like a lecture. "But maybe most importantly you must have a way to say it." Normal Boy looks distraught at such a thorough answer, as though he can't believe I've actually thought about it. "Love me," Normal Boy says. "Why don't you?" He is the most handsome of normal boys and he's not used to girls treating him like this.

Normal Boy looks lonely, and there's nothing I want to do or can do to help him. Even if I could be in love with him, and I can't, he would still be completely alone with the hundred pages of his novel. I want something other than that, I think to myself. "I wrote *Delirium* ten years ago," I tell Normal Boy, who's twenty-three. "I'm thirty now. The world is spinning away. It's going so fast we don't even know it's moving." At least still it for a moment, I think to myself, still it with an image if you can. Or at least a little soiree in the Den.

The invitation read: "Please come to a nocturnal Gathering of Women in the Den at 11 p.m." My hosts wore harem pants, scarves. We drank cognac in bowled glasses and smoked hashish in the stone room. A scent of spices. A flash of dark hair. They were all there: the Minister's Daughter, the Young Beauty, the Contortionist, the Handywoman. The summer finally slowing up here. Cigarettes rolled by hand. The smell of blackberries. The touch of silver birch in the moonlight. Of smooth, smooth skin. And I knew finally, looking at all those liquid women in the half-light as we flirted and joked and napped and purred and smoked and sighed, that this was the secret, but real, life.

In the sky Virgo, Cassiopeia, Andromeda, Cygnus. In the sky Venus rising. Then light. It was my first dawn, the whole world on fire. The light caressing this familiar and beautiful landscape, the ferns, fantastic, alive, at my feet. The fierceness of tiger lilies, cattails, the heavy hydrangeas, the smell of camomile and thyme—all my senses keener somehow, on end. The tractor. The wood piled up by my neighbors, the Thayers.

It must be very early because it's still quiet over there. The sheep they are sheep-sitting for their daughter graze in the backyard. No one is awake yet. I near my door.

The baaing of a few sheep floats over on a sweet breeze. Then all is silent.

"Lamb of God who takes away the sins of the world have mercy on us," I whisper and enter the cool dark house.

I roam around in the kitchen a bit. Summer. Mice jumping out of cereal boxes, mice in the plastic in the ceiling's insulation. Mice dancing on the kitchen table and one lazy cat named Edward.

In the Frazier kitchen a notice posted:

Writers and Artists:
—Virginia Woolf did her dishes.
—Annibale Carracci did his.
—Proust probably didn't do his, but hell, he was richer than
   God.

A clean kitchen is a creative kitchen.

I run into a painter who has just gotten back from the dump
run. "You'll never guess what I *found*," he says. He shows me a
weathered archery target wrapped in newspaper. "And the
newspaper," he says, "is from the day I was born!" I wonder
what I am to think of this. "Great, that's great. Neat." I know
someday in his open studio we'll be seeing circle after obsessive
circle in his work. Something entitled "Birthday," no doubt.
Here, we turn everything into art.

I prefer sometimes what I believe is the simple life of the
Thayers: Leon, deaf now, riding his tractor across the expanse of
green. Olive filled with life, still, at eighty-five, snipping flowers
from her cutting garden, almost skipping to the mailbox. Drinking in the day's sun. And the sun is only the sun. Her grave waits
nonetheless, just a few yards away in Dawes Cemetery. The
stone up, already engraved.

Leon D. Thayer
1895–19

Olive M.
1898–19

Here at the Community, where there is so much life, the
graveyard still at the center. I go in there this morning and sit.
There are many good stones.

I've done lots of grave rubbings with the children. Quiet Cora
and John Snow, Doctor Royal Joy, the Philbricks, whose joined
hands shake farewell against tiger lilies each July. And of
course, the Abolitionists:

Can you see this picture, Max? I heard you gave your eyes to the eye bank. It is so much like you. The thing you treasured most, those intelligent, pale, all-seeing eyes. So I repeat the question. Shall I hold this photo closer to light or away from light? What's better now?

Shall I write you an epitaph? You who have no stone?

Scholar, Teacher, Father, Lover. You who insisted on being cremated and having your ashes sprinkled around the Guggenheim Museum. "That museum addition is not going up if I have anything to say about it," you once said. "Over my dead body."

I don't know, Max. This is just your sort of humor, but it's not all that funny. The Guggenheim for a gravestone.

"Max Chrysler was cremated and his ashes whirled around the Guggenheim by his son David. There was no official ceremony." Sometimes I could kill David for taking you so seriously.

And Mother—with no real stone either, no place to visit. Buried secretly in some unconsecrated piece of frozen ground in Quebec province, her parents hurrying her "home," *mon Dieu.*

I remember a flash of dark hair. I remember her standing in a garden. Her white hand clenched.

Mon coeur, mon petit fromage, mon oiseau, you called her. I like to think of her now somewhere near the Hotel Frontenac, in the *belle province* where you first met her, where you spent your first night together. "It was carnival. There was twenty feet of snow."

These things I have memorized. "I was there for a conference on the relationship between beauty, love and art in the twentieth century, and there she was." No wait. That's not right. He was a painter then who followed any celebration, anywhere. He was just out of college at the time and in some sort of despair. "I found her parked in a snow bank, laughing hysterically in the ten-degree cold. I don't think they had windchill factors then. She was saying over and over, 'Le bonhomme vivre.' And 'Qui suis-je?'—a game from her childhood. 'Vous êtes une femme magnifique.' I asked her what she wanted to do. She said she wanted me to take her to the Hotel Frontenac. Jesus, what a night."

I think of her death curled inside her from the start like a fiddlehead fern.

" 'I love the ice sculptures,' she kept saying.

'Oh my sweet, petite Veronique. Mon ange.' "

Max.

Scholar. Teacher. Husband. Father. Lover.

"She was so beautiful. So extraordinary."

Did you try to paint her into a life?

I count the Thayers' sheep, fourteen, fifteen, sixteen.

Tired, I drag myself up the hill and to my room. I dream myself to sleep, counting sheep.

Lamb of God who takes away the sins of the world, have mercy on us.

The sheep on their way to a sheep show are dressed in hoods and coats, medieval executioners.

I open her clenched hand one finger at a time.

Lamb of God who takes away the sins of the world, have mercy on us.

When I wake up it is late afternoon. As I walk through the woods I see the Young Beauty strewing pinecones she has painted white. She is hanging white muslin from the trees. In the studio she is building clay pieces the size of herself. She talks of her move from paint to clay. She talks of going deep into herself and bringing back shapes. Already she's brought such beautiful shapes into the world. She describes with delight these shapes, amazed as anyone.

"I've got to feel the earth. Do you know what I'm saying?"

I do. I've got to feel flesh, bone, hair, earth, somehow in words. The urgency of flesh, bone, hair. The thousand demands of blood.

I ring the dinner bell. The artists gather. Mimi and the Contortionist talk about Rajneesh, the globe-trotting guru. The Druid and Celtic crowd are not here tonight. They went to look at stones somewhere on the Vermont border.

I open her hand. She holds a spiral in her palm.

Lamb of God who takes away the sins of the world, grant us peace.

The Young Beauty sits next to me. She throws back her head. Her beautiful dark hair. I look at her sculpted face. The tendons in her neck. We enter sexual time. We sit across from each other at the crowded dinner table. The conversation is about bears, I think. What to do if you see one—throw mothballs, could that be what they are saying? Eat garlic? Run downhill? People pass out various useful instructions regarding the plant and animal kingdom—heady stuff for the New York crowd.

Bears will take the path of least resistance, someone is saying. They will walk where you walk. In other words, they will take the path you are on toward you.

"Should we or should we not wrap the tomatoes in plastic dresses? They're predicting frost for tonight," says the ingenious director, who uses bridal veil purchased at a yard sale for mosquito netting.

I could stay warm, I think, with her. They're talking about something else now, tofu burgers or the weasel walk or Julian Schnabel. They're passing out lists of things—poisonous plants, the names of trees. The truth is we have been making love from the first moment we saw each other, at the first residents' meeting. And then last night at the soiree. We make love as we eat. They can't get to us. We won't even engage in bear conversation. She pins her hair to the top of her head. She passes me a porcelain cup, a spoon to hold onto, something to both prolong our pleasure and bring us safely through the meal.

It comes to her as we are sitting there. In her studio she is making a forest of birches to bring back to New York. Each day they grow taller and taller. Figures, yes, but trees nonetheless. It's what I've always wanted. In New York she made little branch sculptures. Here there's been a leap in scale. Our desire helps her understand this desire. It's what I've always wanted. "My life is in trees," she says. "I think I once was a tree," she giggles.

"It's lovely," I tell her, "to think of yourself as a tree." She is making a place to stand. A home for herself. "I want to go further," she says. "Look longer. Harder. I want to go far away." Yes.

We start up the hill to my room in the large white farmhouse in the day's last light, and it seems to me like the first moment of the world. Olive in her cotton dress calls to Leon from her upstairs window, but he can't hear anything anymore. He lingers in the graveyard. The air is so clear this evening, so wonderfully sweet. The hydrangeas bow their sexual heads. I take her hand as we cross the cemetery home, up the hill to my room. Leon tips his straw hat to us, as we pass him standing among the granite stones.

I could think of worse places to lie down forever.

Cygnus

Her mother points to Deneb, the white star in the tail of the Swan. "It can be seen," Maggie says, "any time of the year. It is almost five hundred light years away." Alison nods sleepily.

"Its candlepower must be enormous to make it shine as bright as it does at this distance. It is supposed to be ten thousand times as luminous as the sun."

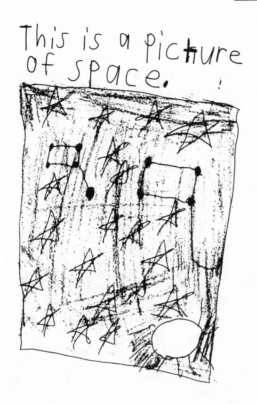

Watch Hill

Sheep graze in a green field. It must be Cummington, I think.
Leon Thayer deep in the ground. Olive, too, I suppose. I hear
the sound of a lute.

Really, a lute?

Yes. A lute: Leon Thayer yet to be born—yet to be born by
a long shot. It's hundreds of years ago. Something in the light
tells me so.

There is the shepherd. There are his sheep. He picks up a
stone and begins to draw something. Yes, of course, it's the
young boy Giotto. My God! He's drawing sheep. He's making
them so beautiful! His angel sheep. Cimabue has not walked

into the frame of this dream yet. He has not yet discovered the
boy drawing sheep in that field. Maybe he's in the next town
still, buying bread, finding a good goat. Maybe he's still at
home, unsure of whether to go out today or not. The boy stands
up and walks toward me. It cannot be easy to do what he will
do. Let me hold him for one moment under the sky's aqua
dome. Let me hold him for one moment now, before everything
is different forever. And something so odd happens as I take
him into my arms, this child of light. As I hug him close, his face
turns into my best friend Steven's face. "My God," I whisper to
him, "you look exactly like a boy I will love thousands of years
from now." He just smiles and runs off, counting sheep.

I open my eyes. "Steven."

"Caroline."

"I must be dreaming," I say. "Steven?"

"Hey, you make a terrific bride!"

I'm wrapped in bridal veil for protection from the mosqui-
toes. I see him through that blur. It's definitely him though.
"Those tulips!"

"For you," he says. They cup the air.

"How long have you been here?"

"Not that long. Get dressed. I'm here to take you on an out-
ing. I've got special permission to take you out of art jail. I'm the
rescue squad."

"My hero," I say, hugging him, happier than I can remember
being in a long time.

"We're going to the sea."

I can't believe he's saying this. "What sea?"

"The sea next to Rhode Island. I've done my research." A
map of blue unfolds to the floor.

"What were you dreaming?"

I dreamt you were Giotto, I think, looking at him. Dark tulips hover, the color of his eyes. But instead I tell him of a dream
from another night. "I dreamt of a bear that would not spare
us."

"Oh God, I knew it was serious. We've got to get you out of here!"

"How though?"

"I've rented a car."

"We're really going then?"

"Look, I've got my thongs on. I've got everything." He puts his feet up on my bed. He unzips his pants to show me his bathing suit. It's true.

"And it's like a miracle. It's my day off. No Octavio, Zoe, Yoho, et cetera. How did you know?"

"It's Sunday, Caroline. Sunday. Sunday's the day."

"Right."

"So let's go. I've packed us a picnic. Champagne and fruit. Some good bread. And I've rented a red car."

"I love a red rented car."

"I know."

We ride with the windows down and the wind blows in our faces like it will on the beach. It feels like we're already there. In the backseat there's suntan lotion, towels, magazines, books, an umbrella.

He talks New York talk to me. He tells me about Max. About the Signs Show he was in that Max curated. "Tell me every single thing," I beg. He does.

I tell him about Normal Boy, the Children's Counselor, the Young Beauty. "Don't leave anything out," he says.

"You just missed the balloon festival, Steven."

"Maybe next year," he says.

He asks about Grey, "the handsome twin," he calls him, even though Grey and David are identical. "Oh, Caroline," he sighs. "Where is your eye?" And besides, he tells me, he likes the moody, brooding type.

"Sometimes, Steven, I'm afraid Grey will just go to sleep like my mother and never wake up."

"I know," Steven says.

I've got the map on my lap. It's almost entirely blue. Sometimes I'm so afraid. Even in bright light. "Sometimes, Steven, I'm afraid that will happen to me."

"I know," he says. "You can talk nonstop to me."

"We're nearly there, aren't we?"

He nods. "Yes."

"Did I tell you about the Inventor?"

"No, I don't think so," he says. He smiles. He knows this is going to be a good one.

"You mean I never told you about my one incredible night with the Inventor—his two Samoyeds, his beakers, his Water Pik?"

He laughs out loud. "No!"

"Have I got a story for you!"

He tells me next about eating sushi with a stranger. That was yesterday. And we're up to date.

We turn a corner and we are there. Suddenly we are at the edge of things. The sea! We gasp. A beautiful expanse of blue.

"Oh, it feels so good," he murmurs, our clothes coming off, the beach already toasty warm. "It feels so wonderful," he says. We know we're drinking in the last hours of summer. "What a truly great idea, Steven." I'm holding his hand. He is my friend.

We sleep in the sun, eat, drink. He sits up now and then. What he sees is sand. Sharks, he thinks, swans. What he sees is everything. A lighthouse, a carousel. Babies in strollers pass by. Kids in water wings. "Cute," he says. A statement of fact as they pass. "Cute. Cute. Cute. Do you ever think of babies these days, Caroline?"

What I'm thinking is I'm afraid they'd all fall asleep like Mother, like I'm afraid for Grey, but I keep it from him.

"How about it, you and me?"

"Why not, Steven?" I smile. A great day. I am simply sitting in the sunlight whispering his name. I am not thinking about rain.

I see two dark women sambaing down the beach and point
them out. "Looking for Latins in Watch Hill, Rhode Island, Caroline?"

We decide it's time to go in the water. We dip ourselves slowly
into the blue. I hold his hand. After all, there is no reason to be
so afraid. Underwater our bodies are huge. It's like we have two
or three bodies each. Big chests, large hearts. We come up for
air, breathless. Enough love to last. It feels so good.

"You look fantastic."

We lie on the beach for hours. We lie on the beach like we've
got all the time in the world. "Some cheese?" he asks. "Some
more champagne?"

It's so bright everything looks white. We picture white
sharks. White horses galloping furiously. Max, that's what the
light looks like.

He talks about eating sushi with a beautiful stranger. We
think of the thousand ways to make love. The thousand ways
to say I love you.

I think of the child Giotto on the verge of his life, in that one
moment before everything is different forever.

"Let's walk," Steven says all of a sudden.

"Sure," I say. We walk a long way. "I was hoping to see starfish," I tell him.

He shrugs. "There's still time," he says.

Down the beach there's a crowd of people surrounding
something. It turns out to be a small whale beached on the
shore. It looks dead to us, but they're lifting it into the water,
trying to help it breathe.

"He's no Lazarus," Steven says and we just stand there and
watch.

Spare us, I think.

We decide to turn around. It's getting late. The sun falling,
the ocean rising high. There's a wall of water. We seem small
when we walk next to it. Then bigger. Suddenly it seems we
might hold it back. For a second we seem that strong, our hands

that steady. We feel that way together: sun-drenched, refreshed, touched by light. We think of No-Lazarus. Then No-Lazarus is replaced by the desire for starfish, children in water wings, dangling earrings, cities in sand reaching up for the perfection of sky.

The sea sprays us. The sea mists us. Steven looks out past me, a young boy intent on sheep, a young man in love with everything. I look into his eyes. What he sees is so much. "Look, Caroline," he says, and he points to the edge of the blackening sea, astonished.

Night Fishing

We caught a lot of fish in the lake, mostly sunnies, which we threw back, but at night we would lay down the line that would sink way to the bottom, the line for the catfish. We would row out to the center of the lake in the boat to the dock. David would take the bait out of the Chinese-food container and put it on the hook on the bobbing dock. Only Grey stayed behind. I had two brothers, one who loved water, and one who loved earth.

I was a little afraid because in the evening we never knew whether the birds were birds or bats. When we were in the boat at night, my mother always wore a scarf on her head, with swirls on it, and as Dad was rowing toward the center she would lean over and put her hand in the lake and she would make a swirling pattern.

Then she looked up. "There's a swan," she said. "There's a horse." And she traced the stars, making pictures in the sky. "And a bear. Everything's up there. There's a fish. Two fish. Swimming in opposite directions."

"At night you can go fishing in the water and you can go fishing in the sky," I said.

That was the last summer of her life. I was six and she was thirty, and the water swirled and the sky swirled.

The Floating Shape

She was wearing earrings shaped like fish that dangled and they swam in the air when she moved her head. We were sitting under a striped parasol. "Parasol," she whispered. She put on a lot of lotion, even though she sat in the shade. I remember her rubbing it into her legs, her shoulders. I guess she believed the sun to be something that could burn her alive, like my father's stare. She leaned over and tied the strings of my sunbonnet. I remember her breasts. Her whole body leaning over. Her suit was red with polka dots. "One, two, buckle my shoe," she sang softly, tying a bow under my chin. "Three, four, shut the door." She put her knees up and looked out at the water.

Dad and David walked along the shore. David was pointing at things and dragging his plastic pail of water. Grey sat further back on the beach, digging deeper and deeper into the sand with his blue shovel. All over the beach children were digging passageways and tunnels and making enormous towers of sand that reached endlessly for the perfection of sky. She put on her hat, picked me up and walked to the water. She seemed very tall; it seemed we were very high up. She pressed me close to her and said, "Don't cry, please, don't cry." But they were her tears I felt on my face, not mine. She sat me down next to her and we let the water lap our legs.

"Swan," she said. "Can you say 'swan'?" and she pointed. We watched a little girl pass in an inflatable white bird. Swan.

We sat there for a long while. She dug into her striped bag and took out a tube of lipstick and put on a bright pink. She blotted her lips on a tissue and showed me the lovely imprint. "Lips," she smiled and gave me a kiss. Lips. For a moment she held the tissue up to the sun, then let that perfect shape go floating out on the lake. "Say good-bye," she said.

Sky Watch | This week at 10 P.M.

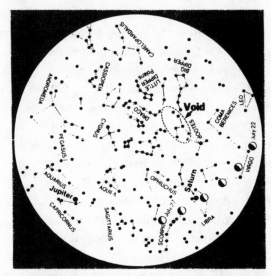

Even if the moon were not moving onto our map this week, we would have a hard time finding one of the most unusual "objects" discovered in recent years: a large, empty hole in space. Almost 40 years ago astronomers at the Lick Observatory in California counted the vast numbers of faint galaxies found in their photos. Analysis of these counts showed that galaxies are arranged in clusters, rather than distributed in clusters, rather than distributed at random. Several years ago, other researchers began trying to determine if the clusters, at least, were randomly spaced. While measuring the speed with which galaxies in three widely separated areas were receding from Earth, they found a vast void, an area 4 million cubic light years, in which there are virtually no galaxies. Theoreticians are now hard at work attempting to explain nothing

To use the map, hold it vertically before you with the direction you are facing positioned at the bottom. The outer circle represents the horizon, the zenith, the spot directly overhead, is near the center of the map. The map is accurate for 10:30 tonight, by Saturday it will be accurate for 10 P.M.

K. L. Franklin, Astronomer Emeritus, The Hayden Planetarium   The New York Times July 21, 1985

Fall

The Renovation of St. Vincent's

Children pass me on the way to the Greenwich Village School,
P.S. 41, my old school. Out my window I can see the tops of
their heads: some hats, mostly not. Rasta curls, ponytails,
braids, lots of braids, carrot tops. All kinds of barrettes: barrettes
with streamers, with liquid goo inside them, barrettes shaped
like bears, like stars. The children scream and yell and sing.
Some days they seem so loud, I'd like them to disappear forever.
Other days I think each little hair on the tops of their heads is
precious, each little sprout. If I stand up, I can watch them
doing things—trading stickers, charms, weird stuff. A red
ET bookbag flies by, a Madonna lunchbox.

A little boy I once knew passes by, clutching in his hand
drawings he's done of his classmates. A little girl walks with
him—silly skirt, knobby knees, dirty blonde braids. "These pictures are so beautiful," she cries." "They look *exactly like everyone*." We are on our way to school, Steven. It's a long time ago,
but I still remember it perfectly. You show me the drawings ex-
citedly. You've made me so beautiful! My best friend forever.
"Will you marry me?" you ask. "Of course!"

Lots more kids pass. Dancing kids, sullen kids, kids with
mothers, kids with nannies. Kids already at 8 a.m. in some kind
of trouble. Studious kids balancing science projects, frogs in for-
maldehyde, the planets.

I notice there's a lot of noise other than the regular kid noise.
I look past the kids into the air and notice they're renovating St.
Vincent's Hospital. Actually they're building a whole new wing.
Max, you would surely complain about this. I don't seem to

mind the noise, though. I imagine this means whole lives will be saved.

I go outside to see exactly what they're doing, what they're tearing down. I try to imagine what will be there when it's over. I wonder what kinds of machines they'll roll in, what sophisticated team of doctors. Maybe they could have saved you, Max, right here, twenty feet away, where now I dream they are making room for the most incredible cerebral-hemorrhage detectors, early-warning systems, all kinds of ways to extend your life past sixty-five.

"What's going to be there when it's done?" I ask a woman passing by.

"The hospital," she says, "what do you think?"

"I mean what part of the hospital? The maternity ward or the coronary unit or what?"

She shrugs. "How do I know?"

All the children are bumping into me like I'm invisible. "Hey, I was once a brat like you," I shout to them.

I see him in a red cap, blue scarf, black sneakers on the first day of school. I see me in a red jumper, white sweater, patent leather shoes.

A hand touches my shoulder from behind.

"Steven."

"Caroline!"

"I was just thinking of you!"

Neither of us is really surprised.

"Steven," I say, "I'm dying to talk to you. It's been so long. So much has happened. Max dead, everything."

"I know, I know. I bet you didn't even hear I went to Italy on a whim. It was glorious!"

He looks a little strange somehow.

"Steven, are you OK?"

"More than OK," he says. He winks. "I've got to run, Doll, I've got a date with a handsome doctor."

"Anyone I know?"

He smiles. "I'll call you."

He kisses me and runs off, crossing Seventh Avenue. I watch him get smaller and smaller—a red cap, blue scarf, black sneakers.

I remember the story you told me, Max, about this spot, the one I'm standing on right now as Steven disappears. Would you tell me that story once more?

"She was lost. That is, I couldn't find her. There were some people over at the house. It was late. We were all quite drunk, but not your mother. She rarely drank near the end. Anyway, she had wandered away. At first I thought she had gone up to our room, but when I went to see how she was doing, she wasn't there. So I went out to look for her. The others were too drunk to notice—they were all too busy doing their *Who's Afraid of Virginia Woolf?* maneuvers, or their wild, young painter bohemian Greenwich Village tricks. Why do you keep wanting to hear this story, Caroline? Surely you know it by heart by now?"

Yes, I do. The night you found her kneeling in the street, staring up at the cement cross, the scrolls, the angel of stone at St. Vincent's was not the night she died, but almost. It was the last real "event." The thing we remember when we think of the end of her life. Her legs had turned to stone, her whole torso to stone, right there on the sidewalk of West Eleventh Street.

She was losing detail. She was disappearing into chaos, dissolving, losing all life. Disappearing. Strange, like those sculptures on the tombs done by, oh, I forget who you said.

"I am a big man and she was a medium-sized woman, but I could not lift her that night in the street as she gazed up at the concrete cross, whispering prayers. Her body had filled with cement. She was part of the pavement, dear God!

"It was early fall, and there was a certain crispness in the air, an excitement, everything back alive in the city, the beginning of a new season, the children just on their way back to school. Her legs lightened a little. She was only thirty then, but after the incident outside St. Vincent's she began to get younger and younger, until she was back in her Catholic school frocks, it seemed, carrying around her little missal. She started feeling afraid. She'd never really felt afraid before. But she was so childlike those last few days. Her little fingers saying the invisible rosary, Jesus Christ."

How did you get her up from the street that night?

"Caroline, do we have to go through this again?"

Just once more.

"I finally got her onto my back. Piggyback. 'I can't go on,' she said. She was too heavy to carry, and I fell with her several times, though it was only a short distance. With her legs of concrete. Her stone shoes. Those pointy pumps dragging along the sidewalk, gouging out the road. 'Leave me,' she said. 'I can't leave you here, Veronica!'"

"But she walked again after that?"

"Oh sure."

"How many times?"

"Damn you, Caroline, a few times. I don't know how many. A few times near the end we went to the Lion's Head, I remember that. On her better days she moved her arms and legs against her depression. She spoke through it, though it took such an enormous effort. She was, on her best days, exerting some pressure against it. Don't forget—those were her best days, Caroline.

"She kept hearing a high-pitched sort of ringing sound in he·

ears. Neither of us believed in doctors, but we went on my insistence to one after another after another, but the sound never went away. And no one ever found anything wrong. I'm convinced now what she was hearing was her own depression. It had become so acute that it made a sound. I think of it as a sort of humming gray clay. She pushed against it—but only on her best days.

"The sky opens, Caroline, but only for a minute, only for a glimpse."

I am tired of all this death, Max. I open the paper and see Italo Calvino, dead today at sixty-one. This seems monstrously young to me. *Mr. Palomar* shouldn't have been his last book. And even James Beard at eighty-six seems young. My God, Max, in the paper I read they're auctioning off his cooking equipment this week. Grey would think they should bury it all with him. And how do I know that James Beard is not going to need his whisks and copper bowls?

"He's not going to need them, Caroline."

I'm catching up on all sorts of deaths. Rock Hudson at fifty-nine. What is all this? The candlestick maker, the whole neighborhood dying. And you at sixty-five! And mother at thirty. I have already survived her by three months.

So much death on my mind this early October. Across the street a jackhammer in concrete.

So much death on my mind this early October, the children knocking me over in the opposite direction now, clutching their drawings of the day. *He's made me so beautiful!*

I know this for sure now—that no amount of renovating could have saved her life. No elaborate psychopharmacology department, no master computer system. No team of doctors. Nothing.

No PET scan.

No CAT scan.

No electroshock.

The Reluctant Magician

He walks toward her on a glittering green-blue sea. "I am the tears of my Father," he says, dragging his net of fish. When he gets close he turns into a bird and lands in her hand. He turns next into a fiddlehead fern.

"You're going too fast," Veronica says. "We're going to crash. We've gone too far. I'm afraid now." She sees her name engraved on the palm of his hand.

"Don't be afraid," he smiles, giving her a hug. "Who'd have thought I'd come to love you best?"

She looks up at the moon and sighs. He offers her wine. He makes her a sumptuous meal from his basket of fragments, from a few small fish.

Miserably, he makes the dead breathe again. He pities Lazarus, who now will have to die twice. Everyone claps. He's a reluctant magician. He doesn't like all the attention.

"Walking on water," he says. "It's no big deal. It's not so hard, really. I'll show you how I do it—

"There are these very large, flat rocks at the bottom of the ocean and —"

"Don't be silly, Jesus, don't be ridiculous. We know it's a miracle! We're sure of it!" the crowd shouts.

Veronica too.

"The people who have walked in darkness have seen a great light," she cries.

The Lion's Head

Sheridan Square is still here. The statue of General Sheridan, still standing. The Lion's Head is still here, 59 Christopher Street. I walk down the steps into the bar and watch the legs go by the window.

"We often went to the Lion's Head in those days. And the White Horse."

Still there. It's comforting to picture my young parents in the White Horse Tavern. Or the Lion's Head.

"But no, Caroline," he says whispering, shaking his head. "Those were not the good old days.

"My God, what do you think it was like for her? Everyone around her seeing and hearing and feeling, or she thinking they were. What must it have really been like? Painters, writers, composers, all working—all *engaged* in things. Artists drinking all night, discussing pure form, twelve tones, God knows what. Journalists yacking away into the wee hours about politics, the left, baseball, I don't know what else, singing songs."

A boyfriend and I used to come here sometimes, Max. There is something about the light here, late afternoon, amber drinks, an early snow—it made us say things we never meant before and would never mean again, but we meant them at that moment at the Lion's Head.

"Yes, Caroline, I understand that."

The head of a lion. The floating hands of that boyfriend. I see things in pieces, in parts. A black shoe with a bow where the foot arches. A delicate ankle. A table separates that foot from the rest of the woman. Why do I see so many things in fragments? A whole person bisected by a table. It becomes something too hideous. I look away.

Was it always so bad for her, Max?

"Well, no. It was actually OK for a while. She got worse as she got older, as she entered her late twenties. Or perhaps it was just that after a while I could better see it. Once I got past the bone structure, the elegance of her movements, the dark hair, the sheer perfection of her, she was an all-consuming feast for the eye. Her ever-changing face in those days."

"Something to eat?" the waiter asks me.

"The food was always inedible in those days."

"No," I tell him, "just another drink."

"At the age I began losing interest in 'death,' your mother's interest seemed to escalate. But no, that's sarcasm talking, bitterness. It wasn't like that. I don't think she ever really thought about killing herself. It never actually occurred to her, I'm quite sure. Even that night in the street. 'The people who have walked in darkness have seen a great light,' she kept whispering. My God, how ghastly, the damn streetlight shining on her extraordinary face."

"But the day she finally died, what made that day different? Surely she suffered many, many days."

"She simply couldn't go on. If nothing else, I'm quite sure of that."

"Why did she do it, Max?"

"She simply couldn't go on."

"Couldn't you have stopped her?"

"What do you think, Caroline?"

"But she was a devout Catholic. You yourself have said."

"She was devout enough to believe He'd forgive her."

"Will He forgive her, Max?"

My father laughs loud, as if he's still alive. "I wouldn't count on it."

On the Street

We walk the same ten blocks, know the same faces, the same dogs. We hear the exact same half dozen or so raps from the street people, because they, like everyone else, are territorial, and we become attached to this all, against our will, somehow.

Through a storefront window a man standing on a box. A nun closing the church gate, a bit of Greek, a radio blasting, a saxophonist, fresh pasta. There was another man kneeling at the feet of the man on the box, a hundred images ago it seems. A woman with a stethoscope around her neck, pigeons, a hand in neon, a locksmith, boys on skateboards, Catholic school uniforms, flower markets, pink, blue, purple hair. Black men selling Gucci bags. It comes to me now, the man on the box was getting his pants fixed, the other man a tailor. Artichokes, acorn squash. It should somehow be possible to paint this scene in Father Demo Square with words.

Why one must be poor.

Why one is poor and another is not.

Why you are poor and I am not.

The sign on the telephone pole says, DANCING FOR OUR LIVES, a Dance Benefit at City Center for AIDS Research. I turn the corner and in a window a blonde has her head in a blue machine to make herself brown—a tanning parlor. I pass the Pottery Barn, Angelina's, Cafe Degli Artistes and so on. We are dancing for our lives. Sticking our white faces in blue machines and coming out brown. This is not invented. This is just how it is.

On my street a child's school paper escaped from a bookbag or a hand that held a jump rope or jacks. I pick it up and go inside.

A Man, Humming

A pianist, not so long dead, an acquaintance of Henry's, hums along quite loudly on the recording he made of Bach's Goldberg Variations shortly before he died. The record, left behind, always reminds Maggie of Henry.

As does Saint-Saëns's "Six Etudes for the Left Hand."

At night she runs from room to room of the big house in her sleep, turning on lamps, looking for him, leaving a trail of light.

Maggie has continued to make signs for the trees. It's a good project, for it keeps her busy now that school has begun for Alison and confirmation classes. Alison seems to have adjusted quite well, certainly as well as one could have expected. She worries about her mother, though, who has never spent a fall anywhere but New York. And never without Henry.

"How will we recognize the trees after the leaves have fallen?" Maggie had worried. "And all the labels from the summer are gone?"

"We'll do it again," Alison says.

"Again?"

"It will be fun, Mom."

And so a good part of the autumn, before the leaves fall, Maggie in a perfect penmanship writes once again the names of all the trees. Sugar Maple, Sycamore, Shining Sumac, Black Oak. This time she has the cards laminated in plastic. She labels the Tulip, she labels the Winged Elm. She invents a way to file, an elaborate coding system with colors. She cross-references.

Alison notices that her mother has completely stopped work on her Renaissance book, and this too worries her. Work was important now, Alison knew. Something demanding. Something hard. Her confirmation classes were becoming demanding in that way for her. She was surprised. She had lost a sureness of footing as far as God was concerned. This was a serious matter: to renew your baptismal vows. It was not to be treated lightly; she would have to be sure she really meant it.

The books on Maggie's bed now were of Manet, Renoir, Degas. In Candace's room there was nothing. They both missed Candace and hated the idea that they had lost her because of Henry, that she had become so strange, losing many of her Candace qualities, except for her passion, which was all rage now.

They could not reach her. She always had on the answering machine. "Hi," she'd say, "this is Candace. I'm probably at school and if I'm not there I'm probably at the Cat Club or The Palladium or Area. Leave a message. I'm bound to get back to you." But she rarely got back to Maggie or Alison. They called the number over and over, listening to the voice and the ever-changing messages as they tried to detect what was left of the old Candace. Often she'd try out new last names. "Hello, this is Candace L' Etoile." "Hello, this is Candace Cambridge." "Hello, this is Candace No Name." One time the message said, "Hello, this is Anorexia Nervosa. If you'd like to leave a message for me or for Bates Motel, go ahead."

"Who is Bates Motel?" Alison asked.

"Oh, some guy from England with no place to stay."

Alison was relieved that her mother and Candace did not talk too often. She hated to see Maggie in tears and inevitably Candace would make Maggie cry.

"Fuck Poussin, Mother. Your husband left you for a twenty-nine-year-old. Let's show a little emotion. Stop looking for the perfect order, reason, symmetry. There's no such thing."

The last time Candace called, only Alison was home. Candace had begun going out with a series of new-wave musicians from various bands that played around downtown. The drummer from P.M.S., the guitar player from the Dead Kennedys, the lead singer of the Dogmatics, somebody from the Squirrels from Hell. But this was only small talk, an introduction, Alison knew. Soon it would start. "Oh, how thoughtful of him to wait for Mom to go on sabbatical." And then on to the girlfriend. "She has no brain, I swear. She keeps changing her hairstyle. And she doesn't even like music. She's tone deaf." She went on. "You can follow her 'career' through the class notes of her college alumni magazine. Listen to this: 'Belinda "Biddy" Hansen has just done a big commercial for Sprite. If you turn on the TV during prime time, don't be surprised to see Biddy playing volleyball on the beach in a bathing suit. (The winning team, of course, Biddy informs us.) Way to go, Biddy!'

"Tell Mom I went to a show by a woman named Jennifer Bartlett. Tell her she should come to New York. There's a lot of art around." And she closed, "It is true that I loved him more than any of you."

Henry wrote periodically to Alison, she the only one who would respond to him at all. Alison tried to give Candace news of their father, but she would hear nothing of it. In his last letter he asked Alison if she would make a tape of the wind in the garden blowing through the dried sunflower stalks.

He had recorded their lovemaking, Maggie remembered.

As a little girl, sometimes, at her father's performances, Alison would clap her hands so hard that she'd have to blow on them to relieve the pain. She loved his music so. And it was not easy music, not in any way.

Alison said yes, she would do this for him, and she tucked the letter away.

A dead man hums over the stereo system in the room where Maggie sits, leafing through a book of Renoirs, and she thinks of her husband.

Who Made Us?

Q: Who made us?
A: God made us.

Q: Why did God make us?
A: God made us to show forth His goodness and to make us happy with Him in heaven.

("I'm afraid we made God, Caroline. He did not make us.")

Jesus at the Museum

"This is so fantastic!" he sings, twirling, circling madly, running around the ramps, dizzy. "What's it called?"
   "The Guggenheim."
   "Did I make it?"
   "No, I don't think so."

Alison: Sounds of My Mother Weeping

My father asked me to send him a recording of the autumn wind moving through the dried sunflower stalks, of rain on the tin garage roof, and of the sheep hooves right before a storm. I recorded everything he asked me for and a few things he didn't.

Candace Speaks (Out of Turn)

This dog or, no doubt, variations on this dog will follow you through your life, looking at you with adoring brown eyes, obeying your every word. Imagine a creature so stupid as to do that, but you know it will and that's why you love it. And the thing needs you, depends on you for food, for walks. It needs you, Biddy Hansen. But not my father. He does not need you for anything, but a moment. He does not look at you with adoring eyes. He does not mean it when he says, "I love you." He is unfaithful to the end.

The Sudden Appearance of Animals After
a Few Hours at the White Horse

Max, it is 4:45 p.m. on October 18, 1985, and I am now sitting in the dark bar called the White Horse. There are animals so huge they dwarf the entire planet.

Can you hear me? Can you hear me at all?

"I can't hear you with the Trout Sonata playing."

Max.

"I can't see you with these Poulenc beasts walking so loudly in my head."

I'm over here. Here's my hand.

"I can't possibly reach you with all this Rachmaninoff going on."

Q: Hello. Can you hear me?

Q: Hello. Can you hear me? Is anybody there? I am trying to
    talk to you.
A: What is it? What is it, my beauty, my work of art?
Q: Why is this happening?
A: What? Why is what happening?
Q: I'd like to know why this is—
A: I can't hear you. I can't really hear you with all the commo-
    tion.
Q: Why did you make us?
A: (Silence)
Q: Answer the question. Why did you make us?
A: Have you not read your catechism?
Q: Why am I here?
A: Did you skip page three altogether?
Q: What is the message I am supposed to leave?
A: I'm very busy. Really, you have no idea.
Q: Are you trying to tell me something?

The Dog Series, a Triptych

This was Candace's first project at the School of Visual Arts.
1. The dog divides neatly into sections like a chicken.
2. The dog with training wheels for legs.
3. The dog in the yearbook. (Barker Hansen, class of '77.)
Oilstick on Canvas.

.rib-
... composer of these
works.
●
Two of America's most important pianists, Leon Fleisher and Gary Graffman, have lost the use of their right hands. Both carry on their careers, playing music for the left hand alone. David Zinman, the conductor of the Rochester Philharmonic and the newly appointed head of the Baltimore Symphony, has an idea. Ravel and others have composed concertos for the left hand alone. What about a concerto for two left hands? Mr. Fleisher would be at one piano, Mr. Graffman the other. The two pianists like the idea. Now all that remains i to find a composer and the funds fo the commission.

The Kiss

The man walks forward.
"I'm not sure," she says.
"Believe me."
"I'm not sure anymore," Alison says.
"Touch me then," he says. He shows her his ruby palms and feet. His ruby wound. "Ye of little faith.
"I was betrayed with a kiss," he says. "I was betrayed by the one who dipped his hand in the dish."
"You said you would be with us forever," cries Alison, the one Jesus loved. "I thought it meant you would never leave us. I was confused."

He puts his hand on her shoulder. He takes it away. She moves toward him. He moves back. They make strange jigsaw shapes in order to maintain the void that must always exist between them.

"How can you turn away?" Alison cries. "Stay a little."

She sees her father. He dips his hand into the dog's water bowl. "Dad," she says, "why?" He gives her a kiss.

Cummington in Fall

How the world seemed to be beginning over again! The summer residents gone back to their restaurants, colleges, word processing jobs. The now familiar landscape taking on yet another hue. I watched the same stretch of land: brown, then purple, then green, and now reddening. I knew those leaves were dying, that everywhere things were falling to sleep, but the world in fall always smelled new to me. Pine and burning wood, the land on fire. Now that it was quiet again, deer came to eat the apples off the trees next to the Children's Barn. And the pear tree I'd been eyeing all summer near Frazier was nearly ready for picking. Max, what the light looks like in the pear trees, in October, is a hundred teardrops of gold, the whole orchard weeping.

I went over to the Thayers. Leon flew by on his tractor. Sweet Olive stood in the flower garden. "Olive, hi, I've got a favor to ask. I'd like to borrow the pear picker."

"It's that time, isn't it?" She flags Leon down. "Leon," she says in a loud voice, "she wants to borrow the pear picker."

"What?"

"She wants to borrow the pear picker! The pear picker!! The pear picker!!!"

Leon, deaf as a doornail, nods. "Come with me," he shouts.

I had, of course, never picked pears. The pear picker, it would turn out, was a long pole with a claw at the end of it. My three-hour chore for the week was to pick the pears.

My other chore was to "orient" the new residents. A sort of welcome wagon, I was to show them their "spaces," pass out extension cords and heaters, answer questions and conduct stove school.

He was tall, sort of good-looking, older, a man of the world. He was balding, distinguished, with a twist. Definitely different from the usual Cummington fare. He was on sabbatical for the fall semester. He was getting away from the city, I imagined. He was getting away from a bad marriage, perhaps.

"Hi," I said. "Welcome to Cummington." By then I was tired of the constant comings and goings of artists. I was tired of getting so attached and then losing them. Love and loss in a month. The drama of the fast-motion friendship or courtship was a little dizzying. The pressure on. Oh, it was true that I had loved all of them in some way, not in the conventional way maybe, but in some way certainly. But it was wearing me down. I was cautious with this man.

"Where are you from?" I asked him.

"Boston."

"What do you do?"

"I teach."

"I mean what do you really do?"

"I'm a composer."

"Do you like Mahler, Brahms, Bach?"

"Yes."

"Do you like Talking Heads?"

"Yes."

"Good, that's good. I'm Caroline Chrysler."

"Hi. I'm Eugene Wilson."

"What is all that stuff?" He was carefully unpacking boxes of equipment, speakers, receivers, gadgets.

"It's a Synclavier."

"You mean like Laurie Anderson uses?"

"Exactly."

"Do you like Laurie Anderson?"

"Very much."

"How old are you anyway?"

"Fifty-two. You?"

"Twenty-nine."

"My eldest son is twenty-eight."

"What are you working on?"

"A suite."

I set up the Composer in the Music Shed. I handed him his extension cords, directions, etc. "Dinner is in two hours, at six, in Vaughn, the stone house down the hill. Here's a map. And a list of who's here. Let's see, what else? Oh, I almost forgot. You've got to go to stove school."

"Where's that?"

"Right here."

"When?"

"Right now. I'm the teacher. Have you ever seen a pear picker?"

"No."

"I didn't think so."

I handed him the "Creosote Papers."

We were bent over the stove. We were burning hot. I touched his hand. How the world seemed to be beginning again.

" 'Fire safety,' " I read. " 'Is your stove making inexplicable noises? Is your stove or stove pipe glowing cherry red? Or for some other reason does your stove appear to be out of control?' "

We never made it to dinner that night. We skipped breakfast. "I've forgotten your last name," he said distraughtly.

"That's OK. It's Chrysler, like the car. But it's my night to help cook dinner. I've got to go."

"Will I see you again?"

"You can't help but see me again."

"I could be your father," he whispered.

"No, you couldn't," I said. "No. Not quite." Max, he thought he could be my father.

I imagine for a minute, Max, being one of your women. But only for a minute.

The affair with the Composer followed the routine course.

By the end of the month he was hooked. It would have been the perfect time for him to leave, but he decided to stay on. And I must admit I was happy he did.

Max, why didn't you ask me to come home that month for the Film Festival?

I grew attached to him. More than the others, though there were others that season. Who could resist the Sweater Man, the Apple-Crisp Maker, the Child Prodigy with his endless stories of Madame Boulanger? But it was different with the Composer. I don't know how exactly. He was smart and funny. He knew a lot of things. He liked Talking Heads, the Bush-Tetras, Sibelius, Bartók. He taught me about the Synclavier—the thousand things it could do. He sped up symphonies until they became one note. He put my voice in and changed it, added rhythms, elongated the syllables.

"One night I'd like to record our lovemaking if that's all right with you. I won't tell you when. We don't want any performances."

"Sure," I said.

It was a kind of magic. He would leave me messages in my mailbox: "I hear you breathing. I hear your breath as I work. Your breath is with me still." I started wishing he'd stay for the high winds and heavy snows part.

" 'High winds and heavy snows,' " I read from the "Creosote Papers" that first night. " 'Keep an eye on your chimney, especially during foul weather. Is it still there? If not, don't use the stove. And if the wind is blowing very hard, don't open up your damper to a roaring fire; there is danger from sparks.

" 'Getting stuffy, close, headachy? Try cracking a window. Your fire burns on air. Too tight a space can asphyxiate or give you the dreaded cabin fever.

" 'Emergency exits—Know how to get out of your space *fast*. Find two directions for easy exit.' "

"I've got to go," I told the Composer that first time. "I'll see you at dinner."

When I got to the Vaughn kitchen with its hundred labels,

signs, instructions: No bones in the compost, Metal and wood spoons in this drawer, Round sponges here, Square sponges there, on and on, I came across a plastic yogurt container labeled Fish Tongues. Taped inside was a clipping from the *New York Times*:

> Dr. Jamison examined 47 leading British artists and writers and found that 38% of them suffered from severe mood disorders. (Normally 6% of the population is stricken.) They would go through alternating periods of incredible creativity, sleeplessness and feverish activity. Then they would sink into depression. Fully 50% of the poets surveyed had been hospitalized for manic-depression.

A visual artist's idea of a joke, no doubt.

For dinner a little Gypsy Soup from *The Moosewood Cookbook*. And after dinner always a fire, in fall.

I learned finally, Max, how to build fires and once I learned, I couldn't stop making them. I kept trying to make them look like the yule log on TV at Christmas. There was real wood at Cummington, Max, from trees. Not the kind you spent a·fortune buying on Sixth Avenue in little log packages from some little log salesman from God knows where.

Sometimes I miss you so much.

Mother loved fires, I remember that. She stared into them for hours while you sketched and we ran around the house.

Call me Max, now.

Real wood from real trees. Deer eating apples, Max. Sheep chewing grass. Right there in front of you. Real wood, really. Lots of fires.

We saw the figure 5 in gold.

Fall at Cummington meant lots of fires. Also a lot of tea drinking. Every few hours people would gather for more tea. Tea by the fire. Celestial Seasonings, of course—Cummington's brand—the packages covered with flowers, swamis and symbols on every flap. There was a vaguely Buddhist or Moonie feel to them. There was something you could not trust in all of this.

There were too many messages; you didn't know why you were being told such things.

On the back of the Cranberry Cove tea there was a Dale Carnegie quotation. Like everything, I wrote it down: "Instead of condemning people, let's try to understand them. Let's try to figure out why they do what they do. That's a lot more profitable and intriguing than criticism and it breeds sympathy, tolerance and kindness."

What does this have to do with tea? Max would have asked. "I object to any tea that implies a 'lifestyle' or a value system."

Another story—actually a proposal—the idea is this, or it has something to do with this: woman, or rather Woman, the full October moon and harvesting at night. The photographer asked if I'd help her. "Sure," I said, swigging back some Cranberry Cove. "Shall I bring the pear picker?" I ended up at midnight in a field of puffy white dandelions, bare breasted, hands on hips, shivering. I do not question these things. I am all for letting the Artist do whatever she sees fit. "Now what?" I ask. "Look strong," she says. "Look at the earth." "OK, now what?" "Turn your face this way." In my profile she sees Woman. "Try putting your skirt over one knee. Now take off your skirt." The bugs bite. The dandelions tickle, but it's all for Art. "Now twirl around." At another tea-drinking session we'll laugh about this, maybe.

Joy Adler is painting an arrangement of tea and pears.

A church bell chimes ten times. I have woken late again. I love the early morning, but the clock chimes ten times—it couldn't be eleven times, could it? And Suzanne's been up since six, her requisite three pages for the day already finished.

Mariana walks up the hill and into the woods near the Hexagon. "It reminds me of home here. The wood talks to me like my father once did," she says, "long ago in Germany." Poles, they lived in a refugee camp during the war. In barracks of wood. From the vast black forest in her heart she makes chopping blocks, coffins. She can't forget, she says, her father, who loved wood, or her mother, who cried in the dark barracks. The faces of the Germans everywhere. "Be thankful you are still alive." She makes what look like ovens, bulbs, huts. And this a torture chamber—this a violated grave. "The wood speaks so loudly to me," she says. "Sometimes it is hard to listen." She carves. She chops. She weeps. She carves more. "Those were my parents you did that to," she says into the air. When I look at her sculpture I'm trapped in her past with her. I'm just where she wants me to be.

He could turn the news into music. He could turn laughter or the wind in the trees into music. On the Synclavier he could make sounds from instruments never heard before.

Eugene, on his last day, took a long walk in the woods after packing his equipment. He knocked at my door and handed me a cassette tape. "This is for you," he said. "We have made a shape together, Caroline, and it is ours forever."

Jesus Listens to Verdi

He braids together blades of grass and listens to the music. "Do you hear that music?" he asks Alison.

"Yes, it's Verdi's Requiem."

"It's very sad, don't you think?"

"Yes."

"It makes me a little scared."

"Me too."

He sees hundreds of mouths opening, hundreds of hearts blooming. And the music. "They're all singing for you," Alison says.

"It makes it even harder, somehow."

Van Gogh at the Met

called m...... tors of his menta. breakdowns at the a., long periods of absolute lu. when he was completely maste. himself and his art."

The distortions that arise from downplaying the severity of van Gogh's emotional struggle are just as great as those that result from interpreting his work as diagrams of derangement. To suggest that van Gogh's "illness" was entirely physical, perhaps intensified by too many bars or an unlucky night, is to trivialize him. It is apparent that van Gogh was exceptionally cultured, passionately attentive and utterly unaffected. It is also apparent that he was terribly conflicted and at times painfully difficult and deeply disturbed. He was caught between wild extremes of hope and disillusion, independence and dependence, ecstasy and despair, sensuality and guilt.

No matter how you look at it,

"Crows Over the Wheat Field" is a trapped, claustrophobic painting. To deny the force of the conflicts that had their run of van Gogh means denying the depths of his understanding, the urgency of his synthesis and the almost cosmic dimension of his joy. Without sensing the restlessness that drove him toward unity and periodically drove him mad, there is no way to do justice to his courage and ambition. Van Gogh risked his life in his work, and he knew it.

•

"Van Gogh in St. Rémy and Auvers" was selected by Mr. Pickvance, installed by Gary Tinterow and coordinated by Susan Alyson Stein, the editor of the recently pub- '-n Gogh: A Retrospective." was made possible by ~'~r-

Maggie and Alison Watch for the Comet

" 'Halley's Comet is about 100 million miles off and heading our way at 66,000 miles an hour. Its closest approach to Earth this month—58 million miles—will be on November 27. But tonight there are two opportunities for a preview in Western Massachusetts.' "

They pointed to the sky. Each night from the eleventh to the sixteenth of November they stood hour after hour up in the garden, the place with the best view. They wore sweaters and down vests. They brought a thermos of coffee, binoculars, a telescope.

The comet was to pass through the Hyades and the Pleiades. The Hyades, Alison knew, was a beautiful V-shaped formation of stars forming the head of Taurus the Bull.

Five nights later, Alison read, the comet was to pass through the Pleiades. Her voice rose in excitement. But despite the absence of the moon, the elaborate charts, the binoculars and telescope, they did not see the comet that week.

A Procession of Saints

There before Candace's eyes saints parade by. They are shot through with arrows, strung up and beheaded, thrown into flaming pits, tied to stakes, jailed and crucified. Their heads split by axes. Their vaginas in boxes.

There's Saint Lucy carrying her eyes on a platter. Saint Apollonia with her thong and pulled molar. Saint Agatha, patron saint of bells, her breasts on a plate. And here comes Saint Margaret, accused of seducing a nun. And Saint Marina dressed as a boy. There's Saint Thérèse filled with longing. And Saint Joan— on fire. How they suffer.

Peace, serenity, love, Candace begs.

The Ostrich Fern in Fall

In her best handwriting Alison wrote the sign for the ostrich fern, and then had it laminated. For what are fiddleheads but the curled plumes of the ostrich fern in spring? Now they were nothing but tall brown stalks—dead, it seemed, but really each tufted brown shoot marked a spot. Each one said, Here, here, here, we return. Be patient. Have faith. We will return again.

Poem for Grey

From the earth
I dig for you
everything I can.
Bloodroot, gentian,
earthworm. A bottle that once
held water, a piece of clay,
a doll's leg.
A huckle
a buckle
a beanstalk.

From the earth
I tear from its roots
the Interrupted Fern
to show you.

I don't know what makes you want to stop.

Against this perfect
sky I picture you back.
The land comes out of your chin.
And the trees come out of your head.

I don't know what makes you so in love with death.

In the garden
the hollyhocks
grown from seeds
are almost trees.

In France they grow
golden apples.
Why can't this be enough?

In Italy there are umbrella trees.

I hand you
a huckle
a buckle
a potato, a flute, a cup
from the earth you love.
For you, Grey, my brother
I bring back all these shapes.

Take one.

Jesus and The Lamentation

"Note," Jesus says, "how the very low center of gravity, the
hunched, bending figures communicate the somber quality
of the scene and arouse our compassion even before we have
grasped the specific meaning of the event depicted. With extraordinary boldness, Giotto sets off the frozen grief of the human mourning against the frantic movement of the weeping
angels among the clouds, as if the figures on the ground are re-
strained by their collective duty to maintain the stability of the
composition while the angels, small and weightless as birds,
do not share this burden. Let us note, too, how the impact of
the drama is heightened by the severely simple setting; the descending slope of the hill acts as a unifying element and at the
same time directs our glances toward my head and the head
of my mother."

The Life in the Sky

When it gets dark, Alison asks her mother to tell her about the stars.

Maggie points to the Corona Borealis. "Dionysius gave his bride an exquisite crown studded with jewels," she says. "And when she died, he set the crown into the sky.

"For objecting to the marriage of Andromeda and Perseus, poor Cassiopeia was turned into stone. To humiliate her further, Neptune arranged her in the sky so that at certain times of the year she would appear to be hanging upside down."

"Nice guy," Alison says. "Tell me about the swan next!"

Maggie points out Cygnus. "Reckless Phaëthon, that mere mortal, convinced his father Helius, the sun god, to allow him to drive the chariot of the sun. When he lost control and the earth was threatened, Zeus intervened, hurling a thunderbolt, and Phaëthon fell into the river. Cygnus, who loved Phaëthon, dove into the water over and over and over again in search of the body. Apollo took pity, changed him into a swan and placed him in the sky."

She has saved their favorite for last tonight. "Castor and Pollux, devoted twins, were the sons of Leda. Castor's father was Tyndareus but Pollux's father was Zeus. After Castor's death, Pollux was overwhelmed with grief and longed to share his immortality with his beloved brother. Finally, Zeus reunited them by putting them together in the sky as Gemini."

The Restoration

The rental TV has finally arrived. The answering machine is set up for calls. The Cuisinart is great, and little Oskar, who does the small jobs. My father's cooking equipment is perfection. Welcome to the civilized world. I love the compact disc player, the VCR.

I can go to the Gay Film Festival, the New Directors' Film
Festival, the Polish Film Festival. I can watch Picasso painting
on film. See Chantal Akerman's early work. I can go to the San
Genaro Festival, the Puerto Rican Day Parade, the Labor Day
Parade. I've been away too long.

I flip on the rental TV. Immediately I learn something new.
St. Clare is the patron saint of television. She and St. Francis
were friends and one day she was too sick to attend mass at his
place, but somehow she was there anyway, without stirring
from her bed. For this, the church decided to make her the
patron saint of television. This is no joke.

Suddenly I love the flood of images, the strangeness of this
world. My therapist calls, leaving the second message on the
machine. I've been lying low, but word is out now; it's fall and
I'm back. He will want to know how I feel about my father's
death. What my dreams are. Why I have not called.

Last night I had a dream I was walking a goldfinch on a
leash. I wonder what Max would say about that?

"It means you always felt little as a child. It means I tried to
keep you tame. It means your parents never loved you. Never
took you to the country."

Then he'd start in on Freud.

"You're interested in Freud?" he'd ask. "How about this
then: Freud said that the Surrealists would often send him their
work. He said, 'They think I approve of what they write. But it is
not art.' This, Caroline, is the *kind* of mind we're dealing with
here. Any takers? No thank you, Herr Freud. None for me,
thanks."

I turn off the sound on the rental TV and just watch the pictures. I put Glenn Gould on the CD. You had so many opinions,
Max. And for better or worse, I am my father's daughter.

Oh, there was a certain perversity to you and your opinions.
If I was too opinionated, if I talked too much about one side of
something, even something you yourself believed in or loved—
foreign movies, for instance, me going on and on about Godard
or Fellini or Fassbinder or whomever, you'd scold, "My God,
Caroline, love an American movie now and again, won't you?

Love a *Raging Bull*, or *Nashville*, or something. How about *Love
Streams*? Love *Love Streams*."

You were always for the whole, never for the part. Myopic as
you so often were, you always encouraged those you loved to
take a broader view, and your best self loved the bigger picture,
the picture beyond the picture. When I talked too much or too
intensely about boys, then men, with my "predatory gleam" as
you called it, you'd say, "My God, Caroline, have you no interest in women?" "As sexual partners?" I'd ask. "Yes, exactly."
And then you'd put your arm around my shoulder and say, "Do
I shock? Oh dear, I do not mean to shock. Veronica, can she
really be ours?" you'd ask into the air. "Is this really our child?"
And you, Max, the devout heterosexual, lover of women,
woman-obsessed, womanizer.

About these shoes in the closet, Max. Are the women going
to come back to claim them? With such a variety of sizes and
styles, I could have a shoe sale on the street, set myself up right
next to the incense people. What do I do if the one with the dog
comes? Are those her topsiders in the closet? David always
wanted a dog, as I recall, begged you for a dog, and you always
said, every time, "I have never met a dog I liked."

"OK, Caroline, that's enough."

A sore spot, Max, the one with the dog? What did she think,
I wonder, about you being scattered around the Guggenheim?
Every time I see her, she starts to cry. I understand she's an ac-
tress.

Max on acting: "There are too many young people in New
York who are in love with the notion of struggle. Too many
people in love with the romance of failure, too many making
the deliberate choice of a career they have not the talent, the
perseverance or the luck for, all the odds against it. Too many
working and working on a whim, and what propelled them
into it? A few compliments on a small part in a third-grade pageant, a smattering of claps which became in that childish ear a
ring of applause, the curtain going up and down and up and
down, and all the curtseying and how they caught bouquets of

flowers. But so often there was really no talent, no natural ability. So what was it? A need to be seen, perhaps, a ring in the ear, that's all. Too many were unable to differentiate a good script from a bad one, too many simply did not know. And the tiresome, tiresome talk. 'What is the motivation for this line?' There was no governing intelligence, no instinct. The 'I-feel-guilty, you-feel-guilty' school of acting. The Jill Clayburgh, Diane Keaton, head-nodding, nose-crinkling school of acting. A constant examining and re-examining of 'feelings.' A regurgitation of pop psychology. A smallness. An essential stinginess, when you get down to it—opting for theory—though it masqueraded as something quite other than that."

Are you done yet, Max?

"Because finally there was no way beyond the catchwords. The feeling floated on top, no matter what degree of sincerity or diligence. There was just no way in—the amount of talent, intelligence, wit, simply did not permit it. And so each was doomed to fail, even if the competition was not overwhelming, because they had made inappropriate choices. Don't get me wrong—those who have talent are obliged to pursue it, Caroline, and those who do not are obliged not to."

You always got the last word in, even when it seemed you were not listening. Somehow you always got your say. It was part of your elegance, your brilliance, not as an art historian or a teacher, but as a father.

I think of the things we loved best. Sunday afternoons together. Lunch uptown at Shun Lee West. Chopsticks, fortunes, tea. And a movie at five at one of the Lincoln Center theaters. I loved conversations with you. Your active mind. One day you'd say, "Let's go check out the Philip Johnson building."

"You mean the AT&T building?"

"Yes, well, whatever."

"Let's go see *Kagemusha*."

Let's do this. And that.

"What do you think about the new Peter Brook piece? What about that Mark Morris you like so much?" Your probing mind.

"What about Jennifer Bartlett? David Salle? Karole Armitage?

"Oh, those wretched buildings on Third Avenue . . . Modern architecture implies a value system, undeniably a social one as well as an aesthetic one. Modern architecture was to be a symbol of the ideal city, a new utopia, it was to embrace idealism, and ironically it became the ultimate symbol of the corporate state."

I always assumed everyone's conversations were like ours, based on what you led me to believe was a certain general knowledge. Of course one was expected to know postmodern from modern, orthodox from neo. I wonder what you would think of neo-geo.

"What about the Gwathmey Siegel addition to the Guggenheim?" I asked.

"No. It is not acceptable. No. It is not satisfactory. Over my dead body," you said.

One day we were walking in the museum together. A man and his wife were looking at a Pollock, I forget which one. "*I can paint better than this*," the man said. I looked to you. Your face was contorted with amusement and horror. Your voice rising with the ludicrousness of it.

"Can you? Really?" You were appalled. Delighted. Usually you said nothing, that was your response, the measure of your contempt for ordinary people, for the man on the street. And the man stupidly nodding. You could turn on me too, I knew, at any moment I seemed ordinary to you, unexceptional. You had no allegiances other than to excellence and so were not really a snob. You told me that Vermont butter was as good as French butter. That many dried pastas were better than fresh. That there's a young woman in Brooklyn really making art.

But was I excellent enough for you? I suspect I was not. Though after you read *Delirium* you said, "It's good!" as if it surprised you. "It's energetic and very funny, also a little terrifying," you said. "A little anarchic. It's filled with promise and I'm proud of you." But I had not written the novel that would be better than that one, that would go further, and you must have been disappointed, as I was, having instilled in me your love of excellence.

Do I try to find a manageable shape for you? Do I put my rage for you into art, where it is acceptable?

"Only, Caroline, my dear, if you're smart enough and talented enough."

I open one of your cookbooks looking for something to make. I want to use your fabulous pots, your Cuisinart, your little Oskar.

How about a duck in port wine with figs from our friend Alice B. Toklas, Max?

I put on "Love for Three Oranges" by Prokofiev.

The phone rings. The phone machine clicks on. "This is David," the voice says. "Pick up the phone if you're there, Caroline. I'm not calling from around the corner."

I decide I'd better pick it up. "Hi, David. How's Milano?"

"OK. What are you doing?"

"I'm thinking of making a duck."

"How's everything in New York?"

"Well, if you really want to know—Jesus, David, it's no joke, you threw Max around the Guggenheim without me."

"It's what he wanted, Caroline. He was very specific. And I didn't throw him, I sort of twirled him."

"I don't know, David, it's just not funny."

"Well, yeah, I thought it sort of was."

"Oh, David, you think it's hysterical when the beard on Saint Simon turns out to be a fish."

"You'd have to be here. And it wasn't a fish. What looked to be a part of his beard that was sticking out rather unnaturally has actually turned out to be a section of tapestry from the background. Every vein in his neck is visible now, every fold in the robe and the details of the hands. On the table in front of Simon these incredible still lifes have emerged. A fish with lemon and orange slices. And you can see the curls on Saint Philip's head!"

"So the restoration is going well?"

"Very. It's really wild. You should come over and take a look."

"Sure, David. Have you heard from Grey?"

"Not a word. As far as I know, he's still on that dig in Greece. Nothing from him in a while, though. Look, I've got to go."

"Me, too," I say. "Ciao, bambino." I take the duck out of the deep freeze.

I think of the things we loved best:

Anything new.
What the light looked like.
Chopsticks and tea.
Jules and Jim.
Mom.
The drive down the Hudson after we dropped off the boys.
The figure 5 in gold.
A duck with figs.

After her death, Max forbade us to call him Dad anymore. "Look, you've got to grow up right now," he said, and he stared into our sad little faces. "One 'Mom' or 'Dad' is quite enough to lose. I want you all to call me Max, from here on."

The night you found her kneeling in the street staring up at the cement cross and scrolls, St. Vincent's written in the stone, was not the night she died, but almost.

Found: my mother's childhood Bible.

I put on "For my brother reported missing in action 1943" by John Jacob Niles. On the television a man hacks down fields of beautiful flowers with a machete.

The duck unthawed turns out to be a goose.

I turn on the sound. It's Laos and the flowers I see now, in the close-up, are poppies. It's a story about the heroin trade.

I go out to get the Sunday *Times* on Saturday night, like you. I briskly walk to the corner of Waverly and Sixth Avenue, re-tracing your steps. You liked to watch the pink and green and blue hairs, as you called them, lining up at the Waverly for the

midnight show. It's odd to think I lived a year without the
Times, without all this. How it would have amused you to think
of. Why didn't I ever come to see you, Max? Why didn't you
ever send me that letter? It makes me wonder what else went
unsaid.

When I get there I'll check to make sure all the sections of the
paper are there, standing in the same spot you did. Like you, I'll
go home and immediately begin to read. The Book Review first,
the Arts and Leisure, The Week in Review, the Magazine. You
were always done with the paper by two o'clock the next day.
By two on Sunday the news is stale, you said. Old news.

I think of you in fall, the season of betrayal, out for a walk
to buy the Sunday *Times*. No one, not the woman with the dog,
studying her lines for acting class, not the size-7 pumps, not the
fuzzy slippers playing the CD player and waiting for you, not
the stiletto heels leaving a message on your machine, not even
you have a clue. Only I—barefoot—far off in the country—under a starburst, next to a fire, somehow know, that this will be
the last year of your life.

yields three-quaɪ ᵗᵉ᷈ ᵔ ᵎ.

CORRECTION: Because of editing errors, the recipe for Chiu Chow braised duck in the Jan. 25 Food column is wrong in part. The duck should not be added to the braising liquid until step three, the garlic in step four should be minced, and the cheesecloth bag of spices should not be removed unless the liquid is to be stored for an extended period.

Scholars Re-examining Rembrandt Attributions

By MICHAEL BRENSON

The announcements last week that two paintings in European museums thought to be by Rembrandt are in fact not by the 17th-century Dutch master are part of a widespread scholarly re-examination that has radically diminished the number of Rembrandt attributions.

During the 1920's, more than 700 paintings were attributed to the artist. By 1969, the tricentennial of his death — which sparked the explosion of scholarly activity — the number had fallen to nearly 400. Partly as a result of the momentum created by the Rembrandt Research Project in Amsterdam, the number is expected to drop to around 350 by the end of the century.

The shifting sands of Rembrandt attributions can also be felt in museum collections. "We have about 20 Rembrandts and about 20 pictures that entered the museum as Rembrandts but which we do not regard as Rembrandts now, almost all of them given before World War II," said Walter Liedtke, curator of Dutch and Flemish paintings at the Metropolitan Museum of Art. "Opinions have been changed one by one. It has been an ongoing process. As it stands now, things are pretty clear."

The research projeᶜ ᵇegan in 19ᵉ It consists of fᶦ ᵗ histor᷈
ᵎ ᵃim ᶦ

ers, the art market, Rembrandt's connections with other artists, what paintings meant for collectors and the visual tradition Rembrandt worked in."

But they also reflect the orientation of our particular age. "In the 19th century it was felt that only tʰ genius could produce what was wᶜ looking at," said Egbert Haverkʳ Begemann, a specialist in Dutᶜ and the John Langelʰoth Loeb Ƭ sor of art history at New York ᵗ sity's Institute of Fine Arts. ᶜ painting that seemed Rerᵎ esque had to be by him. Noᵛ that there were lots of ᶠ painted almost as well aᶠ In contemporary life, ᵛ the validity of many p the main movers."

Decisions about ᶠ made after scholarlᵎ investigation. "We ᵃ ing at the image as ᵎ mosphere, or the arᵗ general," Mr. ᵎann said. "We aᵗ ecution of details the material cᵎ painting. Scientᶦ not give an ansᵎ ing is by an arᵎ ᵎxpand the ᶦish the ᵗist.
ᶠ

Sex in the Hexagon

after Wallace Stevens

1.

There are more than six ways, of course,
but this six-sided glass building
with its six different views poses
limitations of its own, challenges.

2.

They were robin's egg blue, your eyes
and also the sky. You spread
open my thighs. Outside I noticed the field
was being hayed. I cut my hand on the blades
of your blond hair.

3.

In my mind as we
slowly rotate you turn from
man to woman to faun to wood
nymph and back again. Man.
Woman. Bobcat, bear, swan.
Dolphin, under and over and under me,
then you change again.

4.

How lucky we were to be facing
west when the sun set. Your
head sinking to meet me. No
regard for the bed.

5.

I confuse early spring for winter.
It's easy with you gnawing on my neck.
I confuse my blood with the crimson sun

which has long ago set but
still burns in my head. I confuse
the red with the firetruck as you move into me now.
I confuse my own screams of pleasure with sirens.
With terror.

    6.
Think of something fast—a story
in the dark to prolong this sixth pleasure:
For uniting what were their names?
Delphinus, the Dolphin, was placed among the stars.
To humiliate Cassiopeia half the year
She must hang upside down.
Repeat.
The Dolphin was placed in the sky—
it's no use, to think of the spring sky
with your fingers on my own beating
Spring. The stars pulsate.
You and me and the stars are one.

Candace

This is a chance not to be missed, because only Halley's Comet gives us the opportunity we need. Though it remained unseen between 1911 and its recovery in 1982, we have always known its exact position, and we have been able to make plans well in advance. The Americans have missed their opportunity — their Halley probe was cancelled on the grounds of cost, which seems an almost incredible decision (if you doubt me, compare the cost of a comet probe with that of half a nuclear submarine). However, five probes remain: two Russian, two Japanese and one European. The Russian and Japanese probes will bypass the comet at fairly close range. The European spacecraft, Giotto, will — we hope — actually penetrate the comet's head, and send back direct pictures of the nucleus, about which we still know very little.

Why Did God Make Us?

She opened her catechism.

Q: Who made us?
A: God made us.

Q: Why did God make us?
A: God made us to show forth His goodness and to make us happy with Him in Heaven.

Jesus' New Face

An orange becomes whole, a gleaming knife appears, then miraculously there are two slices of fish and a piece of lemon. Saint Matthew's dark matted hair becomes brown curls before my brother's astonished eye. Half of Saint Simon's beard returns to shadow.

His gaze moves toward the head of Jesus, not yet touched. What, once they get to it, will the new face reveal? A debate, I imagine, arises, at different tables in small restaurants all over Milano. A debate arises, What will the real face reveal after layers of overpaint have been removed? Is it exclusively a narrative, a drama of the moment when Jesus says, "One of you shall betray me"? Or does it also include a moment when Jesus, anticipating his death, "took bread and gave it to his disciples and said, 'Take, eat this, for this is my body.' And he took the cup and gave it to them saying, 'Drink, all of you, for this is my blood which shall be shed for you so that sins may be forgiven.'"

Will the face be resigned and suffused with transcendence? "The eucharist," a man shouts across the cafe at another. A man walks across the floor, takes the other man's shirt in his hands and whispers, "It's the betrayal." "Sacramental," an elegant woman in black states, lifting her veil.

"You are all right, it is simultaneously about both. That is what's so marvelous. That is Leonardo's genius." The old man puts down his vermouth and smiles.

The face of Christ will look like a star.

What?

A star for a head?

"My God, no!" "Yes!" "No!"

"Take, eat, for this is my body."

And he took the cup and gave it to them saying, "For this is the cup of my blood, the mystery of faith."

"It is said," David reports, "that Leonardo had great trouble conceiving the head of Jesus. A fellow artist told Leonardo, 'It is your fault. You gave such divine beauty to apostles Philip and James the Elder that now you can do nothing else except leave the face unfinished.'"

"Is the face unfinished? Could Leonardo not paint it?" a man with tears in his eyes asks.

Sighing. Weeping. "Fool!" the others cry to the man with tears in his eyes.

Quietly, a young woman says, "A passive man of sorrow will appear."

"I fear," David says, "that the features of Christ have vanished. It is possible that all that remains is the glue and paint of restorers, of people like me. Caroline, it is possible the face of the Savior is blank." He laughs a little—his stupid sense of humor.

"We are doing all we can to save the painting. Dr. Brambilla expects a beautiful recovery of Christ. We'll see."

An old woman stands on a chair. "The Christ's face is not resigned, nor is he a man of sorrow. There must have been something divine, superhuman in that face, a great serenity. An island of tranquillity."

I picture my brother standing on a scaffold balancing solvents, water, colors, in front of the enormous Jesus. He looks closely at the overpainting. Hands reach out toward the Savior from every direction. The eyes seem partially closed, the mouth slightly open. In this state he could be a man or a woman.

"There are things that we will inevitably lose: part of his hair, a bit of background, but the blue of his robe will be vibrant, and the red mantle," Dr. Brambilla says.

David looks under the microscope at the shadow below the lip of Christ. He enlarges the power to forty. A tiny area becomes an enormous expanse, resembling land, with its many shades of brown, sloping hills and valleys. A solvent is applied, and we see through the liquid many more depths. He takes his tiny surgical scalpel now. Under the microscope is something huge. He hesitates a moment. Underneath this shall be the real Leonardo, obscured for centuries. He carefully lifts the patch of brown and sighs as it gives way to a rose color, filled with light.

The Box in the Sky

You are still, it seems, a member of the Film Society. A few days ago I received the advance announcement for the Twenty-third New York Film Festival. How we loved to mull over the calendar. This year there's Godard's *Hail Mary*. A British documentary called *28 Up* that looks interesting, and a lot more, of course. We never missed a year, not for all those years except last year. I did not come home from Cummington; I missed it, and you, Max.

The Film Festival always felt like a new beginning somehow, the changing of bad times for better times, a wind from the north, the smell of chimneys being used for the first time of the season, a movement inward. It felt like fall, as much a beginning as school was, and you dressed us up each year and took us to the opening night party. "Daddy," I said. "Call me Max now," you said. We scuffed our feet across ballrooms with the likes of Buñuel and Antonioni. It was a childhood not to be forgotten. You, such an elegant man those gala opening nights in your tuxedo, and your unlikely entourage: two grief-stricken twin boys and a small girl. You, with your unfiltered Camels at the time, talking to beautiful women with deep waves in their dark hair and such white throats.

We were well behaved. We did not follow you too closely; we entertained ourselves. We had contests to see who could eat the most of those tiny sandwiches, the most strawberries, the most chocolate tarts.

Why did you bring us all those years? I can only guess it was for the "visual effect," the standard you measured everything by. About my brothers you said, "I have always loved the visual effect of twins," as if they had sprung from your eye, something perfect and realized, not a random event, a quirk of nature. With you nothing seemed random, everything had its aesthetic raison d'être, even Mother—her illness, her beauty. She fit somehow perfectly into your world view, your particular brand of romanticism, your nihilism, your cynicism. You could bear all of it, finally, but her death, though even you thought she had taken it too far sometimes—her indifference, her detachment.

"You went too far, goddamnit," I heard you yell to her one night after all the dinner guests had left, you alone warming your brandy over the fire. "We have three children and you have been half responsible. From your body, Veronica, like it or not, there has come life. Not an appealing thought to you, perhaps, but true nonetheless."

And you buckling my shoe while I kicked before the first New York Film Festival, she dead only a few weeks then. "They are savages, Veronica, they are little monsters and I do not know what to do." I remember that so perfectly. As you got us ready to go to that first festival to watch films we didn't understand, you buckling my shoe and muttering maniacally, "One, two, buckle my shoe," then pausing, and looking into the distance, "I do not forgive you, Veronica."

I was rather old for you to be buckling my shoe, but it seemed like something you needed to do.

How I grew to love those strange films, their isolated images of tree, snow, field, shattering glass, masks, sex. A montage of peasants. Abandoned cars, children playing hide-and-seek in France. How much I looked forward to each evening, the lights going out, the rise of an unfamiliar language, the sound of hopelessly strange or romantic or melancholy music. The talky French movies, the subtitles I could barely keep up with. Max, I am still a slow reader; I think it's a writer's trait. And after the film was over, how I clapped and clapped until my hands stung, and looked up to see the box where the director and actors sat. I always dreamed of sitting there, Max, in that box in the sky. I think it's the reason I went to film school.

"I loved the festival too, Caroline. When the theater finally darkened and the images—light, dark, light—would appear and you could forget a little, lose yourself in the trees or the field or the shattering glass, in the beautiful camera angles, the distinctive points of view, if only for a little while. The comfort of another language, the solace of subtitles, those little words changing at the bottom of the screen. It was everything while it lasted.

"And then the lights would come up and there were these three small, incredibly sad faces again looking at me, blinking and wondering 'What happened to our mother?'"

How we loved through the years those Octobers. Keep your

calendar free, my cherub, you'd say, near summer's end. I used to write things down in my calendar for every day of the month. One makes lists, fills calendars to avoid falling asleep. I believed that if there were things we had to do on certain days, at certain times, then we would be all right. No harm would come to us because that would ruin our plans. I kept a very precise, orderly calendar, easy to read and filled with events for everyone. If only there were enough places to go, we'd be OK. I loved when Mother put on her lipstick because it meant she was going out. I remember her blotted lips floating in the toilet bowl. The bigger the event, the better, but anything was better than nothing. Recalling those calendars now, all those events and non-events come to mind. *La Traviata* 8 p.m., feed the cat breakfast 7 a.m. and dinner 7 p.m. Meet Andrea for a tea party. Label the trees. Meet Max at MOMA one o'clock. Concert in the Park. Finish novel about pioneer girl.

And each fall when we needed it most, I knew we were safe. At least for a few weeks in September and October, my job became easier. How could we die with all those movies to go to? Opening night, closing night and all the nights in between. Mom died right before the first festival. How much I wished she could have held on just one more month!

Call me Max now, you said.

Maybe it would have been something to live for.

You loved those films. "Dad," I'd say, in the middle of one of them. "I've got to go to the bathroom." "Shh," is all you'd say, too captivated to care. Is that why I went to film school? Is that what I wanted finally? Two and a half uninterrupted hours in the dark with you?

Hail Mary is playing October 7th and 8th. *28 Up* is at 9 p.m. on the fifth. *Ran* opens the festival this year, and *Kaos* closes it.

I wonder if this calendar with its thirty squares, its predictable course, its necessary events, I wonder if somehow it could serve as a blueprint.

Let's look. Let's study it closely. Before the phone rings

again. Before another Rembrandt turns out to be a fake. Before
what's really beneath Jesus' face is revealed. Before one more
person dies. Max. Dad. Max, do you think it could serve somehow as instructions on how to live?

The Message on the Machine

"Hi. It's Steven. Guess what? We're neighbors. I've checked into
St. Vincent's. Doctor's orders. My number is 427-4410. Give me
a call, darling. Bye."

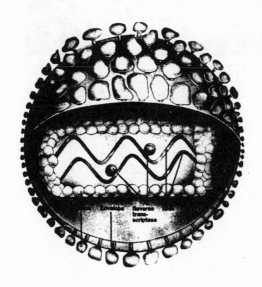

Sky Watch | This week at 11 P.M.

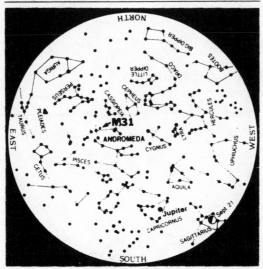

Early this week the absence of a moon allows us to inspect M31, the Great Galaxy in Andromeda. M31 is visible to the naked eye under proper conditions. In the early 1900's a controversy raged over whether spiral-shaped clouds (nebulae) were located in our 'universe' (today known as our galaxy) or at vastly greater distances. Using the 100-inch telescope on Mt. Wilson, Edwin Hubble resolved parts of the spiral arms into stars. Continued observation revealed Cepheid variable stars, the celestial yardsticks, in these arms. The implication was that the 'spiral nebula' in Andromeda was truly beyond our 'universe', suggesting that the real universe was much larger than suspected. This galaxy is the closest to us, yet is the most distant object visible to the naked eye — over 2 million light years away.

To use the map, hold it vertically before you with the direction you are facing positioned at the bottom. The outer circle represents the horizon, the zenith, the spot directly overhead, is near the center of the map. The map is accurate for 11 o'clock tonight by Saturday it will be accurate for 10 30 P M

K L Franklin, Astronomer Emeritus, The Hayden Planetarium   *The New York Times* Sept 15, 1985

Winter

Not Steven

My childhood friend, I think, dialing the first three numbers.
My counterpart—the next four. All these years.

"Steven," I say.

"Hi, Caroline. What's going on? How are you?"

"I'm fine. What are you doing there?"

"Well," he says. He pauses. He is about to say something that
can never be taken back—so he waits a beat. I am being pulled
through a tunnel toward whatever it is he'll say. He gives me
this split second.

"Actually," he says, "I'm not fine."

"What is it, Steven?"

He pauses again, but only for a moment. And I know what it
is. My best friend.

"I have pneumocystis."

"Pneumocystis?" I say slowly, giving myself a little more
time, before full knowledge.

"It's the AIDS pneumonia."

"Yes. I know."

"Caroline."

"Steven . . . Are you afraid?"

"I don't know," he says, "it's not really hitting me. Oh, I've
had my moments. I've already thought about what should be
played at my funeral."

"What?"

"Well, this is only a thought—how about the prologue to *Der
Rosenkavalier*?"

"I have to see you."

"Just call before you come. I'm in the Coleman Wing. I call it the Gary Coleman Wing. The entrance is on Twelfth Street. It's temperature time here, Doll. I've got to go."

"I love you."

I listen to the dial tone on the other end until I hear something. It's my own voice. It says, "Not Steven." Those are the two words I hear again and again. Not Steven.

And a small voice responds. Then who?

"I don't care who. Not Steven."

Death is not only a big-breasted woman whispering over a man whose brain, whose whole body will explode so stupendously; it is also a beautiful man, muscular, faceless, lying on a pier, years ago in the bright sun.

The Teacher in Space

I turn on the rental TV and I think of Steven. It's morning. A blue sky. A sparkling clear day. Freezing temperatures. Seven astronauts waving good-bye.

The first civilian, a teacher, Christa McAuliffe, on board. Reagan's idea. Much fanfare.

I think of my friend and watch the little numbers on the bottom of the screen go by. T minus twenty-nine seconds and counting. The space shuttle *Challenger* poised on the launch pad.

Lift-off.

The upturned faces of the various families with captions under them. The stupid president. The stupid president's stupid wife.

A veering to the right.

Steven.

An explosion in the sky.

Steven.

I do not trust myself on this one. I turn up the sound. "Obviously," a voice says, "a major malfunction."

We see it again.

T Minus 13, 12, 11

"T minus 10, 9, 8, 7, 6—we have main engine start—4, 3, 2, 1, and lift-off. Lift-off of the twenty-fifth space shuttle mission, and it has cleared the tower."

Mission Control: "*Challenger*, go with throttle up."

Francis Scobee, *Challenger* commander: "Roger, go with throttle up."

"Obviously a major malfunction. We have no downlink."

"We have a report from the flight dynamics officer that the vehicle has exploded."

We See It Again

The astronauts are at the last ceremonial breakfast.

The astronauts are entering a white room for the final preparation. Christa McAuliffe is being handed an apple. "It's going to go today," she says. The astronauts stand in front of the traditional good-luck cake. The crew eats the cake.

The crew gets in one by one, waving good-bye. Judith Resnik makes a funny little motion.

Something is said about the future, about pushing the edge, reaching for the stars.

A flash in the sky. If he were here, Max would say that Christa had just taught her best lesson.

We see it again. "T minus 10, 9, 8, 7, 6 . . ."

We See It Again

Ed and Grace Corrigan, father and mother of Christa McAuliffe.
A puff of smoke, a muffled clap. Then Lisa Corrigan, Christa's
sister, hollers and grabs her father's hand. Extreme close-up.
Slow motion. Mrs. Corrigan leans her head on the shoulder of
her husband, whose sweater bears a large button with their
daughter's picture. "The craft has exploded." She turns and
repeats the message to her husband. Screams. Cries.

Red

The entrance to the Coleman Wing is on Twelfth Street. I have
not called, though he told me to. I am afraid he will tell me not
to come, not today. I ask for a visitor's pass at the desk. There
will be a series of doors and elevators to go through, metal
against metal. I am so afraid. I ask the guard which way to go.
He does not look at me but simply points. I want to clutch his
uniform, stop here and simply say it: I am so afraid.

I bring myself down the hall past the first set of double doors,
through a long corridor and up the elevator. There are more
doors, another long hall. I pass a doctor just out of surgery. He's
wearing a shower cap, a long green robe and gloves. My walk is
the longest walk in the hospital. Past more metal doors into the
forbidden zone. There's a nurses' station and then the AIDS
rooms. I look up at the young, young nurse before I go in.
Who thought we would live to see this?

There are a hundred warnings on the door. People in masks.
Enter cautiously. Enter at your own risk. Stay away, I think, at
your own risk.

Bright red. I can hardly find my friend through so much red.
There are red plastic bags on everything. The dumpster, the
wastepaper basket, the tray of food. Touch this and die.

His eyes are closed. How young he looks, like a child, I think, and also how very old. Ancient. Asleep. I look at his sensual mouth. His brown, muscled arms. His handsome profile. He looks so perfect.

I sit on a chair next to the bed.

I think of this disease flowering in his bloodstream like a dark tulip.

He has the softness of a child. Long eyelashes. So beautiful. They flutter. "Caroline," he whispers. "Hi."

"You don't have to say anything."

"I'm so weak," he says.

He is attached to an elaborate IV system that pumps massive doses of medicine into his body.

"All I keep saying over and over to myself is, 'It's making me better, it's making me better.'"

"Shh. It's OK."

He nods. He's too weak. I sit next to him as he dozes in and out of sleep. There's so much red. I can barely see him in the glare the red makes.

"I love you," I whisper. "Hang in there." I put my cheek on his hand, his arm wired to a complicated series of tubes and bags and a metal machine.

I am crying as I leave the room of a thousand warnings. Danger. Stop. Red. The nurse quietly lives in my face with me for a minute. Hers must stay immobile, strong, out in the world. Her face is not allowed to look this way. All of her patients are dying and all of them are too young to die. I stand in the hall for a minute. "They are such nice people," she says. "I never knew." I nod. I walk down the endless corridors. Past wings. Down elevators. Through metal. I give the pass back. On the street my feet assume the rhythm of medicine and blood pumping as I go into the Jefferson Market, into Balducci's, not knowing what to do, where to go. One foot forward, then the other. One foot. The other. It's making me, better. It's making me, better. I bring this message into the world. Write it on the streets. In my steps. I pump the medicine into him. I pump everything I've got into him. I walk miles. Hour after hour. It's making him better.

Again

Steven McAuliffe, his son Scott, nine, his daughter Caroline, six, watching as the spacecraft explodes, showering debris into the ocean. At the launch site all the other astronauts' families as well.

Concord, New Hampshire — Live, students in the auditorium, wearing party hats, blowing into noisemakers.
   "The vehicle has exploded."

If you turn off the sound, all you see is the eerie beauty of an orange fireball and a billowing white trail against the perfect blue. A gorgeous aerial display.

Temperatures in the low twenties.
   "Good morning, Christa, hope we go today," said Ground Control.
   "Good morning, I hope so too." These are her last words.

Chaos

Despite my penchant for order. This is the world. We name it. And what good does it do? We arrange it on a page.
   You were here and now you're gone.
   You were well and now you're sick.
   You were a painting by Matisse, but you took sleeping pills.

More from the Rental TV

Haitians are dancing in the snow in Grand Army Plaza. Duva-
lier gone.

In the Philippines the Marcos-Aquino election. Ballots are
being thrown out the window like confetti, like snow.

A wreath dropped from a helicopter to commemorate seven
astronauts. A group of dolphins in the frame, leaping in unison.

I turn up the sound. A hank of hair has washed up on a Florida beach, not far from the *Challenger* accident. A bit of bone
and tissue wrapped in dark blue cloth.

Better

They took out a piece of his lung, a bronchoscopy, to make sure
it was the AIDS pneumonia and not some other pneumonia.
This I remember now from our first phone conversation, something I remember again as I cross the street to St. Vincent's
wondering, Are they sure it's AIDS, are they positive?

I pass under the stone cross on the street. He will probably die. This is the first time I say it. I pass children on their way home from school, swinging lunchboxes, knapsacks, singing, chasing each other down the dark street.

I enter the hospital, get my pass. I wave to the guard who waves back but does not look at my face. I know my way now. I notice someone in the first hallway that looks like our friend William, but is not. In the elevator I see someone I imagine could be my mother. In the last hall I hear the sound of red. In the last hall a man with gloves on, a green bathrobe, a shower cap.

Steven is sitting up in bed. "Well, well, look who it is!" He smiles, he takes my hand and kisses it. There's a moment of silence. He is brand new at dying. We look at each other curiously.

"What a relief to see you up."

"I feel much better. *Much*."

"How long are you here for?"

"They're not positive. Until my lungs clear up. God, it's good to see you."

It makes it a little easier for me to be next to the red today with Steven sitting up in bed—a death-defying position.

"What happens next?"

"Well, first they've got to get rid of the pneumonia. Then apparently there are a million options. My doctor is very aggressive. I like her a lot. Wait till you meet her." He smiles. "So what's up with you? It's been ages since we've had a real visit."

"Oh, you know, putting Max's house in order. Trying to write a book. Keeping out of trouble."

"That doesn't sound like you, Caroline. Who's your latest love?"

"I've decided to take a break. Really."

"I wonder whether I'll ever have sex again."

"Oh, probably."

"I got this AIDS packet from the hospital, filled with all kinds of info. Parties for people with AIDS, an AIDS dating service. How's the book going? I can't wait to read it!"

"Pretty slowly. I'm having a lot of trouble, actually. It's really just notes toward a novel." I've only just scratched the surface, I think. I'm too afraid.

"You'd better write faster," he says. He doesn't mean to say it—it just comes out. We are so new at this.

I've heard what might happen. The invasion of the blood-brain barrier. Dementia. The inability to read. More. We talk quickly.

He tells me all about his trip last fall to Italy. The Giotto-and-Piero trip, he calls it. He tells me how he meticulously planned it all, exactly where he went. Lunching in the heat of Rome. A villa that had a dumbwaiter. The beauty of the maid. The feel of cool plaster against his hand. A swim he took in a blue grotto with a stranger.

The phone rings. I notice Steven has brought his Rolodex to the hospital. A natural talker, even under the worst circumstances.

Today I am better equipped to say the red means danger. The red means everything is contaminated.

"Was it a shock?" he asks, hanging up the phone. "Max, I mean."

"Not a shock exactly. Something less shocking than a shock. A sort of elongated shock."

"When had you seen him last?"

"One night in late winter. It's strange to think back on now; it seems like we stayed up the whole night saying good-bye. And hello, actually."

"Remember," Steven quotes Laurie Anderson, waving his hand, " 'In our country good-bye looks just like hello.' "

Hello, Can You Hear Me?

Hello, I say, can you hear me? Is anybody up there? Can anybody hear me? I am trying to talk to you.

"I can't hear you with everyone talking at the same time. It's hard to hear you with all the commotion."

Why is this happening? I think of the seeds of this disease with us a long time. I see you with your long arm reaching into your jute sack and planting your seeds.

"You give me too much credit, my dear."

I begin to cry.

"It's hard to worry about you with all these extra people dying."

Why Steven?

"I don't know. Why don't you talk to my son?"

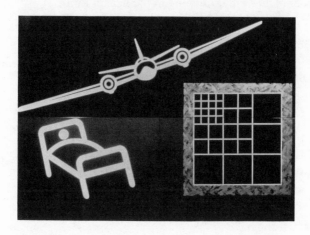

Another Visit

I watch my friend thinning in front of me: a Modigliani. A Giacometti.

He's sleeping, I think. But then he opens his eyes. "Please don't leave me, Caroline."

I flesh him out. I will not turn him into paint and canvas, where he'll be manageable. He won't allow it.

"I'm sorry," I tell him. "I'm here." It's something I learned from Max. To leave like this. How to make pictures of leaving in my head.

I take his hand of flesh and blood. "I'm here, Steven."

"Good," he says very quietly. "Tell me about the book." He is trying to be a good host, even now.

"I don't know." I'm reluctant, but it's what he wants to hear. "The words don't work anymore, given all of this." I look at my friend, thirty-two, under a fluorescent light, dying.

He nods.

Please get better, I say to myself.

"I don't know why it's not hitting me harder. Maybe I don't really believe it yet. It just hasn't sunk in, I guess." He hesitates. "I think this is going to be the big breakthrough year. I guess I've *got* to think that."

His doctor comes in. She is in war paint. She is here to fight this thing. She has told him of all the experimental programs there are to consider. She speaks in the alphabet of hope. She looks incapable of losing even one more person. She walks to the window. Fingers the petals of the fringed tulips on the sill. "These are so wonderful," she says to Steven.

"Oh, *please*, no sexual allusions now," he says to her.

It is the end of visiting hours. A voice makes the announcement. "Please leave your passes at the front desk." I stand up.

"Wait," Steven says.

"*Etienne*," I whisper. "*Qu'est-ce que c'est?*"

"When I was really sick, I imagined this light that protected me, that tricked my body into thinking that I was well. Those days I thought I was dying, I imagined hoops of gold wrapped around me like a Macy's Christmas tree. Isn't that great?"

City of Stars

I like to think it is a city of stars. I go up to the roof. I see no stars. City of small miracles, then. For a star to burn through the lights of the city, the smog of the city. I take my star map up. If we could see stars, these are the stars we would see. It would look like this:

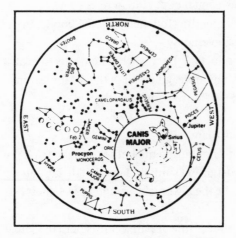

The *New York Times* says so. City of smallest hopes.

I walk up Sixth Avenue with Steven. His lungs are clear and he has been let out of the hospital. We step into a church where Louise Hay is going to speak about her work with AIDS patients.

In the room there are hundreds of people with AIDS and the people who love them. On a neck a purplish lesion shaped like a fish. On a hand a purplish lesion shaped like a heart. A purplish lesion shaped like a star.

A Family of Almost Four

Maggie arranges spices. Alison promises they'll plant tarragon and basil in the spring, and rosemary for remembrance. Alison thought of wildflowers that live for a week.

Candace thought of the childhood stories her father would read her. They were of building a soapbox derby car and winning a race. Becoming a sailor. Being ten feet tall. Crossing the tundra. Being a pioneer. Though there were a variety of characters and situations, all had the same message finally, the same moral: Nothing is impossible, you can do anything you want, the world is filled with possibility. But with the loss of her father some idea of herself had been taken away, the loss of a world she believed in.

Henry thought of Maggie. He pictured the beautiful flush of his wife's face in winter. He worried about her and the wood-burning stove: she was so easily distracted.

He thought of Alison, studying her confirmation questions in dim light. So serious, so determined to get to the bottom of things.

He thought of Candace, who refused to talk to him even though they were in the same city, blocks apart. He wondered whether she had begun her Italian lessons. If he knew her, she was already composing little Italian verses on that swirling marbled paper from Florence, but he could not be sure any-more. He had put those flat Florentine pencils in her stocking one year and she had loved them. She, laughing and dancing with delight. He thought of Candace dancing. What did she dream? Perhaps her dreams were all Piero and Giotto now. Who knows? He thought of his wife's lovely flushed face. And Ali-son.

Candace dreams the family whole—for Christmas.

Alison looks. Alison keeps looking.

Maggie turns the pages.

that separated .
dividual talents?

CLAUDE MONET

Monet's art, almost in itself, spans and crowns what is most significant in Impressionism. In "luminous waves," in "splashes of brilliance,"[36] he set down the moment on canvas. The *carpe lucem*. He was both the virtuoso of light and its willing subject. "When it gets dark," he confided to a friend, "I feel as though I'm dying."[37]

His portraits around the age of thirty-five show him with a well-kept beard and a determined, youthful look. T~harant described hi~ ~kv, his should-

Timid and violent, emotional to the highest degree, Cézanne was an unusual combination of mysticism and positive reality. "We are nothing but a little bit of solar heat stored up and organized, a reminder of the sun, a little phosphorus burning in the meninges of the world,"[57] he said on reading Lucretius. But his intelligence was not content to be deductive; it passed over the things of this world and, strengthened by intuition, arrived at the Christian faith. Gasquet recalls seeing him at Le Tholonet, "after Vespers, his head bare, magnificent in the sunlight, around him a large circle of respectful young people, walking behind the canopy in the procession of Rogations,[58] and kneeling along the way at the edge of the fields with tears in his eyes."[59]

Paul Cézanne. *House of Dr. Gachet at Auvers.* c. 1873. Oil on canvas, 18⅛″ × 15″. Museum of Impressionism, The Louvre, Paris

For him, everything came from inner conflict. "An art that does not have its source in emotion is not an art," he liked to say. But his work does not have the quick accents of Monet, Sisley, or Morisot; it is, on the contrary, patient and deliberate. "How does he do it?" Renoir wondered. "He puts two brushstrokes of color on a canvas and it's already something good."[60]

At Aix, merged with his corner of earth, he did not take his eyes from it until nightfall, in his effort to put "the flow of the world into an inch of matter."[61] Educated in all things, spewing up what he called the "Ecole des *Bozards*," he conceived the course of ⊦ from the bisons and deer engraved on t⊦ up to the steam-filled railway stati⸍ see in painting," he sai⸍ seen, everything h℮ ' man " ⸜ ' ⊦⸍

Maggie saw so many people in double now. People who resembled so closely people she had loved, and she wondered if in some way this was a preparation for death; she did not know how.

Maggie thought of the bear on the path. The family of almost four.

Maggie listened to soloists. Yo-Yo Ma. Glenn Gould. She also did chores, things she had never done before. While Alison was in school she put plastic up on the windows, hay around the foundation of the house. In the afternoon she'd build a fire, and wait for Alison.

A Dog, a Cat, a Rabbit Chasing a Carrot

I turn on the rental TV but keep the sound off. I put Yo-Yo Ma on the compact disc player. I turn on the light board and look at the slides Steven has lent me.

I think of him across the street in a strange place, in a strange room.

I was away too long. I didn't keep up with you. I turn off the music and in silence look at his life.

He's painting on metallic panels, divided into three and four sections. Cool, beautiful surfaces. The drawings simple. Signs.

A dog.

A cat.

A rabbit chasing a carrot.

A house.

An armchair.

A diamond ring.

A division sign.

A cloud and a man.

A hand reaching through ice.

Or a hand falling through ice.

A hospital bed, a patient with a halo over his head.

A horse with wings.

A plane that descends.

The Message on the Machine

The message on the machine, my friend, is that you are back in the hospital, with high fevers, with horrendous headaches. You've got a new phone number and a new room. I get out my phone book and pencil it in. Around your name in the phone book are bits of our conversations over the years. "Review in *Artforum*, May *GQ*. New working hours: M, T, W nights and

Thurs lunch. Opening 15 February, New Museum. Call tomor-
row about blood. Blood in on Monday. Patient info: 790-7070.
Lungs, Chest X ray. What happens next??? FIND COM-
POUND S.

Compound S, AZT, the drug that stops the damn virus from
dividing. It's the program, you explain to me over the machine,
you'll have to try to get into. Call me, you say. Bye.

I am tired of things that divide, that change shape, that become anything other than themselves. I am tired not only of the
sinister magic that changes normal cells into death cells, but of
any magic, the cells in my brain that turn the homeless on the
streets into pink and purple mountains, the cells that turn broken glass into ice. I am tired of any deception. The cells of my
brain that bring you back, Max. I am sick of myself trying to
give shape to all this sorrow, all this rage, all this loss—and
failing.

Friend

I look at my friend hooked up to a huge machine. It should be
possible to say something, to do something with words. But all
I can manage is "I love you." I hold his hand lightly, watch the
liquid drop from its bag into the tube and into his arm. The
nurse comes in, but sees me and turns. I realize I could be his
sister perhaps, and, it is true, I could be his mother. He's that
young all of a sudden today. "I'm just like a pioneer," he sput-
ters, lying there. He opens his childish eyes. Stares at the poster
that hangs across from him. Closes them again. "It looks like a
carnival," he says, "a carnival on a hot summer night." A ferris
wheel—he rode it into fever.

He is sleeping, this pioneer, and I am grateful for that. I
watch him sleep for a long time. No one seems to mind. It's visiting hours, after all.

Max, I don't understand any of it.

I am not mother or sister, wife or lover. Remember how we used to dream of having children together, Steven?

I am your friend.

He's sleeping so soundly. On his night table, *The Vampire Lestat*, *The Face* magazine, *Mr. Palomar*, his Walkman, his Rolodex.

Men with masks and gloves come in. I move my fingers to my lips to say, Quiet, my friend is asleep. They are young men and even in masks I can tell they are good-looking. Like my friend.

Steven opens his eyes. He looks at them as they remove the red plastic bags that are full and replace them. He's thinking, Oh, those cute orderlies, or, Didn't I meet you once at the Palladium? or—I don't know what he's thinking. He turns his palm over. I put my finger lightly in his hand and he folds his finger around mine. He's thinking so many things lying there. He opens his mouth slightly, like a baby bird. It should be possible to do something with words.

"Caroline," he whispers, "I love you too."

Sometimes it is best not to go directly home after a visit to the hospital. Sometimes it is best to go sit in a cafe for a while. Espresso and an anisette biscuit. Lean against some column, some faux marble.

I feel the toll that suffering takes. You are my friend and you are suffering. High fevers, chills. Tests, a bronchoscopy, a spinal tap.

"My brother had a spinal tap once," I tell him. "He said it wasn't too bad."

You are sarcastic with suffering, and then not. When you are not, you sit up in bed, you clip things from newspapers, looking for shapes. You make out bills. You send me the latest fashions in an envelope. You type me little notes.

Then you're doubtful. We find it difficult to talk about the future. All talk of galleries stops. Shows. You are sarcastic with suffering. What gallery would want you with your machines, your chills, your death sentence? You are not old enough to die. This I know for sure.

These things are true about yourself, Caroline:

Sometimes you need to sit in a cafe after a visit to the hospital. You like to watch the people around you, pretend it's the whole world. You sit, even now, with a pen in your hand. You hold it like a paintbrush sometimes. Sometimes like a staff. Sometimes like a weapon. Now and then you still think of Maggie and Alison, of Candace and Henry.

You push your hair to one side of your head, capable of arranging, if nothing else, the way your hair falls.

You are perceived as aloof, sad, a little strange.

"Another espresso, please. Something strong, with a kick."

We used to joke about having children.

"I had a dream that I was making love with my doctor and all of her friends on this enormous bed."

"You were making love with your woman doctor?"

"And all her friends," you add. "All women."

They were saving your life, I thought, biting into the anisette biscuit.

"I called my parents this morning at about six o'clock and told them how much I loved them, how much I appreciated all they'd done, how wonderful they've been. They called back an hour later. They thought I was going to kill myself. End it right here. They thought I was saying good-bye."

Put the ashtray in the center of the table. The little vase with the flower and baby's breath slightly to the left. The sugar in its glass pot to the other side.

The woman at the next table has four cigarettes left in her pack.

My house is about four minutes from here.

Let me amend what I have always thought. I love not things that are certain, but simply things in themselves.

Four cigarettes on a table in a cafe. I love not the future. Not the fact that she will surely smoke them, but that they are here right now. Four of them, in a brightly colored package.

What he was saying was thank you.

What they thought he was saying was good-bye.

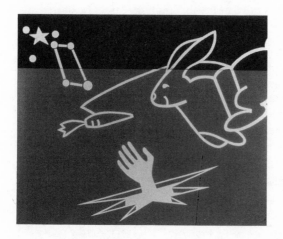

Another Message on the Machine

"Hi, Joanie, this is Celia calling about Boris's surprise party. Meet us outside the Cafe Sha-Sha. Be there at 11, not 11:30. And bring some vodka. See you!"

I do not know Celia or Boris or where to bring the vodka, but I write it down anyway.

I think of my own voice left in fragments all over the city. I wonder if somehow all those fragments could be spliced together and played—would that be the message I finally meant to leave?

The Handsome Face

The sensuous lips. The beautiful, browning skin. No outward imperfections. What I love most perhaps are the lashes, dark, curling on the closed eyes. The dark, dark eyes. The vulnerable chin with its cleft, the perfect slope of the shoulders, the sensuous lips.

I see sometimes now, as I walk down the street or sit in a cafe, or theater or museum, I see now your cleft chin in others, your hairline, your hands, your look. Is this how it works then? Your special way of saying hello and good-bye.

The slightly faraway look in your eyes already.

Good-bye

Thank you. I love you. Alarming things to hear from a grown son somehow, especially from one who is so sick. But nothing compared to good-bye.

Mary, Can You Help Me?

"I don't know, Caroline. I'm not sure anymore."

Mary, please.

"I'm having trouble watching all these sons die. It reminds me of—"

I know. But that was so long ago.

We See It Again

At 6 a.m. the temperature was twenty-seven degrees and the shuttle's orange external tank was white with ice and frost.

At 9:07, after the astronauts were seated in the *Challenger* wearing gloves because the interior was so cold, ground controllers broke into a round of applause. Still, the countdown was halted, primarily to wait for the morning to warm up and melt some of the ice. It was a two-hour postponement.

All this time the crew was waiting in the *Challenger*'s cabin.

Dick Scobee, the mission commander, and Michael Smith of the Navy sat at the controls. Behind them sat Judy Resnik and Ronald McNair. Below, in the mid-deck, were the other crew members, Ellison Onizuka, Gregory Jarvis and Christa McAuliffe.

"Lift-off," announced the countdown commentator. "Lift-off of the twenty-fifth space shuttle mission, and it has cleared the tower."

A second later a puff of smoke from the right solid rocket booster.

"*Challenger*, go with throttle up."

"Roger, go with throttle up."

"Uh oh." These are the last words heard. "Uh oh."

From the *New York Times*, I read to Steven:

" 'At 59 seconds the *Challenger* went through its time of maximum dynamic pressure when the vibrations of thrusting rockets, the momentum of ascent and the force of the wind resistance combined to exert tremendous stresses on the shuttle structure. At about this time, a relentless sequence of events, none immediately detectable to ground controllers or the crew, was dooming the *Challenger*.

" 'A new plume of smoke issued from the lower side of the right booster. Pressures inside the two boosters, which should be equal, began to diverge, with those in the right booster dropping sharply to suggest a leak of some sort. At 60.6 seconds, flame erupted from the right booster. At 66.17 seconds, a bright glow appeared on that booster and merged with the fast-burning plume. At 73 seconds pressure in the right booster plunged further, reaching 24 pounds per square inch less than the pressure in the other booster.

" 'Immediately afterward, at 73.175 seconds, a mysterious cloud spread along the external fuel tank, followed by flashes of light and explosions. The last radioed data from the shuttle, at 73.621 seconds, told of a sudden surge of pressure in the main engines. Intense heat in the fuel pump caused one of the engines to shut down.

" 'Eighteen miles off Cape Canaveral and 10 miles up in the blue sky, a fireball engulfed the *Challenger*. If the crew had any warning, it came too late for them to do anything, even radio Mission Control. The first sign most flight controllers had that anything was amiss came when their computer screens flashed on and off.' "

Obviously a major malfunction.

Uh Oh

Max, if you were here you'd say something about Judy Resnik, I know. Something like "The idea of a life wasted, not just when the damn thing blew up but all along—I don't know. She was a smart girl. People have a responsibility to their intelligence, my God! Some of those others, they were just simple boys, rather mediocre, all in all. They had reached their pinnacle, lived their personal dream. They did well for themselves, simply to be whirled around in space like a monkey or a dog."

A dog named Leika.

A dog named Sue.

A dog named Christa.

An American Child, January 1986

A child points to a toaster. "Is this going to blow up?" she asks. To a cat. "Is Whiskers going to blow up?"

"Are you going to blow up, Mommy?"

Jesus Falls for the Second Time

And the woman whose name was Veronica wept when she saw Christ dragging his wooden cross to the place of skulls. She wept. His purple rag and crown. Sweat pouring from him. He falls and she wipes his brow. And I know the image of his face is supposed to appear on that towel, but there's nothing there this time when she hands it to me except what appears to be a small pink flower. But on closer examination, I see it is the swollen imprint of a woman's feverish lips.

Desire

It is 3:20 p.m. on Sunday, February 2, 1986. I have rented a car for the day just so that I can go someplace—I don't know where. I am driving on the West Side Highway. The Empire State Building is golden and shining, splendid against a steel gray sky. What the light looks like at this very moment is a golden pillar of hope. A flaming cylinder of desire. I am driving fast. Fast enough so that it is ten years ago. A Sunday afternoon in winter as well. He walks into one of the bars that flank the West Side Highway. He is not in love, though he would not mind it. He sees in the dark corner a beauty and moves toward him. How wonderful he thinks this life of desire, this body of desire; it is as large as the heart, as large as the mind. How it pulled him like any wind, in many directions and he simply followed. How wonderful. Sometimes just a passing stranger on a passing afternoon is enough. A bristling encounter. He moves toward it and it takes form. He trembles, he feels the blood moving in his body, he is so alive. And I am driving faster. He shudders. He wants so much. He is so filled with blood and life. The press of loud music and flesh. The smell of hair and sweat and highway. Of heat and cold. Of leather and denim. Of dark and light.

He will go home later to paint. How he loves this life. He is only twenty-two. Just come to New York from Yale and everything seems new. He is a waiter four nights a week, which is bad, but not that bad. He will not become a doctor like his father; he will not go to architecture school, which would be the practical thing to do. He will paint during the day, wait on tables at night to make money, not a lot, but enough to enjoy this passing Sunday afternoon, to buy food and supplies, in summer enough money to spend a few weeks in Italy with a blond boy or some Greek god on the shores of the Aegean.

He is still innocent of everything. Tell him of a ravaging death only ten years in the future and he will bat his beautiful lashes and say, "Please, save that for a Byron or a Keats."

A cleft chin.

Dark eyes.

Black hair.

Steven, forty years before this, in another country, would have received a death sentence as well.

Intellectual.

Homosexual.

Jew.

Max Speaks

I get up. Look for her. No, she's not here. She must have risen early. Such a beautiful face. Gone. Eyes of light.

No note.

I know her passion. I remember such passion from once before.

She's a few blocks away. A phone call away.

That hair I remember so well. It is like yours, Veronica, thick and wavy, only lighter. How you return whole in a curl of hair on the feverish forehead of our daughter.

She's told me she's going to an artist colony for the spring. She came to say good-bye.

Her eyes like sapphires. Her smooth skin.

When she first heard Stravinsky, she said it sounded like zebras walking. My love.

On the table two empty brandy glasses. A pipe. My pipe. A leaf that once wrapped cheese.

Research

Categories have often helped. Research helps.

I make a list of depression clinics: New York Hospital, Mount Sinai, NYU.

A list of sleep clinics.

Electroshock therapy is available at the New York State Psychiatric Institute, Mother.

The new fast-acting antidepressants are Asendin, Desyrel, Ludiomil, Tegratol, Xanax.

Light therapy—that sounds nice. We could go to the Affective Disorders Program, Mom. Rochester is not so far.

He's Hungry

He's starving. He keeps asking for more and more food. Later we'll learn it's because of the medication, but for now it's just a ravenous appetite that both tortures him and reminds him of what it means to be healthy. He's baffled. I bring him ham-and-swiss on rye with lettuce and mayo. I bring him bags of Dipsy Doodles, cans and cans of classic Coke. He gains weight in front of me. His face is bloated. "You look like Robert DeNiro in *King of Comedy*," I tell him. Steven, you are breaking my heart.

He eats and eats, adding pounds, adding flesh to his body. Adding life. I bring him turkey with tomato on whole wheat. I bring him wonton soup. Italian candies my brother has sent from Perugia wrapped in red and silver and gold foil.

I would bring you Tescher chocolates. Reggiano Parmesan. Sushi. Champagne. Goat's cheese and pears. I would bring you anything you asked for.

I bring you *The Face* magazine, hot off the press, your favorite

"Let me give you some money," he says.

"Steven, please."

"Everyone's working really hard to get me into the Compound S program," he says.

"That's good," I say. "What about that drug from Mexico?"

"Ribavirin?"

"If you want, I'll go get it." I would bring you Ribavirin from Mexico.

"Oh, I love it. I can just see you in your raincoat and sunglasses, crossing the border. You'd be so gorgeous. The Mexicans would kidnap you and leave me here to die."

We talk about fashion for hours. You devour all kinds of news from the outside. We gossip, about stars, about friends.

"And how's David?"

"Same. Still working on the restoration. Still bothering me about my book, though he doesn't really want to hear about it."

"Yes, I remember. He always liked the success of *Delirium* but not *Delirium* itself."

He smiles and closes his eyes for a moment.

"You look tired, Steven."

"No, I'm OK. Please stay. Do you want to split a Dove Bar?"

"Sure," I say.

On my way down I notice that there is no thirteenth floor. I hand back my pass. I laugh out loud. He is dying on the lucky fourteenth floor.

Candace, Dancing

He had said that he loved them.

Candace remembers last year at the summer house. They had gone earlier than usual. She was going to dance a rite of spring.

Her father had looked sad, as if with each step she was dancing away from him, but it was he in fact who was dancing away from her.

He had said that he loved them.

She took out her sketchbook and drew a hand. His hand. She

thought that it had meant he would never leave them. She draws a rifle sight on the page and begins to cry.

She would like to kill him and the "actress" and the dog. She would like to kill the dog first.

He had hurt them terribly. He had hurt their mother.

She had thought he loved them. She turns the page. "Fucking Liar," she writes. She draws his hand reaching up through ice and she lets it go under.

"I do not believe we are powerless," she writes. "I believe it is still possible to do something."

She would like to shoot that dopey dog.

She closes her book and gets up. "I do not believe in the limitations of art," she writes with a bright red lipstick across the wall.

"I do not know if there is a heaven, but I do not believe we are powerless.

"I do not believe there are no solutions."

She opens the window that looks out on Eleventh Street. "I do not believe in Ronald Reagan," she shouts." I do not believe in Ed Koch!"

"Neither do I!" someone shouts back.

"I do not believe in Sigmund Freud. I am not smiling when I say this.

"I do not believe in any of the fathers. I do not believe in Science or Medicine. I do not believe in NASA. I do not believe in God. I do not accept that it is a man's world."

"I will not keep quiet," she writes in red. She calls Biddy's answering machine. "Fucking liar," she says, and hangs up.

"I do not believe there are no solutions. I do not believe that we are doing all we can. I do not accept that we are expendable. I do not believe we are powerless.

"I know there are solutions."

She dips her hands into paint and leaves her fingerprints on the walls in every room of their apartment. "I was someone once," she says. "I was here."

"I still believe that anything is possible," she shouts, and she whirls around the house.

CAROLE MASO * 162

Freud Speaks

I dream I am swimming.

   "You are in the birth canal."

   "No, I am swimming in a pool," I say.

   "Very common," he says. The water sac. The birth canal.

   "It's not even a kidney-shaped pool," I say. "It's rectangular, you know, a normal one, nothing fancy."

   He smirks a little. He's heard this all before.

   "It really *is* a pool. I think it means I want to go swimming."

   "Don't be ridiculous," he says.

We have received orders not to move

Good News

```
Dear C,
     In case you hadn't heard the good news - 7 astronomers
(from Carnegie Tech) tell us the Milky Way & neighboring
galaxies (over 350 light years across) are moving at one
million miles an hour toward the same spot near the Southern
Cross. Toward what? An exotic particle? Invisible star? The
densest dark matter in creation? They can't say, but the odd
convergence & galactic rush is causing serious reconsideration
of Big Bang & ghostly architecture of time/space universe. & -
since the Southern Cross is only 150 light years away - you
probably only have 2 or 3 thousand years left to finish the
novel before ...
                    A Fellow Skywatcher

Ps/ I've always been suspicious of Cygnus X-3, myself.
```

Because Silence Has Always Equaled Death

We are singing for our lives.

He's back on track today. We talk about Compound S—AZT. "Oh, where's my blackboard?" he says, as he describes to me how it works.

I read to him from the Science *Times* about the secret language of elephants, and then about concentration: " 'The seemingly simple act of being fully absorbed in a challenging task is now being seen as akin to some extravagantly euphoric states of mind as might be experienced in drugs or sex.' " We laugh. We are wondering who this is news to.

He begins to cough. "So tell me," he says, "is there really a God or what? Where do you suppose I'm going next?"

I shrug. The dream of the resurrection breaks in my heart.

"What does NASA stand for?" he asks.

"What?"

"Need Another Seven Astronauts."

"Right. And what's the only kind of wood that doesn't float?"

He looks at me knowingly. "Natalie Wood, of course. Do you know what Matisse said when he was asked if he believed in God?"

"What?"

"He said, 'Yes, when I am working.'"

"What did Christa McAuliffe's husband say to her right before she left?"

"I'll feed the dog, you feed the fish." He tries to smile. He's tired. "The Salle show is going up soon. Go for me, would you, Caroline?"

"Sure. I'll give you a full report."

"Did you see the sets he did for Karole Armitage? Great, huh?"

We go on like this. "I liked *My Beautiful Laundrette* too. Did you see *Parting Glances* yet?"

"No."

"Oh, you really should. It's about us. Have you heard the new Bronski Beat?" he sings to me. "Have you gotten your dream date yet with Nadja Salerno-Sonnenberg?"

He smiles. He wants to be around for this, if it ever happens.

He looks in the mirror. "God, I could be a model with these angles."

He takes out a pencil and paper and draws a little self-portrait.

We are fighting for our lives.

"Tell me a story," he says, still drawing. "Tell me about Cummington. Tell me about some wolf in sheep's clothing."

"Did I ever tell you about the Baby Grand Larceny?"

"No!" he smiles.

We are speaking for our lives.

A Message to My Mother

Mother, I do not hold still hour after hour, day after day and then die. I do not.

Jesus Learning to Swim

She's helping the baby Jesus put on his water wings. Carefully she takes the tiny dimpled arm and bends it at the elbow. First one, then the other. He puts his face in the water. He begins to cry.

"Don't cry," Veronica whispers, swirling her hand in the water. "Kick your feet. Keep moving. The dark is not so dark."

City of Light

I am back in your city of light, Max. City of dark, city of death. City of beauty and scum. Of saliva, your city of saliva, Max.

"Not *my* city of saliva."

Yes. Yours.

"Please help me."

"I am recently widowed."

"I have no food."

"My house has burned down."

"I am a Vietnam vet."

"I am the Emperor Caesar."

"I have no food."

City of the starving and homeless.

Your city of elephants and lions and horses. Goddamnit, Max, who ever dreamed there'd be so many animals in this urban center? City of parakeets and ferrets on the loose. Lost two-legged dogs. City of pieces. Max, why didn't you ever mention that everywhere around you young men were dying? That you were living in a village of death inside a city of death. How could you not have seen it? How could you have overlooked it? But somehow you did. Never mind the young men wheezing on the streets. Never mind the sudden vacancies in prime downtown apartment buildings. Never mind the unmistakable face of suffering everywhere.

"Why didn't you ever open a newspaper up there, Caroline? Or put on National Public Radio?"

I am back in your city of small hopes. City of faith, of little miracles. City of fish markets and butchers. Of Italian stores and Korean grocers. City of people not willing to give up.

It should be possible to paint with words.

oranges/   artichokes/   tomatoes/   something green/

City of Steven and me.

It should be possible to make the words work.

I LOVE YOU.

Once, Steven, this city stretched ahead of us in endless night. We stood at the top of the World Trade Towers, where you worked. It was all ours, a carpet of light; I have not forgotten, two walls of light, a vast ceiling of light.

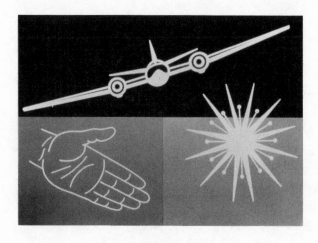

Maggie and Alison Watching

"This is our last chance until spring," Maggie says, as they climb the hill together to their spot in the garden.

"We'll see it tonight," says Alison, "I've got a feeling."

But as the comet passed Jupiter and the thin crescent moon, they saw only darkness. Alison gave out a little cry. Without seeing it, she could feel the comet move into deep space, leaving them there alone on the top of the dark hill.

The Agony in the Garden

He pricks his finger on a rose bush. He begins to bleed. Beads of sweat on his brow turn red. The word "purpura" comes to him.

"The concentric globes of the onion symbolized eternity to the Egyptians," he says deliriously. He weeps at the sight of trillium—all those perfect threes. "One of you," he cries, "shall betray me." He hears the deafening crow of the cock. The hour is at hand.

Now the night sweats come and he knows what they mean. He sees the moon, a luminous wafer in the sky. He gets up, making his nightmare run through the garden. He runs fast, a star blazing on his forehead like some dark horse. He's begging to live past thirty-three. Why must this be?

He stops abruptly and looks at me, bewildered, drenched. "Nothing is finished," he says, "or put away."

"Can you hear me, Father? Can you hear me at all? Nothing is finished. Take this cup away from me."

Qui Suis-Je?

Etes-vous un homme?
Non.
Etes-vous une femme?
Oui.
Etes-vous la vache qui rit?
Caroline! Non!
Etes-vous morte?
Oui.
Es-tu ma mère?
Oui.

Es-tu triste?
Non, pas maintenant.

An Afternoon at Dean & DeLuca's

They're all back this year. The deer and quails hanging from the
ceiling in an elaborate Christmas display. I remember the year
we stood here together and I shrieked as I looked up at all the
feathers and antlers and hooves. "Oh my," you said, looking up
to the sky, to the heavens, past the brown eyeballs, the orange
claws. "Can she really be our daughter, Veronica? Can she
really be ours?" And she is there with him for a minute, the
mother of his children, the subject of all his art, the love of his
life, for a minute.

You said to go to Dean & DeLuca's for smoked salmon, but
that Ottomanelli's has the best game in town and always get
veal chops at the Florence Meat Market.

Standing here, missing you, I think of all the weird things
you and Mother loved:

grouse
pigeon
partridge
pheasant
quail
hen
squab
venison
boar
buffalo
alligator
hare

Cummington in Winter

A wicker rocking chair against faded wallpaper. Those blue
flowers were forget-me-nots, and the orange ones, it's hard to

tell. A rag rug. A steam heater. Swiss curtains. So much depends on this.

Plastic covers the windows. We put it up just in time, our final winterizing chore. It's supposed to keep us safe and warm. The outside, seen through plastic, seems a long way off, unreal.

Winter is the longest season here. It goes on and on. The snow seems like it's never going to stop, there's always lots of wind and ice, trees down, power out. I love this falling-apart place, and in the winter the four of us who are here make up little projects to keep us sane, keep us busy when the poems won't come, when the canvas turns to ice, too slippery to get hold of.

I arrange the spices in the pantry and wonder why I choose such loneliness as this. These ever-darkening December days. Allspice, Anise, Basil, Bay Leaves, Bouillon, Coriander, Cumin, Curry. I discover a strange little bottom shelf of teas: German Camomile, Black Cohosh Tea, Comfrey, Kachina Spirit, Breathing Easy Tea. In the corner, piles of rice cakes.

In the refrigerator: Mushroom Ramen, Buckwheat Ramen, Raw Bee Pollen Granules.

In the bathroom: Tom's toothpaste with propolis and myrrh, a message on the tube signed "Your friend, Tom."

I can hear Max on this one— My friend indeed! He is most certainly not my friend. This is how Max predictably went on often. I think it was something he acquired when he was with my mother, as he tried to fill in the great gaps with banter, muttering, the sound of his voice.

Max, it is December 18, 1985, and it is 2:15 p.m. I am in the Vaughn kitchen at the Cummington Community of the Arts in Cummington, Massachusetts. We are far inland and there is seven feet of snow. But what the light looks like as it falls on the giant butcher block table is two huge fish swimming through pale water. They are there and then gone. And then another swims by. And then no more. It is 2:16 now and the large fish are gone. A wide stripe of shimmering light and then no light. Thank you for fish in winter. The light is there and then it is gone. Max, sometimes I am so afraid.

I walk up the slippery hill to Frazier, the walk I do in my sleep. I love this house. The faded wallpaper. The wicker chair. The windows protected by plastic, the land fading before me, everything moving to gray. Outside only Olive Thayer negotiating her way to the mailbox through the snow.

There are only four artists here now and two of us I hate. What makes me stay? I watch the panes turn from gray to white to ice blue to cobalt to sapphire to black. Only a young Chinese man playing Bach on a cello accompanies me. It's winter and I am alone.

I imagine my husband and our two sons are out in the fir forest cutting down a Christmas tree. Mother, left alone in the house, bathing. I can see them in the rising steam—their red flannel, their high boots, their rosy cheeks.

"How about that one?" my sweet husband says with glee and the boys walk around it. "No, it's got to be bigger," they scream and run to another, a giant, "like this." The littler one, still unaccustomed to being away from me, huddles next to his father, closes his eyes for a second and stretches out his arms and whispers, "You know how Mom likes a big tree." His arms can barely make the width of me, the size still of his whole world. They circle each tree in the forest before choosing. Their dream of perfection is a small one and will remain so. They ask so little from the world. They are so easily satisfied. They are so involved and so happy in their Christmas tasks.

I am thirty this year. These December nights, alone in the house, are so long. My husband and two sons are out Christmas shopping. The older one glides his hand over an antique lacquered box. The younger one picks up a rag doll with no face. He pulls at his father's sweater to question this.

My husband points to a case of rings, and a woman takes one out for him. He runs his finger along the ring's intricate setting. He looks into the center of the stone. Like outside, it is slate blue and white.

I step from the bath. My husband and children are huddled downstairs now in the library, whispering about the gifts, next to a fire.

I take out the L. L. Bean catalog. For my husband, a Penobscot Parka (p. 15) or a Pendleton robe and slippers (p. 36).

And for my sons, Bean's Child's Pull Sleds. They are sturdy, the catalog says, well made.

I drift into sleep. I dream of a large sleigh, a chestnut horse galloping through snow. Clearly it is a vision from the past, but I miss it as keenly as if it were my own childhood.

A woman, a mother in velvet. A muff in her lap. A mustached man in a top hat and bright scarf. Children. Carols. Sleigh bells.

What artist has given me this scene? What painter or poet? Who has made me nostalgic for a past I cannot have ever known?

A racing sleigh moving through the snow toward loved ones on a winter night. One drip. Two drips. A cry in the night. "Mommy."

I dream of the one yet to be born. The one still curled in my womb. The one who will open like a star. I will kiss the stars she has on her hands instead of knuckles. I will make her new potatoes, baby vegetables, potage St.-Germain, oeufs à la neige.

I wear red woolen tights, flannel dresses, clogs sometimes. There are always children around my hips. The kitchen is always warm.

I dream my son hands me a rag doll with no face. "Thou shall not make graven images."

The length of the winter takes its toll. The snow on top of snow on top of snow. How cold it is. How lonely. How long each night.

But then it is light. Suddenly there is the shock of morning. I run to the window. Is that a cardinal in the snow? No, just the tip of Leon Thayer's elbow in his foul-weather gear. But when one wants badly enough to see a cardinal, even an elbow will do. When one needs to see cardinals, somehow cardinals do appear.

Did it happen last night while I slept? We can't exactly say when it happened, only that it happened in winter, and that it

was not until the snow melted and we sent the piano tuner out
to the Hexagon did we know what had happened.

I picture them pulling up in a van. Olive Thayer, parting the
curtains, thinks, This is like the Community, to let these people
who have nowhere to go, stay for the night—it is so cold, and so
late.

They must have looked like lovers carrying blankets into the
Hexagon, where they would huddle for the night under the
baby grand. But instead they *took* the baby grand. Lifted it carefully into the van and disappeared in the night. An entire Stein-
way piano slipped away in the night while the four of us slept.

"There's no piano in there," the piano tuner from Pittsfield
said, his tools dangling at his side.

This is how life is, I have learned—not just at Cummington,
but everywhere. It is a world where it is perfectly possible at any
moment for an entire piano to disappear into thin air and never
be heard from again. Or almost never. On learning the news,
my friend Karen changed this disaster into a bit of art:

baby·grand·larceny

Not everything disappears, I suppose.

I think of Gene. He could change the sounds of our lovemaking into music. He could turn the radio news into music. He could turn the wind in the trees into music.

How odd that only after hearing the music he composed while we were together did I realize how much he had loved me.

I listened to the strange and beautiful composition early one winter morning and knew. The bass line sounded like descending bells. He could make sounds never heard before, from instruments never invented.

"I hear you breathing, I hear your breath. Your breath is with me still," he wrote me in a letter. "I hear your laugh."

It was all there. The way he loved, finally, unconditionally, and with great purity. His wit, his desire, his particular regret, his wife, his children, it was all there . . .

"I have your laugh, your laugh is with me always."

Eugene, I did love you—but only after hearing the music did I realize it.

"We have made a shape together, Caroline," he said, "and it is ours forever."

Forever

I was here. I touched your hand. We loved each other. We tried not to be afraid. You painted. I tried to put a few real words on a page. This is what it meant to be alive.

We lived very hard. We loved everything: flesh, earth, water, sky. We were hurt often. But we loved the world and it was good.

You painted. I tried to put a few words on a page. I learned words I never wanted to have to know—the solid rocket boosters, the blood-brain barrier. We tried not to be afraid. There was red. It was too much. I was frightened of the things there were

still no names for, the things yet to come. We loved each other.
We needed to say something. We did our best. There wasn't
enough time.

When we were young we learned math together. We learned
that two take away one equals one. I am afraid.

We wanted to live long. I put a few words on a page. You
painted—a man, a cloud, a diamond ring, a hospital bed, a
horse with wings.

Max Speaks Again

"My baby girl. My only daughter. My love. I used to sit by your
crib. Watch light move through the slats.

"And later? What was I later but a tired, crabby old giant,
with such a small child to care for. Wife: deceased. Sons: in
boarding school up the Hudson.

"Caroline, I did my best."

Jesus with Palm and Thistle

They wave palm fronds back and forth as he enters the dark city. "Hosanna," they say to him "Hosanna in the highest. Behold, the son of God." Jesus rides through the town on a mule obeying the orders of his moody madman father. He looks through the jail of palm. He feels feverish. "Stop," he says. He feels a little woozy.

"Why have you forsaken me?" Jesus weeps. He's so thin. Dragging his bag of fish. He wears a wreath of rosemary around his head. "That's for remembrance, Mother," he says, delirious.

He's seeing things. He leaves his own face on the towel of a woman. He starts to hear voices. "You are my son and you are dying," his father says. "Save me," he begs. "Look to your brothers," his father says.

He holds a staff of thistle. It has the power, he's heard, to cure any disease, even the plague.

He hallucinates his way across the landscape. He enters the late twentieth century dragging his bag of tricks—his basket of fragments, his fish and thistle.

A star blooms on his forehead like some dark horse. He looks to his brothers, anorectic and dying. "Stay a little," he says, putting his hands on their chests. He waves his thistle like a wand and weeps. "Stay a little." He can't save anyone.

"Wake," he pleads, "wake." He's desperate. He tries everything he can think of. "This is the cup of my blood," he says. He closes his eyes. "Arise." He opens them. "I am the Lamb of God," he says. "I am the Bread of Life." He turns away. "Listen," he says, "you're too young to die." But nothing works.

"Please," he begs, "one more minute. I love you. Today you will be with me in Paradise."

The Black Tulip

"Oude Niedorp, The Netherlands — A black tulip, flowering at midnight, sounds like something from an old Dutch fairy tale. But it happened in the tiny village (pop. 300) of Oude Niedorp, a one-windmill town about 35 miles northwest of Amsterdam. And after a month of newspaper interviews, Geert Hageman, the 29-year-old horticulturist who developed the new black tulip, is still euphoric about this somber variety of his national flower.

" 'It was about 12:30 on Feb. 18,' Mr. Hageman recounted. 'I had already looked once or twice at this group of tulips, and then I saw it. I couldn't tell anybody—my wife was sleeping—so I walked around drinking a beer . . .' "

Steven laughs.

"Mr. Hageman allowed the black flower to bloom for 14 days, then cut it and the foliage off at the base. Tulip blooms take strength away from their bulbs and eventually kill them and the bulb is the important thing in multiplying hybrid tulips.

"The mother tulip, Queen of the Night, is the color of eggplant. The father, Wienerwald, was shorter and darker, but had a white border around the petals. Their offspring, the new black tulip, was 40 centimeters tall—about 16 inches—and nearly opaque purplish-black. Or was it blackish-purple? If so, 'It's a very, very dark shade of purple,' Mr. Hageman said. 'If you were holding my tulip against something pure black, you might say it was a light shade of black. I think it's the blackest tulip anyone's ever seen.'

"Jacques Henneman, the marketing manager of the International Bulb Center, an independent trade organization in Hillegom, said: 'There were two or three black tulips before: La Tulipe Noire, which appeared in 1891, and Queen of the Night, which appeared in 1955. But in nature it is very difficult to breed black varieties.'

"Kees van Ness, a horticulturist at the Laboratory for Bulb

Research in Lisse, took a good look at the Hageman tulip at the flower show. He carefully avoided the word black when asked for his opinion. 'It's a very dark tulip,' he said. 'It's the darkest I've ever seen, but that doesn't mean that it's the darkest of all. But of course, people have been looking for the darkest tulips they can make since 1600.'"

Maggie Reads to Alison

"Mountain View, California, February 10 — In a cataclysmic drama played out once every 76 years, Halley's Comet has swept to within 55 miles of the surface of the Sun, and once again has been hurled back toward exile in the furthest reaches of the solar system, renewing a cycle as old as history.

"Even now, as it begins another 7 billion mile trip out beyond Neptune and back, the famous comet's ice is flashing into hot gas, its dust is being blasted away and pockets of trapped gas are exploding into enormous spectacular tails. The comet is at its biggest and its best.

"Unfortunately, this historic period of perihelion, one of the greatest shows in the solar system, is happening on the opposite side of the Sun from the Earth. The comet will not be visible to Earthbound viewers again until next month."

The Final Shape

There's a shape I've seen my whole life, in dreams. It's changed only slightly through time, but it's definitely changed. It's changing now.

"You are moving toward the perfect shape," a voice says, but I don't know who's speaking. I can't make out who it is.

"It is the shape of your death."

How will I know when I have seen the final shape?

"You'll remember it."

From where?

"It is the shape of your mother's womb."

The Night of Pity and Self-Loathing

It's a bitterly cold and clear night.

Max calls. "What's new?" he says.

"The weather's new. It's ten below," I say.

"That's only with the windchill factor, my dear. We were never as cold until they discovered that damned windchill factor. Now an entire generation has grown up believing in ten below zero."

"How's the East Village?" you ask.

"Same," I say.

"Come over, I'll make you dinner."

"Will Biddy be there?"

"No. She's gone home to Virginia for a few weeks."

"Fine," I say. "I'll see you soon."

I stop by Balducci's on my way. Eye all the weird things you love: grouse, pheasant, buffalo, quail. I decide to buy cheese that's wrapped in a leaf.

This night reminds me of a winter night long ago. The temperatures way below freezing, the wind harsh, the snow kissing us. The street glittering. "Careful, Dad, of the ice," I said, holding his hand. "That's not ice, Caroline, that's glass."

To mistake glass for ice.

He's in a heavy gray sweater. The house is warm. He smells comforting, safe, he smells of alcohol and pipe tobacco. I kiss him on the cheek. I hand him the cheese.

He unwraps it. "Oh, my whimsy," he says. "Cheese wrapped in a leaf."

We go into the kitchen, where he is making some confection. "How about a drink?"

"Sure. What are you making?"

"Oeufs à la neige," he says.

Before my eyes, my father molds meringue with two large spoons into oval shapes, perfect eggs. "Oh, they're so beautiful!" I say. He smiles. "They really are, aren't they?"

He makes me a drink. We settle into our familiar spots, two chairs next to the fire. I love him. I want him to know this and so, though I do not care, I ask him, "How is Biddy?" Also it is easy conversation. It is a way around this impending feeling of I don't know what.

"Ah, Biddy," he says. "She is a young woman intimately involved in the romance of failure, in struggle as an art form. She has made the deliberate choice of a career she has not the talent

or instinct for, and she continues to pursue it, though the odds
are against even a good actor. But the overwhelming need
seems to be the struggle, the starving, the sacrificing for that
noble thing called Art. A whole career or noncareer passionately pursued and founded on a fancy. A compliment from a
teacher in fifth grade. A lead role in an Easter pageant, a smattering of applause, a need to be seen. Of course, this did not
cover up the fact that there was no talent there, no feel for the
thing, no natural ability.

"Oh, it's tiresome, Caroline, tiresome. How much nicer to
have you here tonight. She cannot decipher a good script from a
bad one." He sighs. "No matter what degree of desire, sincerity,
diligence, there is no way in—her wit, her intelligence does not
permit it." He sighs again, getting up, "And yet she refuses to
give it up. Am I making any sense? You look a little baffled,
dear. Do I seem to be making sense?" He pats me on the head.
"Oh, the tenacious nature of some young people! The young are
so stubborn! so fierce!"

For dinner he has made sautéed foie gras with curly endive.
A sherry vinaigrette with shallots, garnished with crescents of
mango. For the main course, garlic-and-thyme encrusted hali-
but, roasted potatoes and braised rhubarb stems. It all looks so
beautiful.

On the CD player: *Der Rosenkavalier.*

"Perfection as always," I say, lifting my glass to him.

"Taste it first, my dear."

"I went to see *Der Rosenkavalier* at the Met last week," he
says. "Do you remember the end of the first act? So poignant.
The Marschallin sits at her mirror, worrying about her lover,
feeling mortal. The curtain starts to fall and there's that incredible cadence Strauss created to accompany its drop—well, inevitably, the other night as well, it was lost in applause. If only
people could actually listen, instead of relying on the condi-
tioned response: they see the curtain going down and they begin to clap their hands. Sometimes I think they're no better
than dogs . . . That moment was ruined for me, at any rate."

I smile. "You are even more opinionated in real life than you are in my imagination, Max."

"Oh my dear, I suppose I'm not the easiest of fathers."

No. He hadn't been the easiest of fathers. That could be said with certainty. But I could not imagine life with anyone else. He made all other lives unimaginable. Dismissable. Those poor slobs who clapped because the curtain went down. I held it against him sometimes, but there was no denying I loved the life he suggested to me.

He was passionately urban, almost archetypically so. He loved Manhattan and what only Manhattan could offer him. He was so relentless, so demanding. "Caroline," he'd say, "what do you think of Ping Chong? What about Robert Wilson? Pina Bausch? Maguy Marin? Charles Ludlum? Liz LeCompte? James Lapine? What do you think is going on in these new David Salles? How about the Jennifer Bartlett show? What do you see? What do you see? What about Martha Clark's *Garden of Earthly Delights*?"

He talks about the death of the riddler, the guy who slowly turns champagne bottles to bring the yeast to the top. "I heard," he says, "that there's a new process that will make riddling obsolete.

" 'It was a lousy job anyway,' those riddlers are saying. 'We're sorry we took it in the first place.' "

He remembers Nixon, still president, in an air-conditioned room, the fireplace going, his bum leg propped up.

We drank and drank and ate course after course and became dizzy with the array of names. Let's talk about this. Now this. What about this? As if talking could save us. "Keep up with me, Caroline, goddamnit."

I rest on the subject of food for a moment. Something he always loved to gossip about. "Did you hear what's just in at Ottomanelli's? Have you been by the Florence Meat Market? At the Italian store they've got mozzarella in corroza . . . Well, it's the preciousness I detest," he says. "The rising intolerance in people like you and me. The need for an extra, then an extra-

extra, then an extra-extra-extra virgin olive oil at every turn. What is wrong with us? Would you like another mango, my dear, or how about a braised rhubarb stem?"

I close my eyes and his oeufs à la neige float before me in the darkness, those perfect, cloudy, lighter-than-air eggs.

You saw the figure 5 in gold, I think to myself.

Sooner or later we get to the fiddleheads, as always. A dream of spring. Invariably I'd ask to hear again about Mother as a small child in Canada eating fiddleheads. "Well, that's how we got them in this country, you know," he'd say. "The French Canadians brought them down." I think of my mother with a handful of emerald spirals. I wonder why this somehow was not enough to make her want to live.

"Caroline, you're drifting off."

"I'm a little drunk," I say.

"Nonsense. Well, I am too, but just a little." He smiles.

I amuse him, I think. He wants to know how the East Village is. If I've seen anything I might call art over there. He wants to know about my psychotherapy. "Don't forget it all started with Freud, that inventor of penis envy, anatomy as destiny, female masochism. Oh, the feminists *do* have their work cut out for them and maybe they will have some impact, some degree of success. But don't expect this therapy business to work in your lifetime, Caroline. It's a primitive art, based on lies.

"You dream you are a tightrope walker in the circus. It means: your father never loved you. You could never please him. You had to work hard to keep your balance. You dream of a field of flowers. It means you want to lie yourself down like a carpet and be stepped on."

"Max, last night I dreamt that a B movie actor decided as a joke to run for president and got elected and then started a zany military program called Star Wars, like the movie, while every-one on the earth was dying or starving to death. A big dome in the sky that would keep out all the bad guys."

"It means that you are a paranoid schizophrenic, Caroline. It means they will lock you away forever."

"I'm going away, Max, next week, to the country for the spring."

"Where?" he asks. I think the idea of the country amuses him.

"An artist colony in the Berkshires—Western Massachusetts." I know the idea of an artist colony amuses him.

"A colony of artists," he says. He raises his eyebrows. "Well now, isn't that a novel, as it were, idea?"

"Don't be sarcastic, Max."

"Are you thinking of writing again?"

"Yes."

"Good. That's good. When did you say you were leaving?"

"Next week."

"Oh, my whimsy," he says, "my cherub. Let's move into the other room, shall we?" We go into the front room and sit next to the fire. "What can I get you, my sweet? Cognac? Biscotti di vino? Figs? Cheese wrapped in a leaf?"

"Cognac, please. And perhaps a fig."

"Your mother had a cat named Fig, you know."

"I was there. I remember that cat, Dad."

Call me Max, you said when I was seven. You were Dad, or more often, Father until then.

"Dad."

"Call me Max."

You ran out of patience often with us, Max. You refused to humor us. Remember the time David came home with one of those weekly newspapers written for grade schoolers with the headline "It can be fun to raise bananas at home." You looked at it and said, "No, I cannot see how it could be fun to raise bananas at home." And David bursting into tears and saying, "If Mother were here," those four wounding words. And you the cruel realist. Tyrant. Monster. "But she is not here." And then Grey would begin to cry, and David in some corner swearing at you, pouring water into various pots, measuring cups, jars.

I appreciated it though, Max, that you spoke your mind when you could, that you did not lie. That you let us know how you saw things; it was something for us to see against, if necessary.

For that was the fact of the matter, as you put it, the fact of the matter: Mother was not here. What one *did* with that information was entirely one's own choice. What you did was offer some possibilities, some clues toward a way to proceed. You tried to teach us something about art, its consoling nature, its transcendent nature, its ability to help distance.

The attempts: to paint her back into a body, lengthen her thick dark hair and climb it, use it as a rope ladder out of here.

The attempts: to look for her in every other woman.

The attempt: to forget her. The attempt: to forgive her. But it did not seem possible to do either.

To look for her in every other woman. "I looked for her in all of them."

"Did you really, Max?"

"Caroline, please."

Ask about his work. "Then your work. How is your work going? I read your piece in *Art Forum*."

"It is a different approach, that is all. It's the process of entering into the understanding that you may be completely off base, and that's all right. I'm working on a method that lets other variables in, things that independently, given a narrow field, would most likely not occur to the viewer.

"You're very beautiful," he says. "That curve there. The openness of the forehead, the lidded eye. The sensuous mouth. If you could just look down for a minute. If you would just move a little to the right, you would be in the perfect light. The tension between your smooth arm and the curtain, the transparency of eye and window . . . If you could move just a bit."

"No, Max. She needed a husband."

"A husband was one of the things she needed, yes."

"She needed you to treat her other than as an object of beauty, of art. She needed you, Max.

"Did you try to keep her at a distance by putting her on canvas, turning her into something else?"

"It's more complicated, Caroline. Painting her brought her sadness nearer to me too; I could feel it more keenly, I understood it better. Until it in some way became unbearable for me too, and I had to stop."

"You could have continued."

"No, I lacked the courage. I couldn't do it.

"I loved her very much. And such a hatred I had for everything after she died! Contempt for art and artists. For women, restaurants, plays, films. My contempt for you children. How I hated your teary faces! My God, Caroline, that one woman could do such damage."

"Come on, Max, that's not completely true. You know that."

"You're right, of course." He lit his pipe.

"I remember her earrings shaped like fish."

"Yes, indeed. A Pisces through and through, your mother."

"I remember her lips imprinted on a tissue floating in the toilet bowl. I loved those lip imprints. She would leave them blotted on a tissue on my pillow at night sometimes. Did you know that, Max, about Mom?"

"No," he said quietly, wrinkling his brow, smiling slightly.

"Ah, *ma dormeuse*," he whispers. "She was dying right there before my eyes and I, like some fool, some blind man, just kept painting and painting her. And don't think she didn't notice it, she saw it—that I was painting her back into a life she could not live.

"There was no going back, after her. The rest were vacant compared to her—their beautiful bodies or extreme kindness was some sort of consolation. She was smart, she was so beautiful, but what good was it?"

"I don't remember her being smart or beautiful. I just remember her being my mother, that's all. I remember her breasts, her lap, her hands moving through water. Her lips. We played Huckle Buckle Beanstalk and Qui Suis-Je? This is what I remember: she cried us to sleep. She prayed to Mary. She loved the stars.

"Did we ever have a garden in the country, Max? Sometimes

I have this image of Mom and I out there growing all kinds of things—vegetables, tulips. Planting seeds. I seem to remember spending hours and hours there with her. Could that be true?"

"I'm afraid not, Caroline. Your mother never gardened. Your mother never grew anything."

"Are you sure?"

He closes his eyes and nods. "I'm sure.

"I continued same as always. Well not quite but—what is nearly impossible to accept is that she changed everything forever. After all these years, Veronica, I still miss you! Though I am not sure I even remember you accurately anymore, or the things we actually did. The White Horse, the Lion's Head. The hours and hours of painting. Even you've faded, Veronica. Now I have trouble remembering precisely what is no longer the same anymore. But then I'll look at the paintings, or some other thing will bring you back. I've only *almost* forgotten. I still have an inkling of what it all meant—long ago when we were young. Veronica, we were sweethearts . . .

"But I have had too much to drink tonight and I am getting morose, ridiculous, as surely these stabs at reconciliation, these stabs at recovering the past, spoken at all are ludicrous—inadequate and too late."

"Was there no one who could have taken her place?"

"Oh, Caroline. Your mother and I were like Canada geese. We mated for life."

"Well, not take her place, but you know what I mean, Max. I always wondered how you could dismiss the women you knew, a whole person, in a few words. With the turn of a hand. 'She is most intelligent,' you said about the NYU librarian. 'She has a sharp mind and wit, but her obsessions are fundamentally uninteresting.'

"And what about Biddy? What contempt you hold her in. What was I to think? How you loathe her! The ready smile, the dog, the thousand changes in makeup and hair, the float tank, the tanning parlor, the total absorption in self, the complete preoccupation with self."

"Caroline, I have been doomed to scour the earth looking over and over for the same woman, your mother, Veronica, the missing one, the absent one, the one who most profoundly betrayed me. I've never stopped looking for her, regardless of how it has appeared. Every choice never a choice *for* something, but a choice made in relation to her. This one's hair is like hers was, thick and wavy and dark, or that one's hair is not like hers was. Or, they would have been nearly the same age, or, no, she is quite a bit younger even than Veronica was then. Or, Veronica would have never thought of this in that way. With mindlessness I tried to wipe out her mind. With blondeness, her darkness. With emotion, her coldness, her detachment. I worked so hard not to miss her.

"I miss you, Veronica!" he yells into the room. "All these years I have missed you!"

He stands. Wavers. Pours us more to drink.

"We are wounded, symbol-making creatures, Caroline." He looks at a reproduction on his desk. "So is this or is this not a Caravaggio?"

"Jesus, was this any way to spend precious time on this earth? To spend one's life quibbling, as it were. My God, was this any way to live? Spewing jargon. The vocabulary of what?"

"She couldn't think of anything worth doing and I detested her for it."

He weeps. "Was that any way to live?"

"Max," I say, nearing him, wiping his brow. He picks up a copy of *David and Goliath*, the painting in question. Groans. Cries. "I think not," he howls, collapsing in his chair.

I too begin to cry. "Oh, my cherub," he says, running his hand through my hair, holding the reproduction in the other hand, quieting down. He kisses me on the forehead. "I think it is finally not a Caravaggio." He smiles a little. Lights his pipe. "Oh, Caroline. Everywhere, betrayal, betrayal, betrayal." He puts his pipe down. Puts his face in his hands. "All the time spent thinking about Cézanne or the way Degas worked. What does it amount to? What does it matter?"

I take his big shoulders. "Max. Dad. That's *all* that matters. Degas standing over a stove, pink softening in his hands as he adds color to a slipper or an elbow. That's all that matters. All that matters, Max, is Chagall painting lovers who could sail over the city in a dream of freedom. Cézanne standing in front of the same mountain year after year. Vermeer!"

He looks up. "You are right about that, aren't you, Caroline?"

"Yes."

"And you are mine, after all. With your free spirit, your feistiness—so unlike your mother's. Veronique, never made for this world. The V in her name, heaven bound as soon as it was put down here, even as a baby, my winged angel. *Mon ange.* V, V, V, V. Flying off even then. But is it heaven she's gone to?

"I'm afraid heaven is just some concoction of the brain, a coping mechanism, a way to continue, through all this mire.

"She wasn't like you, Caroline, with your sturdy C, caught in the early alphabet.

"Oh, Veronica, you broke my heart!

"She simply could not go on. I am quite sure of it."

How he hated her sometimes, and us. "Let's help dress Mommy," he'd shout, clapping his hands and laughing demonically. She was a statue. Like any in New York. "Come on now, Caroline, don't be afraid," you'd say. "Mommy needs help." And Grey cowering in the next room.

"What a mistake to bring children into this!" you said.

"She is not a sack of potatoes, Veronica," I heard you yell at her once, meaning me.

"We used to go for walks at night sometimes. She would look into all the windows of the apartments around the park and wish for any of those lives, rather than her own. She would see people eating, people laughing, people reading, putting children to bed. They all seemed so happy to her. 'I'd take any one of their lives,' she'd say. 'I'd give anything not to always be on the outside looking in.' And then she'd begin to cry.

" 'Carry me on your back, Max. I can't go on,' she'd say, and

I'd say to her, 'But you are too heavy to carry, Veronica.'" He laughs wildly. "'Your legs are too long, Veronica.' The pointy toes of her pumps dragging in the concrete. What a mistake to bring children into this. Me carrying you all on my back.

"There were times she panicked when I had to be somewhere and she would try to prevent me from leaving. She lived in terror of people leaving her. I would be getting into the car and she would follow me down and lie on top of it. Right there in the street, she would put her body over the car's windshield. I'd start the engine, but she wouldn't move. I'd scream at her out the window, but she wouldn't budge . . . It's twenty-five years since her death and every time I get into my car I'm still looking around her armpit to see.

"Twenty-five years of this, Veronica. How does one go on, finally?" He shakes his head. "And you, Caroline, our only daughter, you are partially her, a woman who cared nothing about anything, and partially me, an old man full of self-loathing and pity and contempt. It was wrong of us to bring you into the world."

"I wouldn't agree, Max."

"Me wanting to love you and your brothers, but never having, never having the nerve. I was so afraid. How terrible to be so afraid."

You were always so far away, so distant. What were you afraid of? Did you think I'd betray you too, Max?

"I loved you too much, Caroline."

"I would never have hurt you, Max."

"Ah, Caroline—you have no idea."

"Max," I say, "I am not Mother. I do not hold still for thirty years and then die. I do not."

"I was not about to allow you to break my heart, Caroline, I loved her too much. The heart is not a resilient muscle like the poets tell us. I have not the stamina. Not to be father, or lover, or artist. You know best of all, Caroline—to be an artist is to be willing to have your heart broken every day. I am here only to admire the darings of others."

He puts his head in his hands and rubs his face. "Such a silly man. Sixty-four. Art historian."

"You look tired, Max. I should go. It's late."

"It's too late," he says. "I'm your father, I can't send you into the city at 4 a.m."

"I could take a cab."

He waves his hand in dismissal. "Stay here."

"Are you sure?"

"Of course I'm sure. It's almost four. So now that that's settled, would you like a cognac? I think we could use another cognac."

He pats my hand. "You will break my heart yet."

You're probably right, I think. It is part of the agreement to live.

We have cognac. Oeufs à la neige. Figs. Tears of contempt and sadness run down his face.

One of us will die first. Probably one of us will do unforgivable things to the other. One of us will not be able to make sense of the other. But not tonight.

He takes my arm. He sees it is flesh and blood. He loves me, allows his heart to break into a thousand pieces. He feeds me cheese in a leaf. He rocks me in his arms. Hums along with Glenn Gould. I hear his astounding heart beating in his chest.

"I love you," he whispers.

"I love you, too, Max," I whisper back.

More Winter

Today I'm thinking how we never learned the things they were best at teaching—to look away, to say no, to want only a little.

Was it our mistake—that we loved everything so much? I remember you, even during your last stay at the hospital, shuddering with pleasure when we talked of a certain beach. It came back to you nearly complete and you still wanted it, the sun on your back, the feel of the breeze, the cool ocean and all the love in the world.

Imagine this, Gary, I say: we pack a picnic lunch, champagne and fruit, a little cheese, some good bread, and we leave early. We drive at dawn, right into the sun. You have one arm out the car window and it feels so good. We've both got our Ray-Bans on, we've brought lots of suntan lotion, towels, magazines and books. And now feel the sun, how it warms us inside and out, and the water is so sparkly clear and blue. We are being caressed by waves and light.

"Oh, Carole, it feels so wonderful."

I separate from him only long enough to think, Whoever is responsible for this is not forgiven. Whoever looked on this and allowed it to happen is not forgiven. How could this be allowed to happen? The age-old complaint with God still holds.

But you are still on the beach or in Paris or in front of the Giottos in Italy. Then you are back again, saying you think 1986 will be the breakthrough year, saying you've got to believe that.

Gary, I say, "Picture eggs that grow impenetrable, picture white horses galloping furiously, white tigers, white sharks that will devour this thing."

"I see a horse with wings," you whisper. "I see a horse made out of stars."

I thought if I sat there day after day I could save your life. I thought I could turn my body into a pillar of light.

Gary, remember the dawn at Cummington when we went and watched hot-air balloons being blown up in that huge field. Bright. Striped. Picture this: those beautiful balloons inflating and rising into a pink sky. Think of being that light.

They said the AIDS was moving through your brain. I kept thinking it would be reversible, the damage to your brain. "Is it reversible?" I asked the doctor. "Is it reversible?" She is cautious. "I have never known a case to be reversible."

You lost vision in one eye. "When I get out of here," you said, "I've got to get this dog eye fixed."

You've got a spiral taped to your chest that feeds medicine directly into your heart. You're attached to a machine called an IMED. They taught you how to use it. They said you'd have to be on it every four days of the week for the rest of your life, but you forgot near the end how to do it, it was so complicated.

You were still hopeful then, like a little boy. But this time it would turn out, Gary, that we were small, so very small, and we were fighting something monstrous. You were always brave. You were always brave in the dark, in the hospital, at ten or eleven at night, well past visiting hours, everything quiet, only white shoes against a polished floor—you were so brave.

I am just trying to get some of this down.

When I was away from you, I had become only a person who misses, only the person who is afraid. Nothing else. No one else. When I turn the last corner, I brace myself for whatever you will be like that day. I can't help. I talk to myself in half-sentences, sometimes only in sounds, in groans. How is—but before I complete the thought you are in front of me. You're the same or you're worse or you're a little better. When you're a little better my heart soars. Then it looks to me like you're having trouble breathing; I think your chest heaves. I get the nurse. No, she says, no. I'm so afraid. I sweat. I'm drenched. I've never seen someone so young take so long to die. There is so much suffering in your one skinny body. I don't know what makes your heart continue to beat. You hallucinate yourself free. I have never seen someone suffer the way you are suffering. I am no one but the person who goes to see you. And despite my visits, you are clearly worsening.

I am here to keep you alive, and I am failing so magnificently.

And God is a laughable thing, a child's dream.

They promised me they'd give you morphine at the end, if you needed it. I kept checking. I kept asking if you were in pain. You kept saying no. You didn't ever need the morphine. You started seeing things on your own. "Isn't it fantastic the way they keep changing the paintings in here?" you asked me. "It's really a great museum."

You had been worried. For months and months before you even saw a doctor, you drew hospital beds, a hand reaching up through broken ice, a jet that descends. For months you drew an angel in a hospital bed.

And when the night sweats came at three in the morning and you knew what they meant, you closed your eyes and instead of saying I'm dying, you imagined being somewhere far off in a different place, under lights, a throbbing dance floor, and the way you were sweating and the way you shook when a stranger touched you on the shoulder. That freedom, that pleasure was something we could imagine dying for, though we never thought we'd actually have to.

I remember phone conversations from years ago. You'll love this story, Carole, you'd say, or, This one is right up your alley.

Let me tell you about this beautiful farm boy, Gary, I'd say. I didn't think blonds were your type, you'd respond. Or, When you're done, send him my way. We didn't think living could ever be this dangerous. Such intricate, marvelous stories. A bouncer from the bar whispering over the phone line at 5 a.m., *I must see you now*. Gary, a man takes me out into snow . . .

That handful of days, when you still had the whole world and not just the world of St. Vincent's. Those four white walls, those diamonded pajamas with the V for Vincent over the heart. They were made of cotton. They tied in the back. And finally the ties that kept you latched to the chair because every time you'd try to get up you'd fall over from being so weak. "Untie me," you'd whisper.

I am trying to get this down, Gary.

In your sleep, tied to the bed, you'd kick your legs madly. There is a home movie of me as an infant doing exactly the same thing. But my legs were pink and chubby. Yours are the skinniest legs I have ever seen. You were ninety pounds.

I am trying to get this down.

Your arm slung around my shoulder as I carried you and your IMED around the fourteenth floor. We'd stop at the large window that looked out high over the city. There's Seventh Avenue and Greenwich. There's the coffee shop, I said, where I sometimes wait for visiting hours to begin. And then a few weeks later when we stood at that large gray window, you said, I know exactly what's out there but I can't see it anymore. You were going blind. When the doctor came in I'd sit out in the hall and look out the window and watch in miniature a woman on a rooftop walking a dog. Watch an arm out a window pull in wash from the line, a world where normal things were still going on, same as always, a world beckoning us to enter. But I knew I was too large and too far off, hovering above the dark city, and the neurologist about to come out with his bad news.

The virus had crossed the blood-brain barrier. I kept asking what would happen. I asked the lovely nurses who had grown to love you too. How beautiful they were—the twenty-year-old nurses who did whatever they could—unflagging, attentive, diligent. "How are you feeling, Hon?" they asked you. "Oh, sweetheart, what's the matter?" I think of my own mother, and I love her so much in this instant, once a twenty-year-old woman like these women, in a white uniform, thinking she could save anyone.

The future: I could imagine it only too well. The nurses' faces are grave as you struggle for breath. It's what they've warned me about. When the disease enters the brain stem your breathing will shut down. That's one thing that might happen. And many people, they told me, die from the drugs, from the medication.

I am trying to get this down for good.

I hugged your legs. They were so skinny. "Aren't these the bees' knees?" you smiled.

I fed you. I didn't know how big to cut the pieces. So I cut them tiny, tiny. "Well," you laughed, "this certainly gives bite-size a whole new meaning."

In my phone book next to your name, the jottings of years, as we talked and talked . . . M, T, W nights and TH lunch, reviews in *Artforum*, May *GQ, NY Magazine*. ARC. Chest X ray Fri. Cryptococcus. Call tomorrow about blood. Fri 11, Memorial Service, Society for Ethical Culture, 2 West 64th Street, CPW. A life in shorthand. These abbreviations. You were fine, you were well, and then you were not. Suddenly you were dying.

A cry in the night. Gary, half the time I don't know where I am. Half the time I jump up wondering if it's time to go visit you yet. I think about what I can bring to you. I could talk nonstop into your one good ear. "Remind me," you said, "to get my ear fixed too."

I know, Gary, to write it down is always to get it wrong. But here, wanting you back, it's the closest I can get to heaven— where I like to picture you.

But is it heaven you've gone to?

"Do you believe in God?" I asked you. "I don't know," you said. "Do you?" "Yes, and I'm praying for you." "That's good," you said. "Thank you."

I've always prayed to Mary, but I only ask her for help when I absolutely need it. To help me out of a debilitating depression. To save you. But now I've got to say I don't know if I believe in God anymore or his skinny son and all that rising up. I am short of faith when I need it most.

We hold a dish under your chin while you spit up pills.

We're going to need a miracle, my friend.

From your hospital bed you built churches. You measured the lumber in your head. You transported everything you needed from site to site. You described the altars to me. Talked to me about Le Corbusier. It was all so real. I was with you. "I don't know if I can get them all done in time, Carole." "Let me help you," I said.

I think of the light that flared starlike in you for a fraction of a second in the history of the planet.

Gary, I am trying to talk to you.

You were put in an oven and cremated. I don't know where your ashes went.

What keeps going through my head are bits from the Bible. Faces of Sunday school teachers. Miracles. Things I think I used to believe.

You thought a lot about Rilke, my cat. "What did he look like when he was dead?" you asked.

"He looked like he was sleeping," I said.

You spoke a lot about children. In your last months you spoke of babies, dreams of babies, of adopting a small black boy and girl. "I ask you, Carole, what am I going to do with two small black children?"

My chest began to hurt. I imagined the lining of my heart to be inflamed.

"Maybe you could have the bed next to mine," you said. "My brother is moving in too." Gary, I wanted to say, I've already moved in. I live in a city named St. Vincent's with you. I know the streets, the neighbors, the merchants, I know what's for dinner.

"A city named St. Vincent's," you said. "They certainly are megalomaniacs, aren't they?"

Like you, I start confusing your stays in the hospital. I can't remember one from the next. In the beginning we talked a lot about art. You were in the Signs Shows with Jenny Holzer. I gave you a report on David Salle at Castelli's. One of the most beautiful flower arrangements I have ever seen arrived from Marcia Tucker at the New Museum. Your window there was so fantastic. You were still disappointed your bunny plates didn't do better. You've got a show, you told me, for 1987. You said 1986 was going to be the breakthrough year. You said you had to believe that. You said you were just on the verge of some-thing large in your work, you had begun working with computer images, you were excited about all your stuff at the lab. You told me all of this as we walked around the fourteenth floor, you dragging your bag of blood. These must have been from earlier stays. By the last time it was all churches and pyramids and children. Trips to the south of France and Florence and Greece and then finally nothing. You could barely speak. I'd call your answering machine just so I could hear you talk in your old voice. Stringing words together, the way you did on your message, seemed a miracle now to me. "This is Gary Falk. If you'd like to leave a message, wait for the beep tone and I'll get back to you." I could almost believe that you would. That's what the message said. You always called it "the beep tone." Your mother told me that you left a message saying good-bye to your own machine. "This is Gary and, well, I guess I won't be needing you anymore, I guess I'm saying good-bye."

"*Je suis Gary Falk*," you said. You thought you were in France. "Gary," I said, "today I've got the map of Paris around my neck." I took off my scarf and showed it to you, "Just in case we need it, OK?"

"Great," you said.

"May I talk with you?" the neurologist said to me. I am not sister or lover. "May I talk to you for a moment in private?"

"All right," I said.

"Does he know who you are?" he asked.

"Yes," I said, "he does."

"Does he know where he is?"

"Yes, he knows exactly where he is," I said, lying, protecting you and me. "Yes," I said, "he knows."

"There's no hope for your friend," he said.

I came back to you. "Oh, hi, Lorraine, I haven't seen you in ages! Did you see that doctor who was just here?" you asked me. "Yes," I said. "Well, he knows nothing about anything."

You're right about that, Gary, you knew. You picked up on him immediately.

I sit next to you. I know about the blood-brain barrier. It was a term I never wanted to know. I know everything that will happen.

From your hospital bed you painted in your head. On a field of slate green. You told me what you were drawing, where the lines intersected. What it would look like in the end.

I thought my desire to keep you alive would keep you alive. I got confused.

You have become my child. I race to you when you cry. I arrange your blankets. I fix your pillow.

Your bones began to glow. Each day I could trace your bones more easily as you became more and more skeletal. It became impossible for me to look at old photographs of you. I couldn't recognize you in them anymore. I put them away. After a while it became impossible to call your answering machine.

Just a month before, we had watched a beauty pageant. You in your loft and me in my apartment. We would call each other during the commercials. "I think it's going to be Germany or Greece," you said. "No, it's going to be Miss Brazil." "Oh, Carole, you've always loved those Latins," you laughed.

We talked about movies. The last ones you saw, I think, were *My Beautiful Laundrette* and *Mona Lisa*. What else? There must have been others.

I heard what happens is that you're put into a wooden casket and then the whole casket is put into the oven. "Please," you'd say, "you're making it sound like a recipe."

In April you read my book *Ghost Dance* in galleys. You understood it like no one else. You told Helen not to tell me, but you found the book so intense that you thought it was making you sicker. You knew, and when you tried to remember certain parts and couldn't anymore, I began to cry and then grow ferocious. "Don't die," I shouted selfishly. "What?" you said, nearly deaf. "Please, don't die," I yelled and the nurse ran in thinking I needed help.

By the time the book was bound you could no longer read. I was thrilled with how beautiful it looked. I carried the first copy of the hardcover to show you in the hospital, but you just went on with your dying.

You worry about your catheter. You're afraid of wetting the bed.

I kept feeding you. "What am I eating?" you asked, as if it were a natural question. When I told you, you said, "No, to me it tastes like veal, very simply prepared, veal piccata, I think. And how elegant and understated this restaurant is. Have you been here before?" Sometimes you thought you were in a hotel. Sometimes you said, "I'm so tired of traveling."

Your bones glowed. Each day I traced your bones more and more easily, the head so much bone, the flesh melting. It seemed as if the flesh were melting from your face.

You were never as angry as I was. You maintained your hope, not only for yourself but for those you loved. Even at the end, when your parents would call, with your voice you tried to reassure them. It was your life, Gary, but you didn't have the energy for rage I had. Rage was a luxury of the well.

I am trying to talk to you.

Your eyes are black tulips, something beautiful and strange, something so rare, so unlikely. So lovely. Your eyes float separate from your illness. You are incapable of giving up. It's the part of you that is not anchored to the floor. The part of you that is really you. The part of you that lasts forever. The part of you that never burns.

You're not ready to die at thirty-two. It's a breakthrough year.

Room 1433. I pace. Pace. Pace. With the part of you that gets up. With the part of you that can't be tied down. So bring in the cameras, the teachers, the priests. Bring in the man on the street. There are people everywhere who say it's deserved, who say that it only goes to show. They say they are not surprised, are not sorry. They tell us we deserve it.

I'm afraid, Gary, that somehow you might think you deserve it. Once you said to Helen, "Oh, Mrs. So-and-so"—a friend of the family's, I can't remember the name—"do you know what I have?" She nodded. "Can you believe that this has happened to that nice boy Gary Falk?" you said, with bitterness.

It should be possible to do something with words.

Gary, it is not your fault.

I get up with the part of you no doctor can touch. The part

that will live. More tests: spinal tap, CAT scan (it's like going through a giant bagel, you say). The best of modern medicine.

Gary, I'd have gone to Mexico for the Ribavirin. I'd have done anything.

They dipped you in blue. They dipped your skinny, childish body into indigo dyes. I saw your small shrunken genitals. Your nearly transparent hands. Your eyes bulging in your bony head.

I am told that there are certain bones that burn slower than others. They can be fished from the ash and crumbled by hand. There are parts of the body that burn slower, the foot, for instance, the breast bone.

I am so afraid. Still.

"Nothing has been finished," you said, bewildered, "or put away."

That last morning you kept saying, "My father loves me, my mother loves me." Then, "Tekka maki," you said, "kappa maki, hirami," filling your mouth like a child with pure sound, delighted.

Your parents called often: "Is he better or worse? Is he eating? Is he coherent? Carole, you must be tired. How are you doing?"

I tell them that all summer my friend Louis has sent the daily revisions of his poems to me. I have watched a word move from one line to the next, watched a comma appear or disappear, seen a stanza rearranged. It's helped a little, I said.

Sometimes I close my eyes, I tell them, open my eyes and you are whole. Not coughing. Not skinny. Just you. Painting. Out for a walk. Or having dinner somewhere in the city you loved.

In your obituary they wrote you died as a result of AIDS. They were not ashamed. They would have loved you just as much if they had known you were gay. You doubted that and kept it from them until you got sick. It hurt them that that was the case.

I talk to your parents now long distance and it reminds me of talking to my own parents, both on the line at the same time. One upstairs, one downstairs. One listening, one talking, then

an interruption and they are talking simultaneously. It's how
they talked to you those days we sat in the hospital and then
to me in the hospital after you couldn't talk anymore.

I am in Provincetown now and it is freezing cold. There's more
snow here than there's been in thirty years. You arrive between
thin cardboard that once held pantyhose. The Bloomingdale's
b-line, sheer-to-the-waist sandalfoot. This I know would amuse
you. Your mother has sent me two photos: in one you are posing in a studio, a professional shot; in the other you are sitting
in the brightest sun on a beach somewhere.

Gary, I've got a studio here near the water. There's a lot I'd
like to tell you. I've been seeing more of that woman you met at
my book party.

There are some nice people here. I think you'd like Scott, the
photographer, a lot. Helen is well. It is snowing again. There's
more snow this year on the Cape than in the last thirty years.
I've said that.

At the very end, with great effort, you moved your hand over
mine and patted it, not because you knew who I was anymore,
but simply because you saw someone in deep distress and you
were so kind—comforting a stranger even as you were dying.

One more minute, Gary.

We thought we had all the time in the world.

I've got your dishes from Paris. Your champagne glasses.
Your green watch is now mine. I've got your copies of Calvino's
Folk Tales and *Mr. Palomar*. Your bunny plate.

A rabbit chases a carrot forever across a plate that lies on my
bureau in Provincetown, Massachusetts.

I have a recurring dream. You are walking down a long
boarded walkway to my studio at the Fine Arts Work Center.
You are wearing your St. Vincent's pajamas and slippers.
You've got a three-day-old beard. You're attached to your
IMED. You've got a little spiral taped to your chest.

You slowly pass Studio One, Studio Two. I am in number
three. It's winter. The ocean is rising behind you. Sometimes
you stop and disappear into the water. Sometimes I walk with

you into the water. Nothing makes this dream stop. Sometimes you point to the spiral and say, "It goes directly into the heart." Sometimes you say nothing. Sometimes you put your hand out to stop me. Sometimes you motion for me to come.

Nothing has made it stop. Not the ocean, not the dunes, not the screams of the seagulls. Not the Slovak poet and his moody translations of Trakl. Not the Dewars or the Absolut. Nothing makes it stop, Gary. Nothing. Not the writing of this. Not the writing of *The Art Lover*.

You are telling me to come. You are telling me not to come. You are dead. You are not really dead. You are walking to my studio, it is winter, you are in your pajamas, the V over your heart. You are dragging your bag of blood. You are so thin.

It means: I miss you.

It means: I can't believe this happened to you.

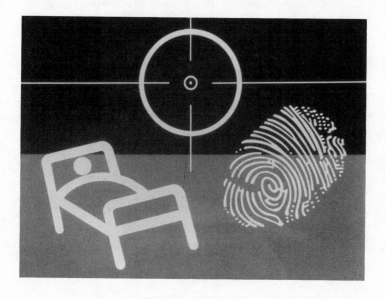

Spring 1986

First Signs of Whirligigs and Hiblinkas

It's still March, but today is the first genuinely springlike day and I am in sitting in your park—Washington Square Park, which you walked through so often to get from home to office and back again, a stack of books and papers under your arm. Dear Father.

People seem happy by this intimation of spring, its mere suggestion. Two lovers sit on a bench, genuinely moved by the warmth in the air. Or is it some little love song that has made them believe this is their time, the spring, on a park bench.

A radio goes by. Madonna sounds so perky. "You must be my lucky star, 'cause you make the darkness seem so far."

People seem more willing to talk to each other. Really. Something relaxes in this false spring. In this spring.

The music in the park today is loud, celebratory. And why not? The temperature near seventy. The sky a sky blue. "Lived in a brownstone, lived in a ghetto, I've lived all over this town," David Byrne sings. Turn your head another angle and you can catch Grand Master Flash saying, "I am somebody!" What a day!

The police car is making its endless slow rotation but finds no trouble.

It's spring, regardless of the date. There's a lot of dancing. People are carrying cameras of every size and shape.

"I know you," someone says, snapping my picture.

There's a lot of dancing and why not? Soon the fire-eaters will be returning. The sword swallowers, the jugglers, the three-card montes, people to draw your picture. There are bicycles galore. Roller skates, skateboards, shopping carts, wagons— every variety of wheel. It's the shopping-bag ladies who have the shopping carts. They are the most grateful of all for spring, I think.

You can see bits of green on the boughs of the trees if you really concentrate.

No matter how nice the day I still do not like pigeons, though what you have heard is true, Max, I have become a bird watcher.

People open their lunches on the benches. Small, modest picnics of sorts. People lift a can of this or that to welcome spring.

The police have found someone to tell to turn down their radio.

Lots of sunglasses.

Lots of hats.

Some babies.

How lovely the townhouses bordering the park look. It is 1:15 p.m., March 11, 1986. They look like red-and-white checkerboards in this light. Like flags.

And the rosy NYU library you came out of so many times. Muttering mostly. I remember that librarian you were seeing for a while. By this time of course we had stopped asking, "Will she be our stepmother?" We had gotten the idea. I remember you walking across the park with her, she in her business suit, you in your sweater. Later she told me, as if I were her friend, she thirty when I was twenty, "We liked it best on my large desk. We would lock the door, during lunch hour. He liked taking me from behind. He said I had lovely earlobes."

The man next to me has one wish for his life. Lots of people are talking to each other today. He wants to die in Brazil. He says it's the country this country could have been.

It's 1:50. The light looks like a flag from a country this one could have been.

It's 2:02 by the digital. The light looks like a tablecloth at a picnic.

There are winos still. Beer bellies. Over the years you developed quite a belly yourself, Max. I remember it crossing the park, your arm crooked to hold those papers and books. Muttering, mostly.

There are a lot of students here. Students in love. Students in love with life, each other, the sweetness, the warmth in the wind. With art.

An NYU film school crew is out making a film. Moving the tripod from here to there. Getting out the trusty Ariflex. Soundman with headphones carrying the Nagra. And how is Laslo doing these days? I wonder. Nice weather for filmmaking. "Light. More light!" the director cries. The aperture opens. The director, just a big kid, passing, says, "Hey, you'd be perfect for this one small part. Do you want to be in my movie?" "Maybe," I say. "Call," he gives me his number. It would be for next week. "Great face," he says. "Thanks," I say.

The dinner is tonight. I must not forget the champagne on the way home. Tonight, only the best champagne. We'll be drinking the stars, as the little monk Dom Perignon said.

People are smiling and dancing. They are glad Halley's Comet is back. There's still a chance we might actually see it.

Children in the distance going up and down on the swings make a pretty pattern. Children going down slides. Children on seesaws. It's the motion that's so pleasing. Children playing on things I have no real names for—doughnut-shaped objects that twirl. Whirligigs, you'd call them, zephyrs, hiblinkas. You were not so old to have to die, especially when I think of you sitting on one of those benches with me and saying, "Look at that kid riding a hiblinka."

They have found an empty spacesuit from the *Challenger*, I've heard. Slowly the ocean gives up the heroes.

Some very professional-looking bike riders pass, with all the equipment—helmets and pads. Yes, this is a dangerous place, there is no doubt, even in spring.

Drug dealers whispering cocaine, cocaine, cocaine. Police circling.

A few girls in short skirts, tee-shirts, the styles of spring. Lots of pinks and yellows. Some probably art history students. I can't believe all the girls you're missing.

An empty spacesuit. This year's model.

The camera crew is looking through the lens at the bouncing and bobbing children. There's lots of wild sound. The light meter is out. Light readings are being taken.

A flag draped over the remains.

People wear buttons, but I can't really read them. "Victim of the press" is a popular one.

Often I feel like I can't quite see in. Never really a part of things. "Ah, Caroline," you'd say. "Never underestimate the gene pool. It's the luck of the draw. Your mother often felt that way."

Grey feels that way, even more often than I do. Though he digs and digs, he can't seem to get dirty enough.

"Ah, the luck of the draw."

David called to say that Grey has checked into a hospital for depression in the south of France. Van Gogh's hospital, *peut-être*? Spring was always hardest for him.

The light comes and goes. It's time for home. Must not forget to see if your librarian is still there one of these days. It's something she should know about you, if she doesn't yet. Nearly a year already now.

If you really concentrate, the light in the trees at 4:30 in Washington Square Park on the 11th of March looks like the first leaves, tiny hands, stars.

Right now Giotto moves toward the nucleus of the comet. Right now Giotto is drinking the stars.

Tonight we will drink bottle after bottle of champagne. Tonight there will be stars in our mouths.

Jesus in the Garden

"Transplant seedlings in the evening, Caroline. If you put them
in during the heat of the day they will wilt," he says, walking up
to the garden at dusk. "They may not survive the shock." He
pauses. "Or you can plant them on a cloudy day. Or just after
rain."

He holds the first seedling in his hand. "Careful not to break
the delicate roots," he says.

"All winter, collect toilet paper cores and small orange juice
cans. Gently slip them over the plants and press them into the
ground. They should be snug around the plants because at night
the worms come up close to the stems.

"Protect my beauties, my firstlings, my primeurs, from the
frost. My asparagus and artichokes. My tender sweet peas,
green beans, early spinach. Sorrel, carrots, beets. Take along
newspaper hats, fruit baskets, burlap blankets. Anything to
hold the warmth from the earth around the foliage through
the night." He touches my hand. "This is the word of God."

Jesus Among the Trillium, Weeping

He is sitting on a rock. He is surrounded by scarlet trillium. He
picks one. Three petals, three perfect leaves. He's inconsolable.

"Why are you weeping, Jesus?" Candace asks.

"Because soon I will have to die and still I do not know why."
She nods.

"Nothing is finished or put away," he whispers.

"I know."

"I'm going to miss the columbine this year."

"How terrible. Never to see columbine again," Candace says.
He looks up. "I'll see it again."

"Are you sure?"

"Oh yes," he says. "I'm sure."

The Beating Leaves

Monica has lost her ferret. I picture it running wild through this city, its small ferret eyes darting here, there. Monica crying out in the night, inconsolable. *Where is my ferret?*

"Oh my. Poor Monica," you'd say, with a certain tenderness and cruelty.

I understand now, Max, that you were heartbroken. I understand there were no suitable words for you to speak, given the enormity of your pain. Given your line of vision. It's my problem too. How to continue at all, how to speak, given everything.

"Yes, but it is the pursuit that is beautiful, my dear. You yourself have said."

Sometimes I'm not sure anymore, Max.

"My darling daughter."

One of Cézanne's last letters. It was to his son: "Finally I must tell you that as a painter I am becoming more and more clear sighted in front of nature but that with me the realization of my sensation is always very difficult. I cannot sustain the intensity that is unfolded before my senses. I have not the magnificent richness of color that animates nature."

Edward Snow on Degas: "The pathos of nearness and distance that one still feels before a Degas—the lingering desire of the artist not so much to possess as to prolong, to be there where the vision is."

Psalm 44: "We have been faithful to you, O God, yet you have broken us in the place of jackals."

I will bring lilacs to him because it is spring. Each leaf, heart-shaped, perfect. I am so filled with sorrow and love. How to begin to say this?

My editor, carrying the first copies of *Delirium*, visits me in my apartment. "Here," he says, proudly. We are in this together. I hold the book for the first time. It's the most beautiful book I have ever seen and I tell him so. "You must sign one," he says, "for me."

Nothing unusual. A lovely afternoon, a little wine, the sun shining brightly. I pick up my pen and open his book, not knowing at all what I will say; I let my hand just go and I write, "For John, with my ultimate respect and love." There is something deeply shocking in this. I was unaware of how I felt until it was written. I trust you. I love you. But I had not realized it.

We talked about the next book. Drank a little more wine. He had to go. He left his cigarettes.

There was the package of cigarettes. We were talking. We were talking about art. He had to leave. He was gone. But he left his Camels behind.

And here he is now, in an image of a single Camel walking through a desert with pyramids on a glass table in New York, ten years ago.

It's such a strange life, Max.

Many years later in Massachusetts, lying on a beach, I look up across the Swift River into the center of a single pine tree and miss her. Her face does not come back, nor her figure. Not a single fragment of her voice or anything she ever said. But I miss my mother, looking at a tree. It is only a tree. A lake. A sound of a body moving through water, a wave.

Sometimes, Max, it feels too sad to have to go on.

Steven gasping for breath, some months from now.

"Feel appalled, Caroline. Feel like Picasso."

In Picasso's by-now-famous last self-portrait, the artist resembles an old Roman warrior. One eye seems in this world, almost popping out of his head in its eagerness to see. The other eye is a beady dot that appears to have glimpsed something that does not allow itself to be seen. His expression as a whole is one of stupefaction. When we arrive at this painting, we are as scandalized as he that even the old warrior, who in his late work seemed to have devoured nature itself, would one day have to say good-bye.

"Oh my, I don't mean to tell you how to feel. The absurdity of it. How queer. You know what death looked like, Caroline? A young man in a shower cap and a bathrobe leaning over me and reciting numbers.

"Who the hell is this guy? I wanted to ask. The whole world disappearing."

Sometimes I think we live in an unbreakable code. The world refusing to give up its logic. As much as I turn it, it remains indecipherable, a cloudy bowl of blue water half-filled. A New York winter. And I am afraid of all that is opaque, viscous. It's so difficult to really see.

The starburst was the shape of your death, of so many things. I know that now, but to be truthful, at the time I thought it was only the shape of pleasure, the shape of orgasm.

To mistake glass for ice.

"That's OK. All you have to do is keep looking," says Max.

And to keep feeling, Max, regardless of the consequences.

Steven, here, now, still.

I love you.

Because he was saying I love you, something he had never said to them before, they thought he was saying good-bye.

Because it is spring I think of lilacs. I think of bringing you lilacs, of inhaling them deeply as the elevator rises up to the Coleman Wing where you sleep. The leaves shaped like hearts. Each one beating for you.

I pass the Korean grocer. Everything feels heightened. Each vegetable and fruit, they're greener, rounder, riper. I look at the Korean grocer's old face. I am afraid. Everything feels over. I hand him an avocado. It's greener. A peach. It's rounder. I hand him the world. I can feel its delicate skin. Its softness. A plum. A pear. A melon. Its infinite variety, smell, shape. I begin to cry. He had no language for me. We were from opposite sides of the earth. But it's over. Everything feels over.

One more minute, I beg.

I open the avocado. I put the apple in my mouth. I would bring parsnips to your lips, tender raspberries, asparagus. I eat oranges and figs. I devour all the things of this world.

I dream everything. There is nothing I do not dream. I dream of a shining city rising up from an island if only for one moment in the history of the world. Steven, I dream of your blood in my bloodstream, which is death, and I dream of the lilacs I bring. I dream of the way to speak of all of this. First, we are seven, you are drawing my picture in class, and then you are dying on the fourteenth floor of St. Vincent's Hospital. We are on a beach. We are moving our hands through water. There is a camel. A stone cross. A sunburst.

I hand the poor old woman who sits on the park bench a bag of plums.

I eat the peach. We are eating to live.

We are in a disco, Steven. We are dancing for our lives.

We dare to write it down, to make a mark on a page, to utter something.

I love you.

We are speaking for our lives.

The Lady Fern

There were so many different kinds of ferns, and now they were on the verge of fern season again.

The seeds ordered in January from catalogs had arrived. The names they dreamt of all winter long now had shape. Alison took packet after packet out of the box, a small weight in her hands.

The Maestro Peas. The Champion Radish. The Jubilee Sweet Corn. The Early Wonder Beets. The Ace Pepper. The Hungarian Hot Wax. The Young Beauties. The Ruby Perfection. They had all arrived.

The garden shed was cool. They collected the tools and put them in the wagon: hoes, shovels, rakes and the pitchfork. Slowly they climbed the hill to the large patch Alison had covered several weeks earlier with manure.

"What shall I do?" Maggie asked.

"I'll show you, Mother. It's not so hard to grow things. I'll teach you everything I know."

It was a warm day, really the first warm day of the season and already their NYU sweatshirts were off. "Let's turn over the earth first, take out any big rocks. We should probably just get a feel for it. It seems like it's been such a long time."

"My farmer," Maggie said. From her back pocket Alison took out the map of the garden she had planned on paper.

"How did you decide what goes next to what?"

"Oh, it's very well thought out."

"I'm sure," Maggie smiled.

"I put the root crops together because they use a lot of potash. Leafy greens, cauliflower and cabbage use more nitrogen, so I decided to put them next to the peas and beans, which put nitrogen in the soil. If you keep moving plant families around, the bugs and disease will have to travel. Mostly they're not up for the trip. Last year the root vegetables were there. The peas and beans there. It's best to rotate."

"We've lived through almost a whole year without him. I think we're going to be OK," Maggie whispers.

Alison opened the first packet of seeds. The Early Wonder Beets and the Black-Seeded Simpson Leaf Lettuce. Maggie watched Alison's tiny fingers make the first row, indenting the earth and then emptying the seeds into it. "Alison," she said.

"What is it, Mom?"

"It's nothing."

"Come on. Why don't you help me? Here, start another row. Right here next to me."

Maggie lightly pressed her finger into the earth and let out a small sound.

"Are you all right, Mom?"

She pressed her hand into the soil and let out another sound.

"Oh, Alison. It's so dark. It's so very dark. And warm. I didn't expect it to be this warm and dark."

"It's kind of nice, isn't it?"

"It's very nice. No wonder you're always up here."

Alison smiled.

"We're going to be OK, aren't we?"

Alison nodded.

"Candace, too?"

"Sure, she'll be OK."

"Do you miss him, Ali?"

"All the time."

"I thought so."

"Candace has seen him."

"Really?"

"She's bumped into him a few times."

"Was he—"

"Yes, he was with Biddy."

The name sounded ludicrous to Maggie, but she did not allow herself to focus on the woman. It was Henry. She did not complete the sentence even in her mind. But it was Henry she hated. She stood up straight on the dark, turning earth, felt dizzy, lost her balance and then regained it. The world seemed to open up with emotion and she marveled at the breadth of her sudden rage. There was no other word for it. She shouted into the open earth, "I hate you for what you've done."

Alison quietly moved down the row, bending over the plot, gently covering over the seeds she had just sown.

"Candace says she despises him. She says she always will and that she'll never forgive him."

How oddly this moment of hate, Maggie thought, however fleeting, made her capable of a different sort of love as well. She looked at this daughter and loved her with an intensity she had never before felt.

"Candace is coming home," Alison said. "Back for the summer, soon as school is out." Maggie thought of Candace again, her angry, passionate daughter, the fierce child of fire born in July under the sign of the lion. She had decided to paint. Who would have thought?

Alison thought of the three of them here for the summer.

"It's all so wonderful."

"What, Mom?"

"The world. All this dirt everywhere. And cow shit. My God."

Maggie breathed in the warm air. Alison moved to another plot of land, plot #2 on her plan.

From this place in the garden Maggie could see now how grown-up Alison had become in this last year. Her body catching up with the rest of her. If love had a body, she thought, it would take Alison's shape.

Such a sight. Her daughter. And the painting she could now see in her mind's eye. Mary Cassatt, she said. Why had she never thought of Mary Cassatt before? Or any of the others? Vanessa Bell, she said to herself. Frida Kahlo. Sonia Delaunay. Georgia O'Keeffe.

There was Rosa Bonheur, Paula Modersohn-Becker. Florine Stettheimer and Käthe Kollwitz. She thought she had barely known their names, but now they all came back, in an instant.

Alison turned to her and whispered, "She's much better now,

Candace is, since she's made the decision to paint. She seems much better."

"My hunch," Maggie said, slowly getting up, "is that she'll be very good."

"She wants us to come to New York and go to some galleries with her. She wants you to see Barbara Kruger." But who, she wondered, was Barbara Kruger? "Georgia Marsh. Louisa Chase. Nancy Graves. Ida Applebroog."

"I'd like that."

"She's sure to run us ragged. You know Candace."

But did she know Candace any more than she knew this girl/woman laughing now, rolling in the dirt?

"I'm so happy it's finally spring. And it's here early. Soon there'll be fiddleheads again. And Candace will be here. Aren't you happy, Mom? Spring!"

"I'm not sure. It will mean it's been a whole year."

"We've done all right, Mom."

There are wildflowers that live only for a week, Alison thought. You must love them while you can.

"When is Candace coming?"

"Soon as she finishes her final project."

"What is it?"

"I don't know, she's being pretty mysterious."

"Why hasn't she told me anything, Ali?"

"I guess she thought you just wouldn't be interested. She wants to be a Guerrilla Girl."

"Does that mean she's a lesbian?"

"Mom, don't you know what a Guerrilla Girl is? They're 'the conscience of the art world.' A group of women artists demanding attention."

"Really?" She had neglected them all.

"Don't be so hard on yourself, professor."

"I've been absent a lot. I've nearly missed you girls growing up completely."

"I never held it against you."

"And Candace?"

"I don't know."

Alison looked far out at the dark-green edge where the field met the forest. She thought about those spirals of green about to curl from the earth. "Fiddleheads," she said. She had read that those miraculous ferns were brought by the French Canadians who could not live without them. "Let's go check the asparagus bed."

For the first time, it seemed, Maggie realized the beauty of her surroundings—the gorgeous spot this garden was in, high on the hill overlooking the barn and the garden shed. The apple trees and the field. Past that, the forest. And the bluish Berkshires far in the distance, an ocean in this light. She allowed herself over and over again the pleasure of simply bending in the dirt. She felt the tender tips of the young asparagus on her palms, her wrists. Those purple patterned heads. She felt the pleasure of simply sitting in the dirt with a view like this on a lovely spring day with Alison. For a moment she did not try to name or arrange anything. Side by side, they weeded the long bed of asparagus in silence. It was getting late.

"I love when the ferns come," Alison murmured, rubbing her eyes the way Maggie remembered she did when she was a little girl. They packed the garden wagon and slowly, one step at a time, went down the steep hill.

"The ostrich plume fern," "the maidenhair fern," she said with their steps. "The lady fern."

Alison's Dream

Despite a long Saturday in the garden with her mother, Alison had a hard time falling asleep. First she thought of the day's work and wondered whether she had done the right thing putting the early potatoes so close to the peas. Her father had always done the garden plot arrangements. Plant sage among cabbages because it gives off camphor that repels the cabbage moths. He was good at it. He enjoyed it. He always said it was a rather musical task.

Since the garden slopes from dry to moist, the celery and cukes should go below and early veggies go on the warm upper level. In the spots that don't receive the full sun put cabbage, peas, spinach, lettuce, radishes. In the open sunny areas put the heat-loving tomatoes, eggplants and peppers. Of course, pole beans and corn should not be placed on the south end of the garden because they will cast shadows on the rest of the plants.

She missed him. His jokes, his lightness, his love. He must not have loved them. How could he love them and do what he had done? She worried about the garden. Had she done things properly?

Her confirmation was in two weeks. She recited the things she had learned until she fell asleep.

"See that you do not despise one of these little ones. For the Son of Man came to save what was lost. If a man had a hundred sheep, and one of them stray, will he not leave the ninety-nine in the mountains, and go in search . . ."

And there were many stars, but the path was still dark. She walked a long time in darkness, not knowing where she was. Someone took her hand. She hurt so badly. "Dad," she said finally. "Is that you?" She thought she recognized him but she wasn't absolutely sure. And he was not holding her hand, as she first thought, but someone else's. Or wait. He was holding her mother's hand and her hand too, she thought. And Candace was huddled around his feet. "It's the bear," Candace whispered. "Shh shh." But it was too dark somehow for Alison to see, floating, yes floating as she was in some strange and wonderful shape. It was so dark. "Daddy, the bear," Candace said. Alison saw nothing. But the feeling of her father there protecting them against bears and then the absence of the father made Alison shiver. Hearing her father say now, "Do not worry, I will take care of you forever," as he was saying now, "even against bears," made her shudder with sadness.

"Where's the bear, Candace?" Alison whispered. "Where?"

"Higher," Candace said. "Look higher."

She looked up. "Where?" She saw her mother's full breasts.

"Higher," Candace said.

She looked up and saw her mother's enormous head, like a globe on her shoulders.

"Higher."

Past the universe of her mother's head, Alison saw lights. Beautiful lights in the sky.

"That's right," Candace said, helping Alison slowly navigate her way. They found the Big Dipper, tipped, and with their infinitesimal fingers they connected the stars. In the handle now she saw the tail and in the bowl, the back. She heard her father's voice louder, clearer. "I will protect you forever. I will keep you safe from all bears." And baffled and angered and aching, Alison continued. "I will never leave you." There was the giant head, the body, the paws. And finally, with great effort, she cast it into the sky, Ursa Major, the family bear, and cried.

Jesus, Dancing

Jesus dances among the lilies of the valley. He pats the lambs on their heads. He picks a jeweled fruit from a tree. Someone is playing a lute. He hears a cock crowing; he doesn't think much about it. He thinks he would like to learn how to cook. Maybe he'll be a chef, he thinks—he forgets for a minute. He imagines the day he will feed the multitudes and it makes him smile. He's whirling, twirling, a young man in the years before thirty, when no one knows exactly what he's doing. He looks up to the perfection of sky. He says it to himself; he tries it out—*I am going to rise.*

Reading Steven to Sleep

"'The last spacecraft to encounter the comet will be the European Giotto mission. It is to fly closer to the comet than any of the others.

"The actual encounter will take place between 13 and 14 March 1986 and will only last 4 hours at a possible flyby distance of only 310 miles. At this time the comet will be 90 million miles from Earth and the flyby velocity will be 42 miles per second. If the spacecraft encounters any cometary debris at this speed, the result can only be catastrophic.'"

A Letter from Henry

The letter she had composed hundreds of times over in her head through the past year arrived quite unexpectedly one day. In the past few weeks she had let down her guard, entering the garden with Alison and staying there. In fact, she had not thought of the letter at all since that first day in the garden. Yet here it was. She recognized the handwriting at once.

She knew any word from Henry would arrive in the form of a letter. Henry had always conveyed all really important news in writing. Would you marry me? he had written on a cream-colored card, bordered in gold. And who could have resisted such a man, sending out a formal invitation to live a life together? Over the years she would learn that his proposal was no one-time romantic gesture but just the beginning of a series of notes he would write to her. "I want to have a child." "Bless us with another daughter." It was the one truly odd thing about him. She remembered the morning she woke up to an envelope he had placed next to her on his pillow. "Mother is dying. I must leave for Vermont." He was there in the room dressing, putting on his tie and jacket; he could have spoken to her. In the mirror he watched her open the envelope. He could have said something; he was right there. But writing was his way of coping with the most intense of experiences. Ordering them. Perhaps it made them seem more real. "I'm sorry," she said, kissing him as he left the room.

She should have known that the letter she had waited for would be as simple as those earlier ones had been. Will you marry me? Mother is dying. I have fallen in love with another woman. Not elaborate, as she had fantasized, not filled with explanations, rationales, testimonies. No paragraphs about his new life in New York, pages about what went wrong. She opened it slowly. It was a brief note, and as she read it she could picture him writing it, and she did not know how she could have imagined the note any other way.

She grew angry for a moment. She imagined him writing "I love you" to her on a napkin in a cafe. He had said he loved her. "I have fallen in love with another woman."

She looked at the handwriting she knew so well and grew calm again. The handwriting of good and bad news. "I want to come home." That was the line that stood out, though there were others around it. "Terrible mistake," "miss you," "the children." "I want to come home." "I want to come home"—but she did not know what she thought about that anymore. Her hands were trembling. "I love you. I miss you. I want to come home. Forgive me."

But certainly he did not expect her to forgive him just like that, did he?

She tucked the letter into the pocket of the cardigan sweater she was wearing.

"I love you."

But she did not know if she loved him anymore.

Her response, she thought, might be, Why didn't you ever teach me how to make a fire, Henry? But why hadn't she ever thought to ask? she wondered.

How could he have left her when she loved him so much?

"I love you. I want to come home."

She had come to love not only the names of the trees but gradually the trees themselves. The white bark of the birch. The smell of pines.

"Was I shocked into the world by you or do I still give you more credit than you deserve? I can't say. But things have changed here, and I don't know if I love you anymore."

She looked out the window into the meadow where the cowslip and bloodroot had begun to bloom. She watched a figure out of the distance come nearer, grow bigger.

"There are fiddleheads for lunch," Alison said with delight, entering the kitchen. "And the first asparagus." She got out the steamer, singing. "Oh Mom, please, can't we go out in the boat tonight?"

The Last Dream on Earth

In the last dream I ever have this is what I hope would happen: we are all there, Max and Mom, David and Grey, Steven. We're somewhere far away in a large room. "It's so dark," Steven whispers. "Don't be afraid," I say. "The dark is not so dark."

I put Steven where David usually is—it's surprisingly easy. I can't get him out of his pajamas, though, so I guess his pajamas will have to do. But he is not skinny and he is not coughing. He puts his foot on the first rung of the ladder. He climbs up slowly, one rung at a time. Grey speaks. "We've saved this for you, Steven," he says, and he hands him a scalpel, a tweezers, some solvent, a brush. Grey dozes off. I cannot press him into a life he does not want. David sits down and looks at this remote image of himself. They are Castor and Pollux and one day they will be together forever in the sky. Made of light. But for now—David gets up and moves away from his silent twin. "The restoration," he tells me, "reveals the colors are radiant, like Vasari said."

"It's true," Steven says. "The colors are much less tawdry. And there is more movement."

Max nods, standing at the entrance of this womblike place. Holding his arm is a young woman of exceptional beauty. I'm thinking to myself that she must be my mother. In fact I'm sure of it.

"Christ's face is baffled, unbearable, serene," she says. "Believe me, I know."

"One of you shall betray me," He says.

Hands move to the heart. Hair flies. "Is it I, Lord?" "Is it I?" Palms open. Nostrils flare. Mouths. "Is it I?" There is a terrible space between shapes. A finger points to the sky.

"After this there will be a kiss," she whispers.

I see her lips floating on the black lake.

One of you shall betray me.

She shuts her eyes. She seems to be drowsing on Max's arm. "No, Mother, not tonight," I say to her, and I nudge Grey awake too. "No sleep yet. No gorgeous, drugged slumber. Not yet. Hold on one more moment." And Steven is in his pajamas, still climbing one by one each rung of the ladder. "Stay a little."

"It takes so long. It goes so slowly," Mother says.

"Don't fall," I tell Steven. "Don't worry," he says. "I won't."

In the daily dream I tell myself he is not sick. He is not going to die. But that's only some days. Other days he is already in heaven. Some days he speaks to me. Others he is silent, ashes in the ground.

Sometimes I think I know what the black tulips mean. Other times I have no idea.

Steven stares at the scene in front of him.

Max laughs. "The beards are trimmed. The table reset. But perhaps," he says, getting closer, "most importantly, there is a rearranging of hands. Come, take mine," he says, and we fit together for a minute, just as we are, in our intricate, quirky jigsaw shapes.

"One must integrate each fragment once it has been cleaned with the fragments next to it, fitting the pieces together." Max and I are still holding hands. "See that flake of blue, Caroline?" David says. "It has migrated from where Leonardo originally put it as part of his color for one of the apostles' robes." I can't believe this is David, helpful for once, the person he might have been.

I stare at the molecule of blue floating across the wall past Steven. I think of a flower seeding itself in another part of the garden. I think of the cells of blood. I think of one breaking away and changing shape.

David continues. "Just before beginning restoration on Christ's face we had to stop work because of the humidity level." He enters another time. "There was so much water. People must have traveled here by the canal that once flowed outside these doors," he says, like a little boy loving water.

"A man named Innocenti invented a wall of forced air that now exists between the painting and the viewer," David tells us.

"Pure oxygen," Grey says, revived.

Steven motions for me to come up the ladder. I climb to him, breathing the perfect air. Max and Mom follow. Then Grey and David. Steven brings his trembling finger to the beautiful lip of Christ. He tentatively begins to remove a bit of overpainting. There's a possibility we'll be staring in the end into absolutely nothing, like David says, Max. Like you've said all along.

"His face has not vanished," Grey says. "I do not think his face has vanished."

"Yes, a full recovery is possible," Steven says. "What we'll see there most likely is a good man." He smiles. "But only a man."

As for me—I do not know what we'll see. I am simply grateful to be having such a dream. I'm so high up, standing on the scaffold with Max and Mom, Grey and David. With Steven . . .

I guess I'm still hoping we might rise. Or maybe, just perhaps, holding hands here through this final fiction, we've already risen.

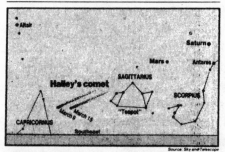

Sky Watch This week at 4:30 A.M.

Source: Sky and Telescope

This week and next, the moon cooperates in our efforts to find Halley's comet, which has returned to the sky after hiding behind the Sun for several weeks. However, the comet will be visible for only a short period before dawn, and will be very low on our southeastern horizon. The farther south one travels, the higher in the sky the comet will be. For those who cannot go south, the period March 10-20, when the moon is absent from the morning sky, may give the best viewing chances until the year 2061, the next time the comet is scheduled to pass our way. The comet, which is notoriously variable, is brighter than originally expected — about 2.5 magnitude — but the first twilight of dawn will obscure its growing tail, now about 2 degrees long. By comparison, the diameter of the moon is about half a degree. To see the comet, get up well before dawn and get as far away from city lights as possible, to a place with an unobstructed view of the southeastern horizon. Give your eyes at least 20 minutes to get accustomed to the dark. Binoculars will provide the best view. The comet will rise shortly after 4 A.M. this morning, or about an hour before morning twilight, and it will rise a few minutes earlier each day thereafter. The best viewing time will be in the half-hour or so before twilight creeps into the sky. By 5 A.M. the light will already be interfering. The comet will be to the right of the faint constellation Capricorn, the goat, no higher than 9 degrees over the horizon — the width of two fists held at arm's length. Its wispy tail, however, rises higher, pointing up and to the right toward the top of the "teapot" in Sagittarius. The comet makes its final bow next month, when the best moon-free viewing period will be from the 2d to the 13th. After then, the comet will fade rapidly as it streaks off to the far reaches of the solar system.

Dr. K. L. Franklin, Astronomer Emeritus, The Hayden Planetarium   The New York Times / March 9, 1986

Jesus, Mary and Alison

She smells of melon. Of ripe fruit. Alison looks at her and touches her own breasts, just budding. "Mary," she says. A flourish of hips. "Why are you weeping?"

"Look to my son," she says.

He's wandering through a field of trillium. He quotes Roethke by heart:

Snail, snail, glister me forward,
Bird, soft-sigh me home.
Worm, be with me.
This is my hard time.

"Jesus," Alison whispers. "What's wrong?"

He holds her tightly. He loves her so much it makes him shudder. "This is my commandment: that you love one another as I have loved you. Greater love has no man," he smiles, "no woman, no child than this, that ye may lay down your life for your friends."

Alison nods. "Of course," she says.

"Oh, my," he says. She's weeping.

Alison gasps. "Will I ever be beautiful like Mary?" she asks.

"Alison," Jesus says, "look at you—your hair the color of nutmeg. Your almond eyes. Your perfect human soul. How beautiful you are right now. Not child and not yet adult, you are at that tender age of becoming." He smiles, pleased with the phrase he's made up. He says it again. It sounds good. Maybe, he thinks to himself, I am going to live.

The Sky at Night

They are taking out the boat for the first time this season. They push it off its rollers under the dock's roof, where it has been kept all winter. Alison gets in the boat, Maggie stands at the lake's edge.

"You'll be cold in just your cardigan, Mom."

Maggie touches her sweater pocket. "Dear Maggie, I want to come home." She wishes she could scream. Suddenly she's afraid of everything.

"What a clear night," Alison says evenly.

It is not a large boat; it is only a rowboat and the smallness of it makes the lake and sky seem vast. It is just the two of them, Maggie and Alison, and as they push off from the shore, Maggie dips her hand into the cold water and swishes it back and forth.

"It hurts," she says. "It's too early to be out."

"We won't stay long, Mom."

Alison rows tentatively at first but then finds a rhythm and the boat moves slowly forward on the smooth cool dark.

It's making me better, Alison says to herself, in strokes. It's making me better.

"I don't know what to do, Alison," Maggie whispers. "I'm lost."

"Look, Mom," Alison says, pointing to the sky. "It's Gemini."

"Oh yes, the twins."

They are clearly visible tonight, back again for spring.

"Do you remember the story of Castor and Pollux, Ali?"

"Tell me again," Alison says.

"They were the sons of Leda. Castor's father was Tyndareus, the king of Sparta. Pollux may have been the son of Zeus, which would have made him immortal. After Castor's death, Pollux was overwhelmed with grief and wanted to share his immortality with his twin. Finally, Zeus reunited them by placing them together in the heavens."

"It's a beautiful story," Alison smiled. Alison had never realized before how much she had missed her mother. She had loved spending this last year with her, difficult as it had been. She and her mother building fires, gardening, rowing together in the boat. And she realized only this year that she had been missing her mother her whole life.

Maggie watched the oars slip into the black water, move back, come around and dip into water again. She thought she saw what van Gogh had described as "a note of intense malachite green, something utterly heartbreaking."

She watched the movement of her daughter, her arm extended then bent, her weight forward then back, forward again. She watched her small sneakered feet, lifting up occasionally, her toes remaining stationary and pointed.

Alison stopped in the center of the lake and looked up into the jeweled sky, that masterpiece. Who made all this? Alison wondered. God made this.

How much Maggie loved this little girl. How much she loved Candace. How much she missed Henry.

Maggie looked up at the spiraling sky, the transfigured, the throbbing sky.

"Such a starry night," she says.

The spiral in her hand, now a star, now a galaxy.

"I am a stranger on this earth," was the psalm van Gogh preached from at age twenty-three. "Hide not thy command-ments from me."

Maggie latched herself on to one of the spirals and spun with it. "I'm dizzy," she said. "I feel sick."

She did not know if she loved him.

Alison held her mother's hand. "Mom, it's going to be OK."

"Do you really think so?"

"Yes."

"Henry, you broke my heart."

For a moment Alison imagined him with them in the boat, humming. She put Candace next to him, completing the family.

Max, come back.

You were not that old. You were elegant, graying, distin-guished, with a slight paunch. I remember. You had many lov-ers. You were not old.

Obviously a major malfunction.

"Sometimes I'm so afraid, Alison."

Alison looks up to the Bear in the sky, but she can't find it. The sky is vast, heartbreakingly beautiful, huge with mystery and longing.

There is so much pain in the world.

The question remains how to speak above all the red in your hospital room.

"There is so much pain in the world," Alison cries. "Why?"

An empty spacesuit flies by.

A man covered with papers and rags trudging through the street.

Young people dying around every corner.

You are in your St. Vincent's pajamas and slippers. Dragging your bag of blood. So thin.

Why have you forsaken me? Can you hear me? Can anybody hear me at all?

"Yes," He says, "I hear you."

"Then do something, dear God."

"No, Caroline. *You* do something."

We have been faithful to you, and you have broken us in the place of jackals.

Maggie cries out in the night. She is angry now. She does not hold still and then die. She stands up in the boat and looks up to the sky.

Did he expect her to just forgive him? How could he have left them?

"Let's go further," Maggie says. "I'll row now."

Maggie rows harder, faster.

"Are you all right, Mom?"

"Yes," she says evenly. "I'm all right now."

She stops rowing suddenly, the lake on fire. "I didn't think they'd be so black. I didn't think they'd be flying so fast. The field so ripe. The sky so wide." Maggie begins to shake. "I didn't think they'd fly this fast. I didn't think they'd swoop and dive."

Everything moving toward us. The whole world moving toward us. She feels the longing for everything in this world. She shrieks and shrieks: "Why these roads? Why these crows?"

He struggles against the perspective that diminishes an individual object before his eyes, Max says. He loads on the pigment.

Maggie screams. Feathers everywhere. The birds beating against the boat.

The wheat so sharp. So beautiful. The sky so dark.

Van Gogh in a wheat field lifting his brush to forestall collapse. To resist disintegration.

Van Gogh taking Maggie's hand now and allowing her through his vision, into the world. The boat rocking. Into the pain of the world. The lake so dark. The sides of the boat peeling. The oars hard in her hands, splintery. The smell of seaweed. The smell of early spring. The sound of water lapping against the boat.

She gasps now looking at Alison. She takes her hand. It is warm, smooth. It is flesh and blood.

"Look how beautiful the sky is," Maggie says. "How it goes on forever. Light and dark intermingled. Together. One world. The sky is enormous, filled with mystery and love."

"My dear one," the mother says, "as a baby you must have thought my sobbing was a song."

I nod. "I know that you did the best you could. I believe it: you simply could not go on."

"*Oui, c'est vrai.*"

Maggie looks at Alison and she begins to cry. She holds her daughter tightly. They rock back and forth, back and forth in this small boat in the middle of the night.

Actually it is not night, it is more like the few moments right before dawn. The comet they had hoped so much to see now veered into deep space. They thought they could feel it as it moved further and further away, and they held each other tightly, and rocked each other with what seemed a steadier, more predictable rhythm.

Alison's heartbeat grew louder and louder. The whole world seemed to pulsate with it. She looked up to the cometless sky. She could barely talk above her own heartbeat. She shuddered.

"Do you think," she said, trembling, looking up to the sky and then into her mother's eyes, "that He really led them—by a star?"

The Hieroglyphs of Hope

Tonight there is champagne because we are celebrating. Not the first springlike day, but that Steven's lungs, while not completely clear, are almost clear, that he has been accepted into the Compound S program and also it's a belated birthday celebration—he turned thirty-three in the hospital several weeks earlier. We are celebrating the fact that he was born and that he got himself out of the hospital with what Max always called his "extraordinary resourcefulness."

I get out Max's cooking equipment: his knives, his presses, his whisks. I am making my friend butterflied leg of lamb. I have marinated it all night in olive oil and rosemary. I am making new potatoes for him, baby carrots.

He arrives, slightly out of breath, holding tulips. He puts *Der Rosenkavalier* on the CD player and settles himself in Max's chair. I look at my friend surrounded by the history of art. He takes a book from the shelf.

In a copper bowl I swirl together sugar, eggs. I add butter to hot milk, add flour. A soufflé. I take the candied violets from the pantry, break them into small pieces and make a wreath for the top—because it is spring.

"I've never seen these drawings before," Steven says, from the study.

"I found them in the closet. Max did them."

"They're really good. It's your mother, yes?"

An arm raised, an arm down, no hat, then a fringed hat. The woman smiling. The woman holding a tambourine. The woman turning away.

"Yes."

"I believe the lamb is ready." It comes perfect to the table. New potatoes, baby carrots. We eat the spring. He praises the braided ring of bread I've made. I open the champagne. We drink the stars. I tell him about the spiral galaxies. He reaches for his heart, the small spiral taped to his chest. He talks about all the new treatments there are. He talks about the work he's got at the lab, his computer pieces.

"I must show you something." I get up and from the desk drawer take out a picture. "I found this in Max's stuff," I say.

His hands tremble. Red jumper. Patent leather shoes. Long flowing hair. "You made me so beautiful!"

He smiles. He pours more champagne. He drinks little. He eats small portions now.

I do not mean to cry.

"Do you remember when our breath had shapes?"

He nods. "Of course."

I am so afraid.

Max hands me three eggs, oeufs à la neige, though it is spring. I pass Steven a perfect oval and he swallows it, another, carefully. The last one. I love you.

"I saw the figure 5 in gold," I say.

He laughs.

"We'll need more champagne soon," he whispers. He makes an elegant turn, reaches slowly for another bottle and opens it.

"Andromeda is a spiral galaxy that we can see, Steven, but it is so far away that its light has been traveling for 2.2 million years to reach us. M33 too."

He senses I need his help. He gives me his mouthful of alphabets: S, AZT, AL 721, HIV. He gives me a smile, a sigh.

When I close my eyes he is still there. When I look away he is still there.

As he begins another story I let down my guard a bit more. Probably he will hurt me more than I can possibly imagine. Certainly we will never be the same again. But it's OK. He's well into another story. I listen to the rise and fall of his beautiful, deep voice. I notice the slope of his shoulders, the arc of his arms as he speaks, his brown hands, his handsome face in candlelight. I will not leave his side. I will stay with him through whatever is to come. Of this I am sure. I will love him even more than I do now. He is my brother, and looking at him and knowing all of this, I realize it is as perfect a moment on earth as I can expect.

I close my eyes and picture the hieroglyphs of hope:

A Z T
S
friend

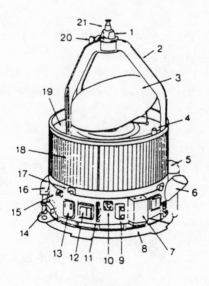

GIOTTO

They are not hard to decipher. They are not really in code.
Do not be afraid, my friend. I am with you.

Giotto approaches Halley's Comet. I move my hand toward
yours across the dinner table.

It is not nearly over.

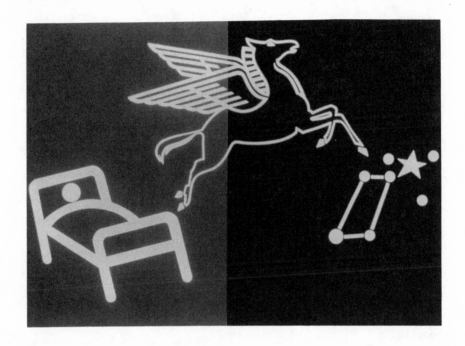

Data Shows Nucleus of Halley's Comet Blacker Than Coal

Darmstadt, West Germany, March 14 — Elated scientists at the European Space Agency said today that the spinning Giotto craft that streaked past the heart of Halley's Comet early this morning revealed the comet's mysterious nucleus to be extremely dark, rough and irregular, and bigger than had been thought.

"There's no question that the true color of the nucleus is black, absolutely black, blacker than coal, almost like velvet," Horst Keller, an agency scientist, told a crammed news conference called to give preliminary results from the Giotto probe. "It's very dark, the darkest dark you can imagine."

What the Light Looks Like

Father, it is 9:30 p.m. on the 29th of March and I am standing outside of 154 West Eleventh Street, where you once lived. The light is warm and I wonder what meal you have just finished eating and what book from the huge library you are about to pick up. What the light looks like is your life. You are all alone, wearing your slippers, smoking your pipe.

It is 3:45 and it is raining lightly, a gray afternoon in late November. What the light looks like is an angel. What the light looks like is a cross and a man nailed to it. What the light looks like is a woman on her knees turning before our eyes, as the light changes, into stone.

Max, sometimes I'm so afraid of what the light looks like.

It is noon in August in Greece. His hands pull from the earth shards, scrolls from the lost world, and he turns them over and over in light.

We are in a disco, years ago on Twelfth Street. A place that allows women in as well as men. We are still unused to doing things separately. We're just eighteen. Drinking age. There's a ball at the ceiling that cuts light and spins it in a thousand directions. You are moving through a thousand specks of light. You are dancing through smoke and space and light. Each gesture frozen for a fraction of a second by the action of the strobe. What the light looks like is the entire galaxy, you unattached, moving through space, your one head larger, more perfect than any planet, than any star.

It is 2:00 in the morning in early spring. I look up and I see a bear in the stars. I look up and I see a teacher in space. I look up and I see a box in the sky. I look up and I see a green monkey in a tree. I look up and I try to picture paradise.

It is 8:35 on the 3rd of June and I am walking uptown on Seventh Avenue carrying a bottle of champagne. I am a little late, but not too late. What the light looks like is hoops of gold wrapped around your body like a Macy's Christmas tree.

Author's Note

In the end I was only hands to him. The last thing I ever heard him say was, "Are these Carole's hands?" My hands on his hands. "Yes," I said. "I am trying to help you with this. I wish I could help you."

He had lost the hearing in his left ear, then sight in his left eye, which he liked to call his dog eye. A few months earlier he had winked at me with that eye, as we stood with a person I wanted his opinion of. "Did you see me wink?" he asked later.

His left hand went numb and began to curl like a claw and he put that on the list of things that needed to be fixed. There were other things he had to do. There was a suit he had to pick up at Barneys, he said. A dinner party somewhere. There was a church he had to finish building.

A few days before he died, he said, "Carole, you'll never guess what." He was so thrilled when I came to visit him that day. "What is it, Gary?" I asked.

"It's the most miraculous thing," he said. "I can see again!" I put my left hand on his left hand and waved my other hand in front of him and realized that both his eyes were darkened now with his wonderful and perfect sight.

Acknowledgments

I would like to express my love to the following people without whom this book could not have been written: Lillian and Charles Falk, pillars of courage; Michael Boodro and Patrick Goodman, who held my hand in the dark; Helen Lang, who taught me how to say good-bye; Ilene Sunshine, in love with light; and my parents, Rosemarie and Kenneth Maso, who showed me that the dark is not so dark, and the stars are not so far.

My gratitude to those who helped realize this project: Barbara Ras, my editor, who was always smart, meticulous, and best of all not afraid to break the rules; Amy Einsohn, who understood what I wanted; David Bullen and Amy Evans, who did the design and layout; and Louis Asekoff and Barbara Page, who read the manuscript first.

My appreciation to those who helped hold back some of the chaos for a while: Zenka Bartek, Robin Becker, Georges Borchardt, Christine and Ben Brown, Joan Einwohner, Nancy Fried, Angela Galardi, Cathleen and Jay Giannelli, Judith Karolyi, Michelle and Ken Maso, Kristi and Michael Maso, Kit and Douglas Maso, Laura Mullen, Christina Schlesinger, Dixie Sheridan, Jack Shoemaker, and Daniel Simko.

My thanks to the following for their generous support: The W. K. Rose Fellowship of Vassar College, the MacDowell Colony, the Provincetown Fine Arts Work Center, the Cummington Community of the Arts, the New York Foundation for the Arts, and the National Endowment for the Arts.

And for their courage and vision, my admiration and respect to Jean-Luc Godard and Max Frisch. And to Donald Barthelme, Jean-Michel Basquiat, and Thomas Bernhard, in memory.

Credits

Page 9: Photograph of farmhouse door. Courtesy of the author.

17: Detail of *Noli me tangere,* by Giotto. Courtesy of Alinari/Art Resource.

24: Detail of *Noli me tangere,* by Giotto.

27: From *Giotto and the Arena Chapel Frescos,* James H. Stubblebine, ed., copyright © 1969 by W. W. Norton and Company, Inc. Reprinted by permission.

29: Details of *The Last Supper,* by Leonardo da Vinci. Courtesy of Alinari/Art Resource.

30: Photograph of fanlight. Courtesy of the author.
   "Sky Watch," *New York Times,* June 23, 1985. © 1985 by The New York
   Times Company. Reprinted by permission.

34: "The Red Wheelbarrow," by William Carlos Williams, *Collected Poems, Volume 1, 1909–1939,* copyright 1938 by New Directions Publishing Corpo-
   ration. Reprinted by permission of New Directions Publishing Corpora-
   tion.

37: Sign language card. Courtesy of the author.

39: Photograph of wooden gate. Courtesy of the author.

40: Lost parrot poster. Courtesy of the author.

40–41: From "The Great Figure," by William Carlos Williams, *Collected Poems,
   Volume 1, 1909–1939,* copyright 1938 by New Directions Publishing Cor-
   poration. Reprinted by permission of New Directions Publishing Corpo-
   ration.

43: Sign language card. Courtesy of the author.

49: Detail of *Noli me tangere,* by Giotto.

57: *Woman in Blue Reading a Letter,* by Vermeer. Courtesy of Alinari/Art Re-
   source. Rijksmuseum, Amsterdam.
   Head of a Young Girl, by Vermeer. Courtesy of Giraudon/Art Resource.
   Mauritshuis, The Hague.

58: Text from *A Study of Vermeer,* by Edward Snow, University of California
   Press, 1979. Reprinted by permission.
   Detail of *Head of a Young Girl,* by Vermeer.

60: Lost dove poster. Courtesy of the author.

64: *Untitled,* by Gary Falk. Courtesy of the Gary Falk Estate.

71: Photograph of Brown tombstone. Courtesy of the author.

75: *This Is a Picture of Space,* by Kristi Maso. Courtesy of the artist.

82: "Sky Watch," *New York Times,* July 21, 1985. © 1985 by The New York Times
   Company. Reprinted by permission.

87: Photograph of fanlight. Courtesy of the author.

90: *Young Woman Sleeping in Rumanian Blouse*, by Henri Matisse. Copyright Succession H. Matisse/ARS N.Y., 1989.

94: Math workbook page from *Math Subtraction 1, Grades 1–2*, © 1984 Western Publishing Company, Inc. Math by Matthew Dawson.

97: *The Dance in the City*, by Auguste Renoir. Courtesy of SCALA/Art Resource. Musée d'Orsay, Paris.

100: From "J. S. Bach . . . ," by Harold C. Schonberg, *New York Times*, November 24, 1985. © 1985 by The New York Times Company. Reprinted by permission.

108: From "Van Gogh at the Met, the Artist Triumphant," by Michael Brenson, *New York Times*, November 28, 1986. © 1986 by The New York Times Company. Reprinted by permission.

119: Detail from *The Last Supper*, by Leonardo da Vinci.

120: Correction to the recipe for Chiu Chow braised duck, *New York Times*, Magazine Section, February 15, 1987. © 1987 by The New York Times Company. Reprinted by permission.

From "Scholars Re-examining Rembrandt Attributions," by Michael Brenson, *New York Times*, November 25, 1985. © 1985 by The New York Times Company. Reprinted by permission.

122: *Untitled*, by Gary Falk. Courtesy of the Gary Falk Estate.

123: From *The Arrival of Halley's Comet, 1985–86*, by Paul B. Doherty, Barron's Educational Series.

129: Illustration of an AIDS cell, *New York Times*, March 3, 1987. © 1987 by The New York Times Company. Reprinted by permission.

130: "Sky Watch," *New York Times*, September 15, 1985. © 1985 by The New York Times Company. Reprinted by permission.

139: *Young Woman Sleeping in Rumanian Blouse*, by Henri Matisse.

142: *Red Desert*, by Gary Falk. Courtesy of the New Museum of Contemporary Arts, N.Y.

144: "Sky Watch," *New York Times*, January 31, 1988. © 1988 by The New York Times Company. Reprinted by permission.

145: From *Impressionism*, by Pierre Courthion, 1974. Reprinted by permission of Harry N. Abrams, Inc. All rights reserved.

146: Text from *Impressionism*, by Pierre Courthion. *House of Dr. Gachet at Auvers*, by Paul Cézanne, courtesy of the Louvre.

151: *Untitled*, by Gary Falk. Courtesy of Charles and Lillian Falk.

152: Lost ferret poster. Courtesy of the author.

153: Photograph of fanlight. Courtesy of the author.

161: Guerrilla Girls posters. Courtesy of the Guerrilla Girls.

162: *Untitled*, by Barbara Kruger. Courtesy of Mary Boone Gallery, N.Y.

163: Letter from lsa to the author.

166: *Homefront*, by Gary Falk. Courtesy of the Corcoran Gallery of Art, Washington, D.C.

168: *Head of a Woman*, by Henri Matisse. Copyright Succession H. Matisse/ARS N.Y., 1989. Photograph courtesy of Art Resource.

173: *Baby Grand Larceny*, by Karen Beckhardt. Courtesy of the artist.

175: *Young Woman Sleeping in Rumanian Blouse*, by Henri Matisse.

177–78: From "A Dutchman's Quest for a Black Tulip," by Alice Furlaud, *New York Times*, March 20, 1986. Copyright © 1986 by The New York Times Company. Reprinted by permission.

178: *Head of a Woman*, by Henri Matisse.

178–79: From "Comet Puts on Biggest Show . . . ," by Sandra Blakeslee, *New*

York Times, February 11, 1986. Copyright © 1986 by The New York Times Company. Reprinted by permission.

192: *I Saw the Figure 5 in Gold*, by Charles Demuth. Courtesy of the Metropolitan Museum of Art, the Alfred Stieglitz Collection, 1949.

206: *Untitled*, by Gary Falk. Courtesy of Charles and Lillian Falk.

215: From "Picasso Survey, the Late Paintings," by Michael Brenson, *New York Times*, March 2, 1984. © 1984 by The New York Times Company. Reprinted by permission.

217: *Self-Portrait*, by Pablo Picasso. Copyright 1989 ARS N.Y./SPADEM. Photograph courtesy of Giraudon/Art Resource.

230: "Sky Watch," *New York Times*, March 9, 1986. © 1986 by The New York Times Company. Reprinted by permission.

From "The Lost Son," copyright 1947 by Theodore Roethke. From *The Collected Poems of Theodore Roethke*, by Theodore Roethke. Used by permission of Doubleday, a division of Bantam, Doubleday, Dell Publishing Group, Inc.

234: *Crows over the Wheatfield*, by Vincent van Gogh. Courtesy of Collection Stichting Rijksmuseum.

238: From *The Arrival of Halley's Comet, 1985–86*, by Paul B. Doherty.

239: Detail from sign language card. Courtesy of the author.

Detail from *Noli me tangere*, by Giotto.

240: *Virgin and Child on Starry Background*, by Henri Matisse. Copyright Succession H. Matisse/ARS N.Y., 1989.

241: *Red Dawn*, by Gary Falk. Courtesy of the Hirshhorn Museum and Sculpture Garden, Washington, D.C.

From "Data Shows Nucleus of Halley's Comet Blacker Than Coal," by James M. Markham, *New York Times*, March 15, 1986. Copyright © 1986 by The New York Times Company. Reprinted by permission.

244: Carole and Gary, Cummington, Massachusetts, 1982. Photograph by Helen Lang.

Special thanks to Katya Stieglitz for her assistance. And again my gratitude to Helen Lang, who went about the huge task of securing these permissions with her usual optimism and persistence.

Design by David Bullen
Layout by Amy Evans
Typeset in Mergenthaler Meridien, Book and Medium
by Wilsted & Taylor
Printed by Maple-Vail
on acid-free paper